The Lady of the Manor

Chris Marr

ROBERT HALE · LONDON

ISBN 978-0-7090-8481-5

Robert Hale Limited
Clerkenwell House
Clerkenwell Green
London EC1R 0HT

www.halebooks.com

2 4 6 8 10 9 7 5 3 1

Typeset in 11½/14pt Erhardt
Printed and bound in Great Britain by
Biddles Limited, King's Lynn

To Barbara

The fountains mingle with the river
And the rivers with the ocean,
The winds of heaven mix for ever
With a sweet emotion;
Nothing in the world is single,
And things, by a law divine
In one another's being mingle –
Why not I with thine?

See the mountains kiss high heaven,
And the waves clasp one another;
No sister-flower would be forgiven
If it disdain'd its brother:
And the sunlight clasps the earth,
And the moonbeams kiss the sea –
What are all these kissings worth,
If thou kiss not me?

Love's Philosophy by Percy Bysshe Shelley (1792–1822)

Contents

PART FOUR

Part One

1

A Day Out

Well, here he was … The best seat in the house. Just for the moment he was standing, but a few well-chosen words and then he could sit down. Really, this must be how it felt to be royalty: all this space either side of him and everyone else having to squeeze in, even an escort (the aptly named Graves) in attendance. On his way up the steps he'd taken a moment to compose himself, prompting Graves to remark, 'First time, is it, sir?' to which he'd barely managed a twitch of the lips. No doubt the fellow wouldn't hesitate to say, 'Chin up, old boy' to a man awaiting the gallows. The advice he'd been given beforehand was that whatever the circumstances, however much his heart was pounding, he ought to present a look of mild perturbation at all times, as though he'd just been informed that dinner arrangements would have to be altered.

'Dinner arrangements?' he had queried.

'Yes, that's the look. Keep that expression.'

So together with all the other actors in the drama he was obliged to play his part as well. Let himself lose his head for one moment and …

Well, there was a sentence Graves would enjoy completing.

Ah, hold on. What was happening now? A man was rising to his feet almost directly opposite. Oh, yes, that was the clerk, wasn't it, about to start proceedings? Just making sure he caught his eye before speaking.

'George Arthur Erskine, you are charged in this indictment. That on the sixth day of July, 1903, at Eveley in Hampshire, you feloniously, wilfully, and of your malice aforethought, did kill and murder one Emily Jane Erskine. How do you plead? Guilty or not guilty?'

All eyes turned in his direction.

'Not guilty, my lord.'

He took his seat between the two warders and bit into his finger-nails. Three months he'd been waiting for this – three whole months incarcerated at His Majesty's pleasure – and all he could see before him was a circus, the proceedings conducted by men in wigs. The jury were called upon to 'hearken to the evidence' and then the clerk sat down, his job accomplished. A subdued buzz broke out in the chamber as the tension eased to be succeeded by a sudden hush. Sir Ernest Hislop, KC, the Attorney-General, was on his feet.

'May it please your lordship, gentlemen of the jury,' he began. 'The accused stands before you charged with murdering his wife by stran-gulation. The Crown will demonstrate not only that Mrs Erskine was murdered but also that the prisoner and no other was responsible for her death. The enquiry, I need hardly point out, is of the utmost gravity, and if this man is guilty of the crime of which he is charged, then, whether you agree with capital punishment or not, you should extend no sympathy towards him.'

George's hands coiled around each other in his lap. Dinner arrange-ments could be notoriously tricky things, there was no doubt about it. A scribbling pad had been placed for his benefit on the ledge of the dock, but there was nothing for him to jot down here. That quiet voice droning on, sapping all hope of an acquittal! The pile of notes on the prosecution counsel's table suggested a huge amount of evidence, painstakingly acquired, and yet no one – certainly not this stranger holding forth – had any idea how he felt about Emily's death, how he really felt ...

'The prosecution thinks that the best way in which to discharge our duty is to narrate the facts in an order which will enable you to observe the conduct of the prisoner, the motives which actuated him, and his behaviour subsequent to the tragedy with which we are concerned. Undoubtedly the prisoner has several commendable qualities, to which we shall certainly bear witness, but his nature is tainted with a terrible jealousy which had its tragic repercussions in the early hours of the sixth of July.'

George writhed impotently in the dock. A vast crowd had greeted him on his arrival at the court building with cries of 'Wife-killer!' and 'Go to hell!' but this approach was infinitely worse. Everything was couched in such reasonable, eloquent language. There was no question he was a monster. It was a fact. And Sir Ernest – humbly, almost apologetically – was at pains to present as full a case as possible, taking as his starting point the moment at which the beast first drew breath.

'George Erskine was born in Hertfordshire in 1880, the second son of a banker. His father died when he was three and he and his brother were brought up solely by their mother. In 1897 he left for Sandhurst as an infantry cadet and, a year later, qualified to take the Queen's commission. In 1899, following in his brother's footsteps, he was gazetted to the Grenadier Guards ...'

The only sound in the courtroom was the Attorney-General's voice as he delved into the prisoner's background, paying reference in particular to his exploits in the South African War. George had been shot in the knee at the Battle of Belmont, at the same time as his brother had been killed, and had spent some time in a hospital in Cape Town. There he had learnt of his mother's death. Returning home with a pronounced limp, he had met his wife at a society ball.

'The marriage was in many ways an unequal partnership. Mrs Erskine came from a rich and privileged background; she moved in what one might call the top echelon of society, being more than once introduced to the King. After the season of 1902, she and her husband lived at Stockley Hall in Hampshire, the ancestral seat of her family, and the defendant was assigned the role of managing the estate. But throughout their relationship Mrs Erskine kept her own banking account and generally handled most of the finances.'

There was nothing new here. George peered at the prosecution counsel over the dock rail, unable to fathom exactly what he was implying. That he resented his role in his relationship with Emily? Not true; simply not true. Even so, there was something about Sir Ernest's manner which was disturbing. He had been addressing a point a few feet above the heads of the jury but now took the time to gaze at his listeners, a gleam in his eye.

'Now we come to a very important part of the case. It is the submission of the prosecution that the inequitable arrangement which formed the public life of this young couple was even more exaggerated in their private affairs. That in their twelve months of marriage they never, once, enjoyed physical relations ...'

There were loud murmurings from the gallery. Journalists' pencils were dancing little jigs of delight. Telltale patches of red flushed angrily on the prisoner's cheeks. A hundred pairs of eyes were now regarding him in an entirely new light.

'… and she never even allowed him the keys to her room, invariably locking her door every evening. Does that not suggest she was somehow afraid of him? That she found his closeness repellent?'

George glared meaningfully at his defence counsel, Sir Lionel Trefford-Letts, but the latter seemed far more interested in disposing of copious quantities of snuff.

'Certainly she never confided in him,' Sir Ernest continued, apparently unaware of the furore he had created. 'She never felt able to discuss her deepest feelings. He always remained in total ignorance.'

The prisoner waited in vain for an objection from his counsel. Surely he couldn't allow this balderdash to continue?

'Now you may hold the opinion that Mrs Erskine was acting unreasonably. That it is the wife's bounden duty to submit to her husband's desires. But whatever your sympathy in that regard, it in no way excuses the defendant's vile and disgusting behaviour during the weekend and in the few hours preceding the murder …'

George sat back in his chair, his arms falling limp at his sides. Well, at least dinner arrangements were no longer a problem. The only item on the menu, in fact, was his goose well and truly cooked. Through haggard eyes he regarded Sir Lionel continue to stuff his nostrils to the gunwales and the words 'vile and disgusting' returned to him. If the latter was hoping to engineer a sneeze and thus distract the jury, it was plainly too little, too late. But then what a farce this all was! If George had any matches to hand, he'd dash over there now and light a couple of flares under the man's nose. The death sentence at any rate would be easier to bear.

Sir Ernest had made his introduction and proceeded with forceful eloquence to unfold the events of the fourth, fifth and sixth of July last. Over the next couple of hours he painstakingly built, in verbal terms, the gallows which he obviously hoped would end George's days. He ended his exhortation with a flourish.

'Jealousy, the green-eyed monster, consumed George Erskine. He was convinced his wife was having an affair and waited until he had received what he regarded as decisive proof.

'No one knows what happened after she had allowed him into her bedroom. Presumably he confronted her with evidence of her infidelity. Perhaps, the hour being late, his state of inebriation advanced, he hoped for some token of carnal affection. Possibly, like Porphyria's lover, he wanted sole possession of her moment of death, her blue eyes shining, the last blaze of colour on her cheeks, as with her final gasp she beheld him and only him.

'He lost his temper, we can be sure of that. And in his rage he killed his wife with his bare hands. Inspired by jealousy and the pangs of rejection, the prisoner felt that she had robbed him of his dignity, his reputation. Incensed that another man could enjoy pleasures earmarked for himself, he put a stop to it forever, extinguishing the cause of his obsession – a young, precious life. Gentlemen of the jury, he deserves no forgiveness.'

And on that note Sir Ernest sat down.

Possibly the only person who hadn't been listening to the last part of this speech was the prisoner himself. Detecting a scent of sweet herbs – sprinkled over the front of the dock before the court had convened – he had slipped away from the dark and claustrophobic splendour of his surroundings, experiencing instead the brilliant sunshine of the previous summer. Head bowed, revealing only his thinning hair, his mind had settled on the week before Emily's murder and the day of the picnic; the day it had all started ...

2

The Picnic

'George … George!'
He was in the bicycle shed, buffing up the machines, when Emily made her entrance.

'Geor—! Oh, there you are. Teddy's just called round in his cart. The hamper's all set. He wants me to head off with him now.'

The cloth he was holding slipped to the ground. She was already making steps to leave.

'But why can't the two of us use the cart?'

'Because it's his, that's why. Besides, he refuses to go by bicycle.'

'Well, let Constance go with him.'

The lines of his jaw hardened but otherwise he remained perfectly composed.

'Don't be tiresome, George. They don't even know each other. Look, I must go. He's waiting for me in the drive.'

One hour later the guests had joined him and the small group had set out in pursuit of Emily and Pilling. It was a Saturday, 27 June. The sun had rolled up its sleeves in preparation for some brisk business ahead, and everyone was bedecked in their full summer regalia, complementing the English countryside.

To begin with they made excellent progress and the cool breeze flicking their faces was most refreshing. The doctor's grey hair flapped uncontrollably in the current, while his wife, Norah, having the foresight to bring a bonnet, sat on her machine with a dignified primness. The other member of the entourage, Constance Appleby, though an old acquaintance of Emily's, was a newcomer to the village. She had moved into Eveley with her mother a month ago – taking residence in the manor house – and it was Emily's idea to invite her along on their outing in the country. Her heels, rather than her toes, were firmly planted on the pedals and her cheeks were glowing fiercely with the effort.

Up and down the winding lanes of Hampshire they careered, intoxicated by the fresh warmth of the air and the smell of the grass. At the crest of a particularly gruelling hill they stopped to admire the panorama of beauty laid out before them, the two women taking up a position a few yards from the men.

'Know what I could do with now, George – what I could positively kill for?' Doctor Wetherington made a smacking sound with his lips. 'A nice cold – very cold – beer. That would be perfect. A nice cold beer in a stone bottle.'

George removed his cloth cap and wiped the sweat from his brow. His knee was throbbing.

'Served up, I suppose, by a beautiful barmaid?'

'M'm.' Wetherington closed his eyes. 'With long fair hair, blue eyes and a welcoming smile.'

'And she says, "Don't worry, Cedric, this one's on the house."'

'Something like that.'

'And whereabouts is your wife in all this?'

The doctor's expression lost some of its rapturous quality. 'What? Oh – er – she'll be somewhere else entirely, living out her own fantasy. At home, I expect, looking after the house.'

'That'll be nice for her.'

Wetherington eyed George somewhat suspiciously. 'Actually, now that I think about it, her fantasy would probably involve that Pilling chap you've invited along.'

George didn't reply, continuing to gaze at the tranquil scene before him. Why bring *him* into it?

'Beats me what women see in him,' the doctor went on. 'Just sits there smiling when it's his turn to buy a round. I told Norah about him not paying his way and all she could say was, "Perhaps he simply lost track. Or perhaps" – listen to this – "perhaps he thought we'd all had a bit too much."'

'What, including him?'

'Oh, no, 'course not. Perfectly happy to accept another one when it was offered. You know, perhaps in future we should all chip in to buy a few rounds for him on his own. 'Least then the rest of us can remain reasonably sober.'

'Ce-dric!' called Mrs Wetherington.

'Uh-ho, off again. Must have heard me talking about her. Coming, my love!'

They hoisted themselves back onto their saddles and headed down into the valley.

What joy! What zest for life! To feel the delicious kiss of the breeze on one's face and see the world shoot by beneath one's dancing feet! And preserve that mood in the face of calamity!

They were just rounding a vast haywain – which took up the entire highway – when a motorcar, coming from the opposite direction, scorching along at no less than twenty miles per hour, turned the corner in front of them, halting abruptly and churning up a huge cloud of dust.

'Ooh-er! Oooh!'

Constance, bringing up the rear, flapped one arm in the air while using the other to steady her hat. Her bicycle, temporarily emancipated, wandered over to the mossy path on the side of the road where she was unceremoniously dumped. She sat there, a few tears smudging her pink, slightly porcine features, surveying her collection of forget-me-nots – now squashed. The doctor hastened to her side while George advanced on the stinkpot behind the wheel.

'Look here,' he began, 'if you must drive that contraption, at least try and point it in the right direction.'

A sharp exchange ensued, the other – without bothering to remove his goggles – suggesting that the young lady took lessons in how to ride a bicycle. It was a little while before they attempted a dignified exit and George found his hands slipping with sweat off the handlebars, the ligaments in his injured knee rubbing together to create a small furnace. He would have defended Constance in any case, but there was plainly a deeper reason for his ill humour. Emily was with Pilling – just the two of them. And though there was nothing untoward in that circumstance, he'd definitely seen a look in Norah Wetherington's eye when he'd passed on news of their absence. What made it all the more irritating was the small doubt which lingered in his own mind about Emily's sudden departure.

Could she have planned everything in advance, leaving him no choice but to agree?

No. Of course not. He was being absurd.

At last they reached a great oak on the edge of Elders Wood and, leaving their bicycles propped up against its sides, they formed an Indian file, picking their way along a dry path leading to their destination. The sun was now irresistible and slivers of gold burst through the branches onto the woodland floor. In the distance they could hear the gentle splash of the stream, soothing and natural, and instinctively George stepped up the pace. Behind him the others, led by the dainty gait of the doctor's wife, zigzagged their way through the overgrown route he'd chosen, and he soon found himself some distance ahead.

What was that?

A murmur of voices – Emily and Pilling's. Definitely Pilling's voice at any rate. Seconds later George saw them, her sitting or kneeling, Pilling walking around her wagging his finger. His whole manner smacked of a certain hauteur – as though he owned her.

Blast! He'd trodden on something. Now they were both looking over.

Well, there was nothing for it. George made his way towards them, not bothering to conceal himself any longer. A moment before he'd given himself away he could have sworn he'd caught the words 'naughty girl' uttered by Pilling.

By now the others had virtually caught up and they reached the opening together, discovering that the two conspirators had separated. Emily was busily shifting the china into various geometric patterns and Pilling, to all appearances, was asleep by the wicker hamper. George gazed down upon the beribboned straw hat which shielded Pilling's face and tightened his grip on his own cloth cap which he'd taken the trouble to remove. Pilling had arrived in the district shortly after themselves and, within no time at all, had married a rich widow, who was an invalid and twenty years his senior. His wife's death three months later had not increased his standing in the village and it was possible that Emily wished to favour him with a public show of support. At least that was the most sanguine interpretation of events. Pilling was their closest neighbour, leading inevitably to the odd encounter, but last week he'd called round when he'd almost certainly known George was out. Indeed, if George hadn't heard Mary, one of the maids, dropping a comment about Pilling traipsing his mud into the house, he'd never even have been aware of his visit.

The other finally tipped back his boater and surveyed George with half-open eyes.

'Thought you'd never arrive, old chap.' He raised himself up on his haunches. 'Your one good leg playing up as well?'

George was saved from replying by the doctor's wife making some complimentary remark about the food, and they all gazed admiringly at the feast laid out for them. In the centre a lobster took pride of place, flanked by two champagne bottles. Smoked oysters, pork pies and strawberries were among the other delicacies on display.

George glanced surreptitiously at Emily, noting the faraway look in her eyes and the flame of red on her cheeks. Seeing nothing, absorbed in her thoughts. All of a sudden she looked up, gazing not at him but further to her right, giving a nod to which Pilling responded with a smile. A sharp pain pierced his chest, as though a long pin had been inserted. He scarcely heard Mrs Wetherington whispering in his ear.

'His hair's wonderful, don't you think? I'd do anything for curls like that.'

She had evidently been following his line of vision. He pointed the sparse thatch adorning his own head to face her.

'Edward's hair,' she repeated. 'Don't you think—?'

'I'd like to run my hands through it over and over.'

Her mouth dropped open and, freed from further interruption (from that quarter at any rate), he resumed his attention to the subject at hand. The secret communication involving Emily and Pilling had ended and she appeared to have regained her poise. Her hair, coiled gracefully around the slim carriage of her neck, looked more lustrous than ever in the midday sun, contrasting with the paleness of her milky-white skin.

As the picnic progressed, George did not notice any further covert operations between the two, and the only member of the party exchanging looks with anybody appeared to be Constance. Indeed, whenever he glanced in her direction she would return his gaze with a doting expression, as though she were about to say, 'Ahhh!'

But maybe the sun was affecting his imagination …

The meal drifted to a close. He had that feeling of having eaten a little more than necessary and needed to stave off the tendency to fall asleep. Perhaps if someone had recited Keats's *Ode to a Nightingale* at that moment he would have slipped quietly Lethewards, a sweet purple-stained smile on his face. A desultory chatter kept up in the background, ranging from such topics as the delightfulness of various Continental watering places to the efficacy of certain stocks and shares and, feeling a sublime sense of ennui, he enjoyed the entertainment of an inquisitive wasp creeping over the lip of one of the wine glasses. The wasp had just flown off in the direction of the river when he detected a definite crescendo in the tenor of the conversation.

'There's all manner of nonsense put about these days. I tell you it won't be long before women are given the vote. The family will be completely undermined.'

'You're doing that, Cedric, by bringing up politics in polite company,' opined Mrs Wetherington, responding good-naturedly to her husband.

'My good doctor, you're becoming quite flustered.' It was difficult to detect whether Pilling was being serious or merely trying to incite an argument. 'Would you like to deny the ladies in our company their rightful say?'

'Of course not,' huffed the doctor.

'If you ask me,' continued Pilling, 'this government's still living in the past. It's high time we devoted ourselves to real issues rather than jingoistic escapades.'

No one said anything for a second while Pilling's eyebrows assumed a noticeable lean towards the centre of his forehead, his head perched on top of an exceedingly high collar. Constance, surprisingly, was the next person to speak.

'How ghastly to have one's rightful say!'

Heads turned in unison, not quite sure what to expect.

'Everyone knows that women control society, deciding whom to invite to our parties, which of our husbands deserve promotion. I intend to subjugate myself to my future husband and thus achieve complete domination.'

She grinned at George.

'What a coup, my dear Constance!' exclaimed Emily. 'That's certainly the way to achieve omnipotence – in the kitchen at any rate. The strings you'll be pulling behind the scenes will be tied to a tread-wheel.'

'I say, that's a bit stiff,' murmured the doctor, stealing a glance at his wife.

'Women will never advance,' pursued Emily, 'until we possess equal rights. That's why I'm a suffragist.'

There was much amusement at this remark, especially when the doctor demanded an explanation from George of how he was keeping his wife for her to hold such views. The real arguments, as always on these occasions, were being conducted along the lines of gender, with women against women, men against men. George, for instance, was still smarting over Pilling's last remark. Jingoistic escapades! From someone who was only twenty-one years old!

'What did you mean,' he turned to Pilling, 'when you said we ought to concentrate on real issues?'

'What did I mean?' replied the other innocently.

'Yes, what did you mean? "Real issues rather than jingoistic escapades"?'

'Oh, is that what I said? Tell you the truth, old chap, I don't recall. Always spouting some nonsense or other, you know how it is.'

'Well, you did say it. I heard you distinctly.'

'Very well, then – if you insist. I'm sure I didn't mean anything by it.'

'I think you did.'

The corners of Pilling's mouth fell and his eyes assumed a dead quality. 'My dear fellow, you mustn't pay so much attention to my rantings.'

'What did you mean?'

'Look. I don't know. Really. I suppose if I meant anything at all, it was that we ought to look after our own people. Not waste money on another war.'

George's face turned very white and he enunciated his words carefully. 'If you think that my brother was killed for no reason—'

'*Shut up, George.*'

He stopped dead, quite unable to believe his ears.

'For heaven's sake, do shut up, there's a good boy. Oh, and hand me a cigarette.'

Now Emily was cooing, but it felt as though someone had just delivered a blow to his stomach. If anyone else had told him to be quiet he would have brushed it aside, probably attacking them with even more venom, but there was something insistent about her voice.

There was an embarrassing silence – and then Constance started laughing. It was more of a nervous giggle, but it was obvious that this woman, who had been gazing at him fawningly for the entire afternoon, now saw him merely as a figure of fun; yet another henpecked husband.

The sun had curled round to its apex in the heavens and was pressing down on them with its full violence. All the picnic things – serving dishes, salad bowls, half-eaten pastries – lay topsy-turvy on the rug beside them. While the others jabbered on, George must have spent the next twenty minutes lost in thought, wearing the sad and vacant expression of cowed manhood. Perhaps the others hadn't read so much into Emily's rebuke, but there'd been a sharpness in her tone which clearly denoted something else. Frustration? Impatience? An expression at long last of her true feelings towards him?

'Coming then, George?'

'H'm?' His head jerked round.

Emily stood up and started walking in the direction of the bridge. The others were grinning.

'Your wife's just going to check on the horses before we play *Last Man Out*,' the doctor kindly explained.

'I'll go and join her then.'

He could see her in the distance, her head held high, her gingham dress, moulded around her slender figure, flowing helplessly behind her. He approached her as quickly as he could, irritated with himself for rising so easily to the bait.

'Emily, wait!'

She turned, her face full of childlike gravity, her cheeks rouged by the effort of walking.

'Oh, good, George. You came.'

'Yes, I didn't quite hear what you said back there.'

'Here, take my arm. I just wanted to talk to you for a moment. To apologize. I didn't mean to snap at you just now. You took it badly, I could tell.'

'It's all right, really.'

'No, let me finish. It's not all right. It's just that I was afraid you'd start arguing with Teddy. Show him up in front of the others. I couldn't think of another way to change the subject.'

'Couldn't you have just let us thrash it out?'

She gave a little laugh. 'It's a picnic, you mad boy. Not a battle to the death. Anyhow, I know what you're like on that particular subject. I daresay I'm the same with the rights of women, but that's constructive, for everybody's benefit. Now, be quiet. And I mean that in the nicest possible way.'

'I accept your apology,' he said with dignity.

He was still somewhat confused, but her obvious contrition soothed him. He patted her hand reassuringly and for a minute or two they stood gazing at the view from the bridge, reminiscent of the balcony of their first meeting-place, the tranquil beauty of Emily investing her surroundings with the quality of an impressionist painting. A solitary angler, living in his own world of emotions and desires, was lowering his line into the thousand strips of silver that drifted by his feet.

In the morning Emily and Pilling had gone as far as they could on the road and had left the cart and pair at the Averburys' house on the other side of the river. The cart was still there in the yard, its shafts pointing disconsolately down in mock homage, and behind the buildings they could see the two greys, their heads sweeping the ground enjoying their own picnic. There did not seem to be any point in calling to ask after the horses, and, after a glance at the windows to check they weren't being watched, they meandered down the lane to gain a better view. Emily pecked him twice, once on either cheek, at the kissing gate, and they walked alongside one field before cutting across another to reach Othello and Desdemona. (They were both mares but one was obsessively jealous.) From here they could even espy the picnic-site and the four tiny specks of humanity. George sat down on the grass and started picking abstractedly at the longer blades, observing how long they needed to grow before keeling over.

'Teddy seems to have got over the death of his wife,' he said, hoping for some sort of consensus.

'He's horrid,' she said simply.

He stopped plucking at the grass. This was quite a shock, bearing in mind how she behaved in Pilling's presence. Had anything happened on their outward journey? Some sort of tiff? But why not let him lose his temper with him earlier?

'I thought it was only me he didn't care for.'

'He has no use for you, that's all. His real love is money.'

'But his wife must have left him a small fortune.'

Her eyes glazed over. 'And now I've got the demands of servants to contend with. Mrs Proops wants to know her future after she retires. She's suggested in so many words we should provide her with a house on the estate.'

'A house?'

'Apparently, it's not such an uncommon practice. Of course I told her it was out of the question, but she then raised the subject of her wages. She's already paid far more than the other servants, but she thought she was worth twice the amount we were paying her.'

George laughed in spite of himself. 'No ...'

'Oh, she was quite serious.'

'Why? What for?' His mood hardened. 'The woman's a misery. I don't think I've ever seen her smile.'

'A good servant – I think you'll find, George – isn't supposed to smile. It expresses a view, as my father used to say.'

'Well, I think if I make a joke they're entitled to smile.'

'Ah.' Emily nodded in an understanding way. 'Well, I'm already paying them not to groan. Smiles, I'm afraid, are just too expensive.'

The conversation lapsed for a moment. He enjoyed their jousting sessions – even if it was he who was invariably lanced – but she had also succeeded in changing the subject.

'So, to return to Teddy ... You were saying that his real love is money. Yet I thought he was fairly well off.'

'George.' She turned her gimlet eye on him. 'Don't be so serious. It's bad form.'

Well, don't be so secretive.

They arrived back at the picnic-site to discover that everything had been put away. Only five napkins, prettily designed as bishops' mitres, stood in a conclave in the middle of the check blanket. This turned out to be part of a game. All save the catcher – nominated by Emily – were meant to hide, but then steal back and retrieve their napkin. There were other rules too, but the real reason behind these festivities was the disproportionate delight Emily gleaned from watching grown adults behave like children, evidently under her spell. Indeed, the doctor, judging by his docile expression, was already a convert.

George really didn't care to exert himself with games of hide-and-seek in the woods. His knee was hurting once more, the rich meal was expanding the walls of his stomach, and he was opposed to ideas involving competition or splitting up the party. He glanced across at Emily and she smiled back, pebble-green eyes sparkling under dark and perfect lashes. He was a fool for love, there was no doubt about it. In the throes of a noble passion, permanently fantasizing about when next he'd be rewarded with some affection.

3

Tapser's Ruin

He knew exactly where he wanted to go.

Tapser's Ruin stood on the eastern rim of Elders Wood, a great sprawling ivy-clad heap long since deserted. He had stumbled upon it once before and the secrets which it obviously harboured intrigued him so much he'd later spent an otherwise boring hour plotting its history.

Its original owner had been Sir Horace Tapser, the famous shipbuilder, who had commissioned his second home to be built in the early sixteenth century. The house was slightly unusual in that it seemed to have been designed along medieval lines – especially the great hall with its vaulted ceiling – and the two turret structures sandwiching the façade looked like gnarled and grizzled warriors defending a giant Gothic beehive. Sir Horace had been a great socialite – retirement providing yet more opportunities to meet people – and the house had been the scene of many grand occasions. Members of the aristocracy would travel considerable distances to grace his dinner table and examples of his wit would then be regurgitated throughout the county and beyond. At the height of his reputation Sir Horace was even granted a royal audience: undoubtedly an important event, but afforded far more significance by the fact that he met and fell in love with one of the Queen's ladies-in-waiting, Maria de Pardo. They were married a month later, in August 1528, the thirty-year age difference feeding the London gossip market for a week.

That autumn they returned to Tapser House fervently hoping that new recruits to the dynasty would be heard scampering along the silent stone passages. In fact they needed to wait eight years before

Maria became heavy with child, and then the most common sound in the house was that of monks intoning psalms or prayerfully conducting their penances. Henry VIII, Defender of the Faith, had split with a papacy which seemed to be promoting Spanish interests, and he and Thomas Cromwell were now implementing a policy of dissolving the monasteries, making thousands of monks destitute. Sir Horace, typically, offered up his abode, not only to provide shelter for the homeless, but to preserve cultural and religious relics which were in danger of being destroyed.

Certainly life at this time was very exciting for the family. No one knew exactly what surprises the future held but there was always a sense that *something* was about to happen. Unfortunately that something was the greatest tragedy of all.

In 1537 Maria died in childbirth.

Horace was broken-hearted. The monks gradually dispersed and he was left to watch the weeds squeezing through the crumbling masonry. The poor man died two years later, as empty inside as his neglected home.

Tapser House fell into a decline in the years that followed, its subsequent owners unable to assuage the sadness that seemed to pervade the atmosphere. It was as if a huge malevolent spider had wrapped its intricate grey web a thousand times around the building and sucked out all the warmth and happiness.

And yet, strangely enough, George found the discarded remains of the house quite reassuring. The spider had eaten its fill and left a delicate shell behind to be tickled by the myriad rays of the sun. All the rooms had been gutted, the furniture and paintings removed, revealing only dusty floors riven with the more tenacious examples of flora. The great hall, once the scene of so many social triumphs, was now a sad monument to times past. The roof had caved in at one end and the gash thus created had been expertly speared by the sun. The heart of Tapser House lay somewhere here, along with the rubble and the litter left by schoolchildren, and along its arteries ran the ghosts of servants and monks, still performing the ritualistic functions they had spent their lifetimes perfecting.

This really was the ideal sanctuary for him away from his companions: peaceful, dreamlike, immense. They could scour the woods for him as much as they liked, yet only he could decide when this farcical day would end. He closed his eyes, experiencing all the feelings connected with the most beautiful word in the English language:

Tranquillity.

He could hear voices, female voices, growing in volume by the second. They were coming towards him – that was clear – but there was nothing to do except await capture. He crouched down like a cornered animal (playing the game as though his life depended on it!) and eyed the doorway. Suddenly they were there, Constance and Emily, and then, miraculously, they were gone, not even glancing in his direction.

He stood up, with no other idea but to follow them. They eventually found their way to the back of the house and sat down on an old marble seat, close enough to the house for him to hear. He was feeling reckless somehow, expecting to be discovered imminently, but also, for the first time, enjoying the game. Unable to stop smiling, he stood at an open window space, imbued with a sense of power. He even guiltily tapped the wall, expecting to be spotted, but only Constance turned round and then somehow seemed to miss him. They were chatting about schooldays and the excitement of secret midnight feasts. Of course he knew the morality of his actions was open to question, but just as he was about to leave he heard his name.

CONSTANCE: Do you suppose they've found George yet?

EMILY: H'm. All I know is the word 'game' is meaningless to my husband. I daresay right now he's wearing that earnest expression down a badger's hole.

CONSTANCE: He's very noble, you know. On the way here I was nearly run over by a motorcar. George raged against the driver in a most becoming manner.

As Constance proceeded to expatiate on the incident, George's smile broadened and his chest swelled out. To have his actions described in such heroic terms and against such a magnificent setting! Somehow he had chanced upon this Shakespearean kingdom in the woods and he himself was playing the part of Puck, rising, almost, above the ground, every word arriving with thrilling urgency.

EMILY: God, how frightful. George isn't lacking in courage, that's true, but I don't think he was just defending your honour. He hates motorcars. Sees them as a threat to civilization. One nearly crashing into a lady cyclist would have upset him beyond measure.

CONSTANCE: I must say the way he treats women is wonderful.

EMILY: So long as you accept the views which go with it, I suppose. His ideal would be for me to darn his socks and warm his slippers.

CONSTANCE: And look after the baby.

EMILY: Precisely.

CONSTANCE: But isn't that what you'd want as well? What every woman aspires to?

EMILY: My dear, I think you and I have very different notions of how to secure dominion over one's husband.

CONSTANCE: George is terribly amusing, though, isn't he? When the men were arguing about politics he was practically shaking.

EMILY: Ha, you saw that then. That was why I calmed him down.

CONSTANCE: Does he have fits?

EMILY [laughing]: Not quite, dear, no. The war affected him profoundly, not just physically. In a way he's like a little chuckle-headed boy who feels he can never win at games because of his leg. I see that look of frustration on his face when an issue crops up. He thinks his first-hand experience of that silly war gives him some expert view of life. But – really, you know, he has no understanding of people. None.

CONSTANCE: But he must understand you.

EMILY: Thank God, no. There's something not quite satisfactory about being understood. Not enough mystery, if you know what I mean. Anyhow, George is too busy wrapped up in little hatreds to assess people properly.

CONSTANCE: Oh dear.

EMILY: I don't mean he isn't a likeable soul. There are only one or two people he doesn't get on with.

CONSTANCE: He doesn't much care for Teddy, does he?

EMILY: No. Well, I suppose they're just very different. Teddy's younger. Craves excitement more than George. He's very attractive, don't you think?

CONSTANCE: Who, George?

EMILY: Con-stance!

CONSTANCE: Oh – Teddy, you mean. Well, I suppose he is. But if you want my opinion, I think Teddy's a bit dull. Always talking about money.

EMILY: No, no. He can be wonderfully amusing when he wants to be.

CONSTANCE: So why doesn't George—

EMILY: Get on with him? Oh, some trifling reason, I expect. Probably something to do with his appearance. I know George would never dress so dashingly for an event like this. He probably thinks in his baggy knickerbockers he's the height of fashion.

CONSTANCE: That's cruel!

EMILY: Then, of course, Teddy has hair. Lots of it.

CONSTANCE: You're shocking!

EMILY: Dreadfully bad form, isn't it? Especially since—

CONSTANCE [taking hold of Emily's arm]: Let's head back now, shall we? Before it gets late.

They sauntered off, conversing still, but with voices growing fainter and fainter until a hush had descended. No movement disturbed the scene and only a lone figure remained, looking with leaden eyes in the direction they'd gone, his body slumped, a huge weight clamped to his chest. At last he sank to the floor, into the dust and cobwebs, reaching out a hand and running his fingers in a line along the wall beside him, feeling the indentations caused by the flaking plaster.

No, there was nothing magical about this place. Nothing. It was simply an old house gone to seed.

The rest of the afternoon passed in a daze, George giving himself up to a victorious doctor, the picnic party breaking up with startling efficiency, the stale platitudes as they prepared to go home.

There was one last note to finish the day.

Emily and Pilling had already gone, leaving the rest of them to wend their way back to the bicycles waiting patiently at the foot of a huge oak tree. After much searching and scratching of heads they realized to their horror that they'd been robbed. Where there'd been four machines there were now only three.

A long discussion ensued.

The ladies must have a bicycle each; the doctor could walk. No, George ventured, it should be him, the party's host, who felt obliged to go on foot. No, the doctor half-heartedly countered, he and George should take it in turns. No, the rest of them concurred, that would just hold everyone up. Why instead, suggested Constance, couldn't the doctor and his wife, as a married couple, take two of the machines, while she stayed behind with George to search for the missing one? No, George retorted, slightly perturbed by that last suggestion (tacitly accepted by the doctor), Constance should go as well, and he would walk, because, quite honestly, he *wanted* to; and, he might have added, 'because I'd prefer to be alone and you're all taxing my nerves'. Amazingly, this self-sacrificing gesture was still not to the liking of Constance.

'But why can't we look for the missing bicycle together?'

'Because, my dear,' the doctor concluded, 'it's gone.'

George watched them weaving their way towards the horizon until, like three little ants, they conquered one of the larger hills. In the distance the drowning sun was firing vivid mauves and magentas into the sky, while the trees and hedgerows took on a delicate blend of light and shade. There was scarcely a sound at all save the occasional owl hooting or the super-abundant crickets with their mating cries.

Over the next four miles his attempts to erase Emily's unbidden words from his memory merely confirmed that he could recall all of them. If one could literally 'paint a mood', then his would have been various shades of black. The most saturnine of these thoughts were saved for the steepest climb of the walk, the most painful for his forgotten leg. He gained the summit with clenched teeth quite prepared to meet his Calvary.

Why, after all this time, was Emily still a mystery? He'd carried the assumption before this afternoon that her mastery over him was their little secret. But not only had she embarrassed him at the picnic, he'd overheard her insulting him to an old friend of hers; moreover, comparing him unfavourably to another man. It was too dreadful to contemplate and he sat down by the verge, biting into his fingernails, attempting to find a more tolerable explanation.

After all, Emily had not said that she didn't love him. Nor had she said that she loved Edward Pilling. No doubt she had left the picnic with the man as a social obligation. Remember: she had accused Pilling of being money-grubbing which, whether true or false, was at least a source of contention between them. A good deal of trust had been lost. His pride had been dented. But he still had the opportunity to change Emily's opinion. Surely she didn't see him in a wholly negative light? What about their history together?

Yes, the key to it all, the answers to these questions, the way through to Emily's heart, lay in the past ...

4

Emily

George had met Emily shortly after he'd returned from the war in South Africa. He'd been staying with Henry Beakston, an old school acquaintance, at his town house in Mayfair, and, through Beakston, had received invitations to various functions – his popularity rising, together with the British Army's, after the Relief of Mafeking. It was the height of the London season, the endless merry-go-round of parties, concerts, famous sporting occasions and the like.

Scattered amid these events, yet nonetheless essential, was Lady Chevening's Ball, a Mecca for the rich and famous, who in that year were licking their lips at the prospect of being introduced to Prince Edward, the future king. If the evening was slightly spoiled through his non-appearance – he finally summoned up the willpower to stay with his sick mother, Victoria – it was more than compensated for in George's case by talking to someone who appeared to be, in her manner and bearing at least, just as regal as the missing guest.

Strangely enough, when he first saw Emily it did not strike him that she was attractive in anything more than a theoretical way. She was dressed quite simply and elegantly, white overlaying white, a high collar boned up to the base of her ears, the only concession to fashion being the sixteen-button gloves which painted her arms. But the second time he noticed her, when they came face to face on the balcony away from the glare of the electric lights, her features seemed to take on a more subtle aspect. Her hair, especially, was beautiful, a swirl of shimmering silk which flopped, almost carelessly, onto her shoulders. She asked him why he wasn't dancing and he explained that he bore a limp and that he felt London wasn't ready for a new dance step which involved hobbling and twisting about in agony – to which she graciously laughed.

It was a wonderfully warm evening with the gentlest of breezes rising up to fan their faces. George would have liked to stay in that spot forever but, to quell concern over the length of their absence, he accompanied Emily back to her chaperon, obtaining permission to pay an afternoon call the following day. Emily was staying for the season at the Belgravia address of an old friend of the family, and George discovered to his good fortune that the lady in question had been an acquaintance of his mother's, elevating him already into the ranks of worthwhile suitors ...

Over the next few weeks his attempts to impress Emily became the central concern of his life. Her laughter, which he was forever trying to provoke, sent a ripple down his spine, and he found himself thinking about her all the time, sweetly at the end of the day as he lay his head on the pillow but with an empty feeling of despair at five o'clock in the morning when he thought of life without her. Always, though, on the way to see her, he felt all-conquering, his body suffused with an unequalled passion – comparable only to the inverted state of his spirit when he made his bedraggled way back home.

It was evident that she was in complete control. Strong and dignified though he tried to be, he felt every slight acutely. She could wait till the end of a perfect evening – giggling hopelessly at his jokes – before saying that she'd spent the previous night in the company of a man who'd made her cry with laughter. At such moments, having made such Herculean efforts to impress her, he felt utterly drained, not to say worthless.

And yet at other times he felt an abundance of confidence. After all, he was the world's leading expert in her life, storing away facts as wide-ranging as her middle name and the date of her birthday to which of her friends she liked that week and why. He would make womanly statements which would astound her, commenting, for instance, on the shapely symmetry of her Russian jacket and how perfectly it matched the plume in her hat. (He'd overheard a friend of hers earlier that day make a similar remark but with qualifications concerning the plume.)

In speaking about himself and his own exploits he'd naturally select the more significant moments – in a life which seemed to veer uneasily at times between comedy and tragedy – and she was especially touched by the story he told about his brother, Geoffrey. The latter had confided to George on the troopship destined for the Cape that he'd been involved in a brief affair a couple of months earlier with a lady who was ten years older and from a much poorer background. Their relationship would no doubt have petered out were it not for the fact that shortly before he'd left the country she'd informed him that she was in the family way. In spite of George's obvious shock at this turn of events, Geoffrey appeared remarkably calm, merely saying that if anything happened to him he'd be obliged if George could pass on the news. The matter wasn't forgotten – although George could never seriously contemplate the death of his brother – but there were other, more immediate, concerns on the horizon.

A week later they were on the point of engaging the Boers for the first time. Two solid days of marching and a trek overnight had brought them to Belmont, where the Boers occupied a cluster of hills. The plan had been to launch an attack on the enemy's flank, but George's battalion had lost their bearings in the darkness and found in the clearing light that they were directly opposite their foe, perched on top of a ridge a thousand yards away. The decision was taken to advance – tactics that had served well enough on India's North-West Frontier – and they moved forward, breaking into a run as the first bullets zipped through the air, stirring up the dust at their feet. George, in the vanguard, had just reached the lower slopes and was fixing his bayonet when he felt a sharp hammer blow to his knee, sending him plummeting to earth. For a moment the world was a blur, every sound muffled, the time stretching out ... before consciousness returned with a rush and a deafening roar burst upon his eardrums. He fumbled around on the ground for his rifle, adjusted his helmet, and hopped the few yards to the next level of the hill, dragging himself up the incline by clutching on to bushes, rocks, tufts of grass. Another bullet hit his forearm and he fell flat on his face, lying in the dirt, panting heavily. Men were going past him now, including Geoffrey, clambering over the rocks a few yards to his right. A shot caught the other in the shoulder, making him rear up, then a second bullet hit him in the chest and he fell backwards down the slope. More and more men overtook George in an action that was to prove successful, but his eyes were averted to where his brother lay motionless, a dark stain showing on his khaki uniform.

The Battle of Belmont marked the end of George's war. He was taken away to hospital to be informed a week later that his mother had recently died of a heart attack. It seemed an age before he left South Africa, but in that time he came to a significant conclusion – indeed, in view of the circumstances he felt he had no alternative. On his return home he would propose marriage to the lady his brother had got into trouble.

'No!'

Emily had sat through his account in respectful silence but evidently could suppress herself no longer.

'It wasn't an easy decision, I must admit. I kept thinking of her, though, waiting for Geoffrey – the agony of hearing about his death. Then, of course, the shame she'd have to go through, bringing the child up on her own.'

He was perturbed to see the beginnings of what looked like tears in Emily's eyes. She rose from the *chaise longue* and gazed out of the window for a few moments.

'You've just proved, George – never mind how – why you're my closest friend. There's something truly wonderful in your nature.'

A deep flush suffused his face and he cleared his throat.

'Well, I'm sure many others would have done likewise. Anyhow, on my first weekend back home I made my way to her address in Walworth. She lived in the last house in a terrace of six, next to a yard.'

'Not a very attractive area?'

'Not really, no.'

'Was *she* attractive?'

'Yes, quite, I'd say.'

'Well, judging by your usual appraisal of women's looks she sounds perfectly hideous.'

'No, that's not true. The – er – bulge was very apparent. She showed me into the sitting-room and I told her about Geoffrey. When I'd finished she lowered her head. He was a good friend, she said, and it was kind of me to pass on the news. I thought all in all she managed to hide her feelings wonderfully well. We spoke a bit more about Geoffrey. Then I asked her one or two discreet questions about her condition.'

'What did you cover? I can't imagine!'

'Dates, mainly.'

'Of what! I'm sorry, George! Forgive me!'

'I think I was playing for time before my proposal. The more I saw of the place, the more I felt for the child she was bringing into the world. There was a damp, sickly smell, the wallpaper was peeling – oh, it was horrible. I asked her how she survived and she said in a perfectly ordinary tone, "Well, there's the pawnbroker."'

'The pawnbroker?'

'Awful, isn't it? She was pawning her possessions one by one and didn't even seem to think it mattered. I told her that I'd heard enough. That I was prepared to propose an alternative to her present situation. I began by explaining the importance of education, how it was essential her child was provided with suitable surroundings in which to study – how, in addition, I was sure I was speaking for my brother as well – when I heard the front door open.

'The next moment this huge brute stood in the doorway – dark hair crawling all over his forearms and across half his face. "This is my pawnbroker," she said with a smile. I tell you I was incensed. Here was the selfish creature who felt he could exploit this wretched woman's poverty. "So you rely on *this*" – I gestured towards him – "to support you?" I wanted the brute to argue his case, but she only looked offended, gazing at him before turning back to me. "Well, he is my husband."'

Emily liked George's jokes especially when he was the butt of them. (No doubt she'd have preferred him to have been beaten to a pulp by the pawnbroker rather than the hasty retreat which occurred.) She soon realized that she could exploit his good nature – he was never happier than when sent on an errand – and for a while he endured constant degradation.

'George, feed me!' she'd say, leaning back on her *chaise longue*. To which he'd retort, 'You can only push an Erskine so far!'

His method of rebellion, in fact, was *not* to disobey her orders – which she eventually tired of giving – but pursue other objectives, little attempts to kidnap her mind. He'd buy small, appropriate presents to let her know how thoughtful he was, or write nonsense poems which brought out the lovable side of his character.

Of course it had to end. He became aware in about their third or fourth week of acquaintanceship – during which he'd contrived to see Emily virtually every day – that she was becoming slightly bored with him, at least that was his impression. He felt exhausted as well, his conversational powers pared to the bone. He stopped seeing her so often – receiving no encouragement or discouragement – and when they did meet up tried to deduce what it was about her which had so enraptured him.

She did have imperfections, naturally. Her teeth weren't flawless. Her hair could look a trifle dishevelled at times – in spite of the fact that it was probably her favourite topic of conversation and she could involve him in clueless discussions about the latest fashions. Her dress sense was a touch conservative too – although, again, this had its advantages when they were joined by the sort of man who could only appreciate a woman when she was half-naked.

It was academic, though, really. She had captured him whole. Love was the strongest and sweetest emotion – the great poets were right! He had discovered his perfect match and the two of them – with their eyes and gestures alone – had made a secret pact which could never be broken. She had shown him a different, more enticing, world to which he was addicted and could never leave.

Furthermore, he had to tell her. Their relationship had so far been conducted within the bounds of convention, but the recent coldness she'd shown him could only be attributed to frustration, her feminine impatience at his lack of enterprise. They hadn't disclosed their feelings for one another.

One afternoon she invited him for a walk and, as they were strolling through the park, his heart pounding, he turned to her.

'Emily, forgive me. I must tell you that I care for you immensely.'

She stopped, gazing at him with a strange expression, a mixture of surprise and pity.

'That's sweet of you, George. I care for you too.'

'No, I mean that I have feelings for you. Beyond friendship.'

He longed to embrace her – *Oh, George, I've waited so long for this moment* ... – but she turned away, her head bowed.

'Oh. I see. Well, I don't know quite what to say. I do care for you, George, you know that. But I've always seen you as a friend. Besides, you don't really know me.'

'But I do. At least I feel that you've shown me enough of yourself—'

'You know nothing. *Nothing*.' She closed her eyes for a second. 'I'm sorry. That sounded harsh.'

She was letting him down lightly. There was no hope. And yet, even as she was breaking his heart, he realized that he was smiling in spite of himself. He had pictured her being overjoyed at his revelation and it was too soon to contemplate any other reaction. When she told him that she didn't deserve him, that his love would be better suited elsewhere, he felt like crying out that *she* was the one, that he wished more than anything to make her happy.

Still, when they finally parted, the world had changed. He was used to great disappointment, but now he felt an overwhelming sense of humiliation as well. His gaudy clothes, worn specially for the occasion, felt sticky and ridiculous – God, *he* was ridiculous! He had been acting the part of a Don Juan, leaving the real him trailing behind. What on earth had he been thinking? What on earth...?

He sloped back to Beakston's house and buried himself under the covers of his bed, waiting for death. You know nothing. *Nothing*. Well, that was clear enough, wasn't it? The scene replayed itself again and again in his mind, the result growing worse with each performance. What had they been talking about? Oh, yes, the effect of the sun on a pale complexion. And he had cut into the conversation, saying to her, more or less shouting, Forgive me! Forgive me, Emily! I must tell you I am the world's greatest buffoon! And the expression on her face, not knowing where to look; the polite but firm response, saying in effect, Yes, she knew, but she didn't want to say anything. Even now his cheeks were burning with the shame of it. Red, bright red, stretching from his neck to his temples. That must have looked good as well ...

Oh, Lord. Oh, heavenly Father. Perhaps that was what she was referring to when she was talking about the sun and a pale complexion. Dropping a hint about his appearance which only the world's greatest buffoon could have missed. Oh, idiot, idiot, idiot ...

Yes, their friendship was over ...

Without a doubt.

5

Emily (continued)

For six long days he saw nothing of Emily, and though, during that time, he spoke to people and they spoke back, it all seemed meaningless, as if they were cameo players in a drama whose main scene of action was elsewhere. How could she be so unmoved by his disappearance? Not try to get back in touch with him at all? It was unjust. He had performed at his best and been rejected. A sickness had taken hold of him, but possibly there was a cure. He would try to forget about her, living life beyond death.

He intoned confidence-boosting aphorisms to the bathroom mirror; placed notes on Beakston's belongings – much to his friend's consternation – such as, 'You are not suffering from a mental breakdown!' and conducted errands for neighbours overcome by his philanthropy. (Beakston was of the opinion that, like himself, George should adopt opium as his trusty mistress.) Remarkably, within a couple of days, his eating and sleeping habits reverted to practically normal and, because he was no longer seeing *her*, he didn't feel under pressure. Indeed, he expected to get better very shortly, fight his infatuation, and eventually wake up into a new post-Emily world, stronger and wiser.

And then she wrote to him.

My dear George
Why haven't you been to see me? I've been missing you, my little soldier! Please call round when you have the time.
Your (hopefully) good friend
Emily

Underneath her name she'd inscribed three kisses, each of which he contemplated for some time after. The letter, brief though it was, had plainly caused her a great deal of thought: the hurt and reproachful tone admitting weakness, coupled with the frank second sentence, then the sweetly sarcastic third. Obviously she wasn't just a friend – they both knew that. She had finally realized she needed him and he was going to fulfil his destiny.

He arrived on her doorstep the next morning and, even though a bridge party was in full swing, she at once excused herself from her hostess and the other guests and devoted herself to him. She looked quite exquisite, wearing a blouse made of the finest black silk, with leg-of-mutton sleeves closely hugging her slender forearms. The temporary break allowed him to see all her faults more clearly – her love, for example, of the most trivial gossip, as well as her insistence on using the adjective 'divine' (which in due course she shortened to 'deevy') – but somehow this only made him cherish her more. They went back to seeing each other on a regular basis and, blessed in his association with such an angel, he felt blissfully happy. While other men flitted in and out of her life – and she'd regale him with asides about so-and-so being terrifyingly good-looking, or so-and-so being hysterically funny – none of them was as hysterically, terrifyingly *dogged* as himself.

A month went by. Much as George wanted to fall out of love with Emily, it never happened. In some ways she reminded him of his mother, the only other woman he'd been close to, and to end their association would have been akin to experiencing another bereavement, just unthinkable. There were moments, too, when she seemed weak and vulnerable, almost dependent on him, when he could see that she valued their friendship. Significantly she invited him to her address in the country to meet her father, a rather dour gentleman with muttonchop whiskers, and in society at large their status as a couple on the brink of matrimony seemed increasingly to be taken for granted. Indeed, the fact that others were talking about them, and that Emily was sensitive to their opinions, was made clear to him on a visit to Covent Garden to see the opera.

'Francesca thinks I'm not being fair on you. She says I'm trying to turn you into someone you're not, just for my own benefit. That I've effectively neutered you.'

They were seated together in a box before the start of the performance. His hands automatically crept along his lap in a protective
capacity.

'She says you always agree to everything I say. But that's not true,
is it?'

He suppressed an impulse to say, 'I don't know, what do you think?'
She was obviously quite serious, perhaps even feeling a little guilty
about her treatment of him.

'What does she know about our relationship?' he asked, hoping to
glean some information on the subject himself.

'Exactly. Anyhow, she's got some strange views on men. She thinks
they're all prey to their base instincts. That within seconds of meeting
someone they're attracted to they'd happily indulge in some sort of
orgiastic frenzy.'

'I prefer to lead up to such things,' he remarked.

'Men are not animals. Not if we purport to be a civilized society.'
She shook her head, letting out a sigh. 'Oh, I don't know. It's not her
opinion of men that's the problem; it's her solution. She thinks women
ought to capitulate to men entirely – give away the one weapon we
possess. That's why she feels sorry for you. She thinks I'm a coquette.'

'Tuh!' said George.

She twisted round in her seat. 'We have disagreements, don't we,
George? There must be times when you think I'm talking rot.
Prattling on about the role of women and the poor while living a life
of luxury and employing servants. Be honest with me now. Do you
ever really disagree with me?'

He hesitated. 'Well, now and then, I suppose. But the way you
express yourself is so charming.'

'Don't ever enter Parliament, George,' she said with a laugh.
'They'll tear you to ribbons. I am serious about this, though. I *know*
you disagree with me over a lot of things. Do you think I'm going
through a passing fad, is that it? Is that why you tolerate my views?
Come on, answer me. Your life would be so much easier with another
woman.'

She was getting quite excited and he felt under bombardment. His
powers of concentration hadn't really been the same since the mention
of orgiastic frenzies.

'Your views are part of you. How can I not take them seriously? In a perfect world there should be votes for women, of course there should. If my outlook is a little more cynical, at least I have you to remind me things could be perfect.'

She leant back in her chair. 'Ah, George, George! I feel sure I ought to find such a sentiment unutterably feeble. But there you are, it still touches me somehow. Who knows? Francesca may even be right about me carrying out an experiment on you. All I can say is, no matter how it looks, I do appreciate you, I really do.' She touched him on the arm and smiled, sending a warm shiver down his spine. 'Have patience with me, won't you, George? I just need more time.'

The curtain was rising and, though she didn't elaborate on this statement, he could have listened to thirty cats caterwauling that night with a blissful expression on his face.

Not that he didn't still suffer the odd setback. On one occasion the two of them were discussing the inventiveness of Thomas Edison, Emily dropping a remark about how she admired intellectuals. He decided to take up chess, determined to teach her the rules and then overwhelm her repeatedly in displays of unerring brilliance, his face a study in brooding deliberation. Meticulously, he played through the games of Emanuel Lasker and Wilhelm Steinitz, but while moving the pieces for both sides a quite novel idea occurred to him. Why not compose a game, playing the moves for Black and White, cunningly leaving a hidden message? Show himself off as a romantic genius! The thought embedded itself so persuasively that eventually he came up with the following *pièce de résistance*:

1. P-K4, P-K4; 2. Kt-KB3, Kt-QB3; 3. B-Kt5, P-QR3; 4. B-B4, P-QKt4; 5. B-K2, P-Q4; 6. Kt-B3, PxP; 7. QKtxKP, B-Q3; 8. P-QKt3, Kt-Q5; 9. B-Q3, Kt-K2; 10. P-QR4, B-Q2; 11. P-B3, Kt-K3; 12. B-Kt2, O-O; 13. Kt(K4)-Kt5, P-Kt3; 14. P-R4, Kt-Q4; 15. P-Kt3, R-Kt1; 16. PxP, PxP; 17. R-R5, P-QB3; 18. P-QKt4, B-B2; 19. QR-R2, Kt-Kt3; 20. Q-K2, R-K1; 21. P-B4, Kt-Kt2; 22. Kt-R2, Kt-R5; 23. B-B3, B-Q3; 24. Q-K3, Q-B2; 25. K-K2, R-R1; 26. KR-R1, KR-Kt1; 27. K-K1, Kt-Kt3; 28. RxR, RxR; 29. RxR, KtxR; 30. Kt-K4, Kt-K3; 31. B-K2, Kt-Kt3; 32. Kt-Kt4, P-R4; 33. Kt(K4)-B6 ch, K-Kt2; 34. Q-R6 mate.

He sent Emily a note with the game inscribed in his neatest hand. And then waited an extra day before calling.

Oh, the anticipation! He walked for miles, gleefully imagining her delight upon reaching the final position, overcome by wonder at his cleverness.

Alas, it was all in vain! Her reaction, when he did pay her a visit, was quite uncharitable. For the first few minutes she did not even mention the subject. And when at last she did produce his note, it was unfolded and examined as though it were an unfavourable medical certificate.

'George, what does this mean?'

'You've played it through?'

'I wouldn't know how to. I couldn't understand what it was meant to achieve.'

'Shall we go through it together?'

'George! Just tell me what it means!'

'Well, you play through all the moves and, at the point where White delivers checkmate, the pieces form themselves into a heart.'

There was a lengthy pause while she looked at him incredulously.

'Do you like playing chess?'

'I think it's a game of beautiful reasoning, immensely satisfying to the logical mind.'

'Did you rehearse that line?'

Infuriatingly, she was right. It was all going wrong.

'You said you admired intellectuals,' he said in desperation.

'Did I? I don't recall. How long did this take you, anyhow?'

'Not long,' he replied, hiding the fact that it had taken him at least four hours.

'But why? I still don't understand why.'

The conversation was exasperating. He had the impression that she was secretly poking fun at him and that later he'd be held up to ridicule in front of her friends.

'I just wanted to see if I could do it.'

She gave out a short, derisive laugh.

'Open your mouth, George.'

He parted his lips.

'No, wider ... *wider!*'

He duly obliged and in one movement she screwed up the note and aimed it at his mouth. He tried to lunge for it but missed.

A month later Emily mentioned his chess game to a friend, telling her just how logical George was. That was all the encouragement he needed to compose a crossword, the clues – a cocktail of wicked and confidential jokes – consisting of events in Emily's life. Unfortunately, again, despite all his efforts, she did not complete it, appearing to be far more interested in what had prompted him to write it.

Clearly, his self-respect was suffering. He was profoundly depressed.

What he wanted to do, desperately, was air his feelings. Again. But on every occasion he tried to raise the subject closest to his heart, she succeeded in deflecting the conversation on to lighter topics.

It had to end. He had had enough. He was leaving, going on a tour of Europe that would last at least a year. He told her in earnest of his intention – a complete fabrication – and awaited her response.

'I'll miss you, George,' she said, a little glum-faced. No tears, no impassioned entreaties.

'The only circumstance which would induce me to stay,' he continued, religiously following his script, 'is marriage. Will you marry me, Emily?'

There was a moment's silence and then a peal of laughter, a positive cascade which seared through his heart, reducing him almost to tears.

'Are you serious?' she asked eventually.

'You know I am.'

'Oh, my, this is a pretty pickle, isn't it?'

His original intention had been to say that she needn't reply straight away, but the words, obviously superfluous, died on his lips.

'I realize you don't feel the same way as I feel about you. I hope, though, that over time you'll come to—' Pity was etched on her face and he choked on his words. 'No, never mind. I can see I'm making a fool of myself.'

He stood up, preparing to leave.

'Where are you going? You were doing so well.'

'You're making fun of me.'

'No, no. It was simply the shock of it all. Please, George. Forgive me.'

He hesitated a moment, breathing heavily. 'Perhaps I should write a letter or something.'

He began to make his way out, but she said after him, 'Are you going to unpack then?'

'Unpack?' He felt obliged to turn round.

'Of course. You didn't expect me to turn you down, did you?'

She smiled angelically; at which point he broke down and cried.

6

Marriage

The marriage took place on 28 June, 1902, at St Paul's in Knightsbridge. The reason for the prolonged engagement was because the feelings of the happy couple were continually ridiculed by the bride's father. Lord Delsey, the venerable Tory grandee – and well-known cuckold whose wife had left him for another man a few years after Emily was born – was against George because he had not heard of him (and therefore could not trust him). True, he was impressed by his valiant services abroad, but then why not consider other young men, patricians, who had similar war records and at least had the support of more respectable families?

With George himself his opposition took the form of trying to persuade him of his daughter's unsuitability for marriage, demonstrating in the process a ruthless disregard for her feelings. Emily, he assured George over the port when just the two of them were left at the table, was a rebellious spirit. Owing to the absence of her mother at a critical time in her life, she had developed her own ideas – dangerous, of course, for any man. Her interest in socialism had taken her away from her own class and produced in her a sentimental weakness for waifs and strays.

Whether this was a reference to George's limp or not, the noble lord proceeded to extend his argument by drawing comparisons between Emily and her mother, the implication being that Emily was equally capable of causing a scandal. It would behove George to think long and hard about what he was letting himself in for and – the upshot of it all – he would not give his consent to the match until a year at least had gone by.

George came away from this interview with the heaviest of hearts, and yet, after thinking about the matter and with Emily's encouragement, he came to the conclusion that it had gone rather well. A year wasn't so long to wait for a lifetime of bliss and, in the meantime, he could make himself useful, acquiring and holding down a job as an assistant editor on the *Boy's Own Paper*. During this time he saw Emily as much as he could, fended off new suitors who appeared on the scene, and wrote numerous letters to his betrothed, buoyed up by a constant hope.

Yet the frustration did not end there. He was just approaching the end of the year when Lord Delsey had a stroke, leaving him paralysed along one side of his body. The doctors, so Emily informed him, said that he didn't have long to live and any shock – such as news presumably of his daughter's impending nuptials to a social inferior – could well deal the fatal blow. If George could only maintain his patience a while longer …

Yes, he could wait. Of greater concern was whether Emily was still resolved on the idea of marriage. The more time that elapsed, the more his insecurities played on him and the more he viewed himself as an interloper in this rarefied world of privilege. Nothing was said to this effect, of course, and he was treated in exactly the same way as all the other guests to Stockley Hall, but he could not avoid feeling a little presumptuous nevertheless. Such an extravagant lifestyle and so many servants, the entire operation running with such perfect correctness! Mrs Proops, the housekeeper, with her old-fashioned style of dress, lips pursed and eyes looking askance, engendered a sense of awe on her own.

In the end Lord Delsey never saw the announcement of the wedding in the *Morning Post*. He passed away quietly, leaving his 900-acre Hampshire estate to his only child. A new life had opened for George and he was immediately taken with his role as land manager, assisting the gamekeeper, Hayes, in his duties. (There was a surprising amount of work to do: the four tenant farms were in a state of disrepair, and the coverts, once the pride of the county, had not been tended for years.) George had achieved his most cherished desire and only one problem remained to darken the horizon.

Within a year of seeing Emily she had confided in him a terrible secret, one which had bedevilled her friendships with men. At the age of twelve she had been assaulted by a friend of her father's. She would not reveal who it was (despite his torturing questions), but this diabolical incident, as well as making her distrustful of the intentions of men, had somehow made her feel ashamed of the sensual side of her nature.

Even in his case her attitude was ambivalent. It was true that his limp inhibited his potential as a threat and, unlike the monster who attacked her, he did not come from the same social class. But he was still, undeniably, a man, albeit one who happened to be her husband.

The condition laid down before their marriage was that:

Physical relations would go no further than if they were the dearest of friends.

This was not an immutable state of affairs, but to help clarify matters the earliest review of the situation would take place after precisely one year of marriage. (Of course, Emily could change her mind any time before then.) Nobody else was to know of this arrangement and she was prepared to accept his word of honour as binding on the matter. Other aspects of their marriage could proceed along conventional lines.

Absurd as it seemed, he was quite happy to comply with these terms. Not only did he sleep in a separate bedroom, next to Emily's, but to show his willingness to respect her privacy he treated her room as out of bounds – an endeavour aided by the fact that she locked her door every evening. (The only other key to the room belonged to the ever reliable Mrs Proops who was permitted to open her door and serve her tea at eight-thirty each morning.)

Thus far his experience with women had been incredibly limited – not going beyond a fond embrace – and he was more than nervous of appearing a novice in the company of Emily. The important aspect was that she felt at ease with him, and, high-mindedly enough, he saw their relationship as one based on thoughts and feelings, rather than ignoble lust. She had assured him that she loved him *because* he wasn't like other men, not prone to the same irresistible desires, and that if he could only wait ...

Unfortunately, it had to be said that the novelty value of her scheme didn't last very long. After a while he didn't want just to nibble at forbidden fruit, he wanted to devour it. The injustice of being locked out every night was especially galling, even if this, apparently, was an ancient habit. (He looked forward to the time when both of them would be locked in her room!) Furthermore, he had overlooked that their chances of having children were, for the time being, postponed. His chief mistake had been to think that she hadn't been altogether serious, that perhaps within a matter of days rather than weeks she would realize her fears were groundless.

Every so often, normally after an especially agreeable evening, he'd make delicate suggestions along these lines, but on every occasion would be cordially rebuffed. His self-esteem, so high in the period directly preceding their wedding, reverted to its old level. Was he even married in the true sense of the word? What if Emily – God forbid – brought a nullity suit? Presumably he'd receive some warning in advance, but the situation wasn't without precedent, was it? He ploughed through all the literature he could find on the subject. In the case of John Ruskin, his marriage was annulled on the grounds of his 'incurable impotency'. Incurable impotency, for heaven's sake! While hostesses promptly struck Ruskin off their party lists, his former wife, as if she had a point to prove, had gone on to have eight children with Millais.

Well, so much for the future. Presumably some people would suppose he simply preferred the company of men, leading to invitations to the odd event at least. Or perhaps his marriage would survive after all and his gravestone would bear the inscription, 'Renowned for his chastity'. But this was hopeless, thinking in these terms! If only he had a greater knowledge of the practical side of lovemaking and it wasn't all so impenetrable. Up till now the sole advice he'd received had come from his brother, following on from their previous conversation on the troopship. The subject of the other's promiscuity was still on George's mind and, finding himself alone with Geoffrey on the first long march of the campaign, he'd tried as delicately as possible to ascertain exactly what being with a woman was like.

'I'll introduce you to one of my lady friends when we get home,' came the response. 'They'll take good care of you, I promise.'

'No, no, it's all right,' George said hastily. 'I'd rather ... you know ...'

'Make an ass of yourself?'

'No. Not that. But these women of yours. They're different, aren't they? They see the whole thing as a pleasurable experience.'

'Well, if you're lucky, certainly.'

'What I mean is, it isn't seemly, is it, for a lady...?' He took a deep breath. 'I thought that any impulse in that direction could only properly be awoken by a husband.'

A smile broke out on Geoffrey's face and he gave George a friendly pat on the shoulder. 'Oh, my dear chap, my dear chap. You're quite right – yes, but of course you are. Look, no one really knows what to do at first. All I knew in the beginning was what Mother told me. I was interested, you see, just as you are. A bit younger, perhaps, than you. Anyhow, she gave me some advice.'

'Advice about...?'

'Yes.'

'She really...?'

'Yes.'

'But this is incredible. What did she say?'

'Oh, I forget now.'

George gave the other a long stare. The sun was burning down on them and he was feeling hotter than ever.

'She didn't say anything, did she?'

'No, no, you're wrong, quite wrong. Ah, wait a minute, it's coming back to me now. Yes ... yes, that's right. She talked about elbows.'

'Elbows?'

'Troublesome beggars. Got to watch where you put 'em.'

'Elbows?'

Even in his naivety George was fairly sure the primary concern of his wife on their wedding night wouldn't be his elbows.

'That's what I said. The point is, you don't want to flatten the poor girl.'

'So is that it, then?' said George at length.

'What do you mean, "Is that it, then"? It's good advice, believe me.' A look of revelation dawned in the face of the speaker. 'Ah, no, there is another thing, now that I think about it. I don't know whether I should tell you, though.'

'Go on.' At last. At long last.

'Well, all right. It concerns Father. When he was with Mother he used to pretend he was Napoleon.'

Geoffrey paused for a reaction, but George's expression remained unchanged. Some idiot had just made a remark of unqualified preposterousness, but nothing which affected him at any rate.

'God only knows where he got the idea. There was no dressing up – 'least so far as I'm aware. Apparently he used to talk about flank attacks, rearguard actions, that sort of thing.'

George wore a heavy frown. His father was a serious-minded banker, a well-respected member of the community.

'Matter of fact,' Geoffrey went on, 'I've tried it once or twice myself, pretending to be Napoleon. Essential to make it clear you're not in earnest, of course. I've found a heavy French accent – the occasional *Sacré bleu!* – is most effective.'

'This is absurd. I'm not listening to this any longer.'

'All I'm saying is it doesn't hurt to jolly things along a bit. Ladies are more anxious about such matters on the whole, so if you can put them at their ease. Just a thought, old chap.'

It certainly wasn't much to go on, but at least it was more helpful than anything he could find subsequently in print. Browning and Swinburne provided no guidance whatever, and Shakespeare's *Venus and Adonis* and the *Sonnets* were equally unavailing. Studying the lives of the great lovers seemed promising at first but also failed to be sufficiently specific. Casanova claimed he could seduce all but the most virtuous women in fifteen minutes. But how? It was all very well knowing that the latter enjoyed nothing more than eating an oyster between a woman's breasts, but how had it arrived there in the first place without producing an hysterical reaction? (And then what was one supposed to do having eaten it?)

In any case, all this was missing the point. Emily was distrustful of such activities after her experience as a child. She needed reassurance more than anything else, a job for which his late mother would have been eminently suited. Eventually George conceded defeat, but the date of 28 June, 1903 – their first wedding anniversary – still loomed ahead like some earth-shattering Day of Judgement, and he'd frequently find himself contemplating the nature of her thoughts on the matter.

Not that their relationship, lacking in this one particular, could be considered in any way glum. Even when he was crying over her acceptance of his marriage proposal she had gently clasped his hand and whispered, 'You are now my slave!' (which he assumed was said in jest). She had once daubed him with her make-up – making Mrs Proops scream – and he would leave little notes, such as the following, under her door:

> *Come, thou fairest masterpiece*
> *Of Nature's work, her golden fleece:*
> *Let me enjoy thee. Flowers will fade*
> *If not refreshed. Die not a maid.*

Which he copied from a poem written in 1640 and which received the sardonic 'Nice try!' as a response.

The physical aspect to their friendship, in any case, was not entirely absent. Now and then she'd grab his arm or kiss him on the cheek. He'd imagine her hair – freed from the encumbrances of pins and pads – toppling down her back; that knowing smile as she let him kiss her slowly on the lips ...

The walk from the picnic-site had, in the end, revived his spirits and he began to look more favourably on events. Tomorrow they would celebrate their first wedding anniversary and the tender subject of their physical intimacy would finally be resolved.

7

The Bathing Party

In fact, on the morning in question George was far more preoccupied with finishing off his anniversary present. This was to take the form of a poem, much longer than his usual little rhymes, aptly titled *Ode to Emily*. He presented it to her with a flourish over breakfast and watched her gobble it up in barely two minutes. Every stanza produced the longed-for whoops of delight and at the end she sat grinning at him like a mischievous child whose pocket money has just been doubled.

'My darling, you are the next Wordsworth!'

He was then compelled, his modest genius allowing, to give a public reading in front of the politely smiling servants. At the stunning denouement – ... *call this veil of darkness bliss* – Emily stepped forward to hand him a fine old cigar box, replete with a small army of Cuban soldiers.

So she did love him after all!

Naturally all his ideas for how they could spend the day were dismissed in a trice.

'I'm going to church this morning. Then I thought we'd have a bathing party.' He was about to ask a question when she added, 'Just you and me – a party of two.'

'Church!'

'Yes. You don't mind, do you?'

He felt slightly thrilled – she hardly ever asked for his opinion – and affected a hurt expression.

'All right, then. I shan't go for your sake.' She turned to one of the footmen. 'Doesn't he look happy, Alfred?'

They chose a spot along the river-bank – not far from where they'd picnicked the day before – and used a weeping willow as a changing-hut. The weather had lost some of its tenacious brilliance, lightly grilling the skin rather than fully roasting it. The weeds on the river bottom were bending over backwards to resist the current while various insects were skimming the surface catching food minutiae in the downstream. George dangled his white-looking feet into the water, resting them on the smooth contours of the pebbles, ripples fanning out from his shins.

'Is it warm?'

Emily appeared wearing a thick woollen bathing dress, pink and white, extending from her neck to her knees.

'Freezing. You can be mad if you like. I'm staying here.'

'George, for goodness' sake! Show the old Boer spirit! Hold my hand. We'll go in together.'

'You first!'

She waded in, stepping unevenly on the gravel, giggling every time she nearly lost her footing. The water had reached waist-high when she flattened herself on the surface, sweeping her arms in wide arcs in front of her.

How things had changed! A year ago she wouldn't have survived without several friends staying in the guest rooms, whiling away the summer months by trumping each other's *bons mots* and smothering the hostess in oiliness. Immense time and effort had been allocated to the bedroom arrangements, cards on the doors specifying which European Count would be sandwiched between which eager ladies (though fun could be had by swapping the cards overnight!). And the manoeuvring at dinnertime!

Personally, he had always found this rather boring – analysing every-body's obnoxious character to death – but now Emily had apparently adopted his opinion. Not only were the two of them cloistered in an outlandishly large house, far too big for their needs, she was also spending more time on her own, often retreating to her bedroom for lengthy periods. Indeed, churchgoing appeared to be her main arena for social activity, and she seemed all in all to be less frivolous. The same dresses were worn not just two or three times but sometimes more.

What had happened to change her? His benign influence, perhaps? His slightly cynical attitude towards socializing?

'Come in, George. Didn't your army training teach you to swim?'
He drew in his breath, pondering his reply.

'Come in, my darling. Let me run my hands over you.'

As if someone was pushing him from behind, he plunged forward awkwardly, swallowed by what felt like liquid ice. Without quite knowing how, he found himself next to Emily and – the most wonderful of surprises – she kissed him on the lips. He raised his hands to respond and, no doubt looking a picture of comic regret, suddenly felt himself sinking. For a couple of seconds he tried to emulate Emily and tread water, but the more he thrashed about, the less impression he seemed to make. Surely there was no chance...? Oh, dear God. The bank was a mile away. He'd still be able to reach it, though, wouldn't he? He swallowed a huge gulp of water. No, no, it was too far. He was going to die – and in such a stupid, avoidable way! Already he was being pulled down and had to throw his chin back at an angle to avoid being submerged. Another gulp of water. He came back up for air and heard Emily's laughter before going under once more. Oh, God, he didn't want to die! And on their anniversary as well! But it was all over now. Best to pass out ... No! – Wait! – A solid surface! He pushed off with all his might. Oh, joy! The world again – and the bank much nearer than he could have hoped. He clambered onto the grass wheezing with the effort.

Everything had happened so quickly that for the next few minutes he could not speak. God, life was so precious! The sky was beautiful, the most brilliant blue. Turning his head to view the scene of his narrow escape, he noted the presence of life in the sprinkling of eddies and bubbles, reflecting the light in dazzling patterns. How innocent it all seemed – how, probably, a thousand petty jealousies were being decided that minute under the calm surface.

He cleared his throat and heard a fusillade of giggles in reply. Emily was lazily backstroking upstream, seemingly without a care in the world. She couldn't realize what he'd been through. No one was that cruel. She came out of the water, whisking up a towel to pat herself down. Her bathing dress was stuck to her body, the soft contours of which were evident underneath, and some strands of her hair had disentangled themselves and hung on her shoulders.

'Everything all right, dearest? You look a bit blue.'

'No.'

Another one of her inane giggles disturbed the peace of the countryside.

'Forgive me, George. I don't know why I like annoying you so much.'

'Perhaps it's because you're a sadist.'

She hesitated a moment, conscious of the new sound in his voice.

'Yes ... I daresay you're right.' She sat down next to him, playfully brushing his cheek with a piece of grass. 'Listen, George. I want to tell you something. Something about my childhood. You will promise to keep this secret, won't you?'

8

Emily's Story

The river continued its sedate journey; timeless and fascinating. A duck would occasionally paddle past, but otherwise Nature took a well-deserved rest. All was serene and the only sound of note was Emily's voice. It seemed she knew exactly the best way to appease him.

'My parents – I'm sure you're aware – didn't get on. They were so intent on fighting each other, they didn't have much time for me. When I was eight they sent me away to boarding-school. We could easily have afforded a governess. But there you are.'

He held her hand. She spoke quietly and gravely, in a manner he found utterly enthralling.

'I went home during the holidays, but things were always the same – the same old rows. Then one summer, when I was twelve, I came back to discover Mother had gone. Father was distraught and Mrs Proops was left to explain what had happened. Mama had "eloped" – the word made no sense to me – with another man. My wish for the fighting to end had come true. But the cost – my God! The atmosphere inside the house was deathly. Father spoke to me even less than before. After a while he turned to other people – not very pleasant types – for company. They'd spend all night drinking, laughing their heads off.'

She paused for a moment, pursing her lips, a droplet of water poised on her forehead. The moment seemed frozen in time.

'One particular friend of his – one of his hunting chums – always looked at me in a queer way. Always smiling, always giving me little winks. Sweating, as well. Always sweating.'

'Is this the man...?'

'Yes, but I haven't given you all the details yet.' She frowned slightly. 'One Sunday morning Father left for the hunt. I discovered this man, quite by accident, in the library. Apparently he'd had some trouble with his horse and was waiting for Father's return.' She tightened her grip on George's hand. 'He was sitting with his feet on the table, his riding crop lying nearby and his jacket thrown over his chair. He beckoned me towards him, making some comment I didn't understand about the book he was reading. I could see his forehead was glistening, but what really caught my eye were these scars on his neck. He must have seen where I was looking because he turned his head to one side, inviting me to touch him there. I reached out a hand and he grabbed it, making me gasp. Then he threw me down on the floor. All I could think was that I'd done something wrong, something so serious and grown-up it was incomprehensible to me. I struggled briefly and then gave in. It was terribly painful. The smell was nauseating. I found myself rising, leaving my body, so that I was gazing at the scene below – at this man and this little girl. When he'd finished he told me to clean myself up.

'"I'm sorry", I said ...'

Emily took her hand away from George's and covered her mouth. The tears were coursing down her cheeks.

'"I'm sorry", I said to him. "So sorry".'

'Oh, darling!' His voice was hoarse.

'I wanted to tell someone about what had happened. I know it sounds foolish and weak, but I just felt ashamed somehow ...' She brushed away a tear. 'In the end, though, I went to Father. He listened for a few minutes but then flew into a rage. He'd known this man for years ... one of his most trusted colleagues ... happily married with children – all of which made him a more reliable witness than me. I can only think he was still affected by Mother leaving him.'

'No, no. It's quite unforgivable.'

Emily closed her eyes, as another tear appeared.

'This isn't easy for me, George. Do you want me to continue?'

He calmed down instantly, nodding his assent. She composed herself.

'His face turned bright red and his eyebrows bristled. He began to explain, quite calmly, why it was dangerous to exaggerate. After he'd finished I went back to my room and thought for a long time about what I should do. The idea of staying there, in that house, was abhorrent to me, so I decided to run away. My plan was to leave at midnight, heading in the direction of the wood. There I'd live on nuts and berries, hide from grown-ups and enlist girls of my own age for company. However, I couldn't resist telling one of the maids about my intentions. She was naturally appalled but, after much toing and froing, suggested another idea. Her fiancé would drive over in his horse and cart, collect me, then press on through the night to Mother's house, thirty miles away. I tell you it was the longest, coldest, darkest night of my life. When I awoke I was in bed. And there, watching over me, was Mother.'

George's interest was tremendously aroused. Emily had scarcely mentioned her mother before, and Edith, he remembered from his own feeble forays into society, was considered *persona non grata*.

'As you'd expect, confusion reigned for the first two days of my stay. Telegrams were exchanged. Solicitors informed. The whole business was very delicate and could have proved highly embarrassing.'

'I should think so.'

'To everyone's surprise, though, Father resigned himself to the situation. Mother was delighted and so was her lover. We survived, comfortably enough, on his small income. No problems arose until nearly a year later.'

She glanced away, studying the river. 'Perhaps I should tell you this another time?'

'No, continue! Please!'

How could she think of stopping at this point?

'Well, let me think. Such a long time ago.' A thin line appeared between her eyebrows. 'I suppose the earliest sign of change came late one evening. I'd gone to bed but was woken up by shouting – Mother and her lover. Suddenly there was a crash, then silence. Someone seemed to be crying.'

'Your mother?'

'Presumably. I think he was insanely jealous, I don't know why. Drink would turn him into another man. The decisive moment between us came when Mother was out of the house. He made his way into my room and began throwing my things on the floor, all the time screaming abuse. (Now you understand, George, why I always lock my bedroom door.) I managed to stay calm somehow, waiting till he'd staggered out. Still, I knew I had to leave.'

'Again!'

'H'm. Back to my old home.'

'But what about the man who assaulted you?'

'He'd gone abroad apparently. Mother was good enough to tell me Father regretted his outburst against me. He was leading a more reclusive existence – no more horse-riding chums. I didn't feel any special warmth for him, but at least I felt I could trust him. He was safe.'

All of a sudden she stopped talking. George waited in vain for her to continue. He had wanted to learn *everything* and it seemed her story had resolved itself a little too easily. Why, for instance, had her mother let her go without more of a struggle? Why – apart from his drunken state – had Edith's lover lost his temper with her? It was difficult to find the right approach to draw her out while provoking the least amount of reaction.

'So your father changed his attitude?'

'Oh, yes, entirely. He told me that for a short period, after I'd left him for Mother, he'd written me out of his will.'

'Ah.' This seemed far more in keeping with the old man's vindictive nature, down to the confession of the crime. 'Who benefited?'

'Really, George, I haven't the least idea. I was more concerned with my own affairs at the time.'

'Yes, yes, of course. Sorry.'

It was unfair. She'd been treated cruelly by both sides of her family and he was probing into pettifogging details.

'You poor angel,' he murmured.

Gratefully, it seemed, she rested her head on his shoulder. He felt omnipotent, all-powerful.

'I do feel better, now that I've spoken to you. You swear not to tell another living soul?'

'Of course, dearest. You have my word.'

In truth, most of her account had been told to him two years since and the only real gap in his knowledge was Emily's staying with her mother. But then was it so important? He'd assumed that whatever she'd been withholding from him all this time – and he *did* suspect she was hiding something – had implicated *her* in some guilty context (to which he'd magnanimously lend his forgiveness). But it seemed that, unless she was still keeping something back, she had nothing to feel ashamed about.

'Do you still love me, George?'

'Of course. You know I do.'

'And if I were to ask you to go away with me, live in America, what would you say then?'

'You mean it, really?'

'I'm just asking, that's all.'

'All right then … yes! Yes, I would!'

'You really do love me, don't you?'

He couldn't stop smiling, almost laughing aloud. 'Till my dying day. Do you love me?'

She proceeded to stand up. 'Ooh, if I don't stretch my legs I shall die. Come on, you spoony old thing.'

9

The Wedding Anniversary

In spite of the exertions of the morning, Emily's idea for the afternoon was a game of golf. Perhaps she wished simply to alleviate the sombre mood that had fallen but, in any case, her suggestion met entirely with George's approval. Here was an opportunity to atone for his inability to swim and demonstrate his sporting prowess!

After a light luncheon, they had played nine holes at the local course, followed, so as to restore male pride, by a game of croquet on the lawn at Stockley Hall – alas, with the same result. Finally, in a bid to retain a semblance of dignity, as George had expressed it, they had played billiards, his favourite pastime, his previous reversals perhaps having an effect on his rather petulant play.

Now, while Emily was immersing her tired but victorious limbs in a bath, he had retreated to the study in order to ponder the success of the day so far. In his main aim – a resolution of the problem of their physical relationship – he had clearly failed. But then what a terrible mistake it had been, reviewing matters after a year! Perhaps he had taken the word 'year' too literally but, in any case, there was no ducking the question now. He could not allow the evening to pass without some reference to the issue.

'Thank you, Hopley.'

The butler had appeared at his side with another whisky and soda. Really, he ought to think about something else, stop going over the same ground all the time.

'Oh, Hopley!' he called out after the retreating figure. 'Don't rush off. Stay and talk for a while.'

The subject of his summons, impeccably attired in black tie and tails, retraced his steps, seeming to make hardly any sound at all. The problems Hopley had experienced in his life certainly made George's own woes appear petty indeed. His wife had died giving birth to their son – a scale of suffering George found impossible to comprehend – and a wealth of experience lay on those wide shoulders.

'Tell me,' George said. 'How's James getting along? I see him from time to time, always rushing about.'

'My apologies, sir, if he gets in your way.'

'Oh, no, not at all. It's nice to have children about the place. It's such a shame he doesn't have a mother still.'

'Yes, sir.'

'Of course,' George added, conscious of perhaps giving the wrong impression, 'you're doing a wonderful job, bringing him up on your own. I didn't mean—'

'No, sir. Thank you, sir. My wife, Grace, was a very remarkable woman.'

A look of pride radiated Hopley's normally inexpressive features and his back appeared straighter than ever. His devotion to his wife was one of the reasons George liked him so much – not just because, as Emily once pointed out, he had less hair than himself.

'She used to work at Eveley Manor, didn't she?'

'Yes, sir. She was head housemaid. She was obliged to sacrifice her career to marry me.'

'Remarkable indeed,' George commented. 'I don't mean ... Well, you know what I mean.'

'Yes, sir.'

'I daresay,' he resumed after a sip of his drink, 'you must have been worried about your own position.'

'Somewhat troubled, yes, sir. At the time, though, the house was in some upheaval. His lordship wasn't quite himself.'

'Oh, was this at the time that Lady Delsey left him?'

'Indeed, sir. Because of the problems his lordship was experiencing, I don't think he was able to give the matter his full attention.'

'Yes. Very well expressed.'

'I believe Mrs Proops also put in a word on my behalf.'

'Mrs Proops? Did she, indeed? Well! Well done, Proopsy!'

The thought of the housekeeper pleading the case of one of the menservants to Lord Delsey – never mind that he should listen to her

– seemed unlikely somehow, but Hopley must know what he was talking about. A misty quality fell over the other's eyes.

'I remember his lordship called me into this room and said, "John, I've decided to keep you on." '

'John?' George lowered the glass he'd just raised to his lips. 'I thought your name was Arthur.'

'Yes, sir, it is. But in those days the first footman was always called John, and the second, James. It saved confusion.'

'Well,' said George doubtfully, 'not if the first footman was really called James and the second footman was called John. Anyhow, that must have been a weight off your mind, even if your wife was treated shabbily.'

'Yes, sir. I felt guilty about that aspect, but she told me later that everything went according to her plans.'

'Oh?'

'Yes, sir. She knew it was likely she'd have to leave service. The terms of her employment stipulated strictly no followers. All along, though, she had confidence – far more than I had myself – in my situation here. Women are very subtle creatures, if I may say so, sir. I think Grace picked me, not the other way round – and perhaps that applies to most men.'

'Yes,' George said, suddenly rising from his chair. 'Yes, you may be right, Hopley. Thank you. I've enjoyed this little chat of ours.'

It was strange that the butler's words should provide such comfort. Emily was certainly not known for her subtlety, but maybe she was more cunning than he'd supposed. After all, on the question of their getting married she had not revealed her intentions until the last moment. Quite probably there was nothing he could say to influence her on the subject of their secret agreement and, therefore, no reason why he should worry unduly about it.

When Emily appeared for dinner she was dressed in black, tight black, her neckline daringly low, revealing the odd fortunate freckle. She looked quite breathtaking, her hair gleaming in the evening light, and George beamed with pleasure as they took their places. She had dressed for him; she did everything for him. They chatted gaily through the meal, laughter never far away, and Emily seemed in an especially playful mood.

'So tell me honestly, George,' she said, 'did you really think you might drown this morning?'

'I'm not going to overdramatize the situation,' he replied. 'All I'm saying is it was touch and go.'

She gave a little giggle and he allowed himself a smile. The intervening hours had helped him to view the incident more favourably – enough, anyhow, to portray himself in a slightly ridiculous light.

'But why didn't you say you couldn't swim? I don't understand.'

'Because ...' – he struggled for an answer – 'you asked me to go in. I thought I could cope. If it hadn't been for, you know, the old ...'

He patted the all too fallible leg, preventing him from performing great athletic feats.

'Oh, yes, of course. Funny, I keep forgetting about that. I know you were really upset afterwards. You were, weren't you? You didn't dedicate your poem to "my wife, the sadist".'

'Yes, well, I suppose I was a bit overwrought at the time.'

The criticism had obviously had quite an effect for her to mention it again. Perhaps she felt guilty over not doing enough to help him and that had influenced her decision to confide about her past.

'I know you think I'm laughing at you, but it's not true, you know,' she continued. 'Remember when I told Father how amusing you were, asking you to tell him a joke? I knew you wouldn't be able to say anything. You just stared at him in horror for a few moments before saying you suspected your humour stemmed not from telling jokes but because you *were* the joke.'

'Yes ... happy times,' George murmured.

'But you see, that's the point, isn't it? You don't take yourself too seriously. A bit seriously perhaps – that's the funny aspect – but it's quite impossible to laugh at someone who sees the joke.'

'You're not a sadist,' he informed her, detecting the undercurrent of her remarks. 'Not a sadist except perhaps – hm-h'm – in one particular area.'

She looked at him curiously. Over her shoulder he could see Alfred standing beside the service screen, gazing straight ahead at nothing. It would have been a hard enough subject to discuss even with just the two of them.

'For the last year you've been withholding ... How can I put this?'

He examined the dinner table for inspiration. Woodcock – no, far too obvious. What were woodcocks stuffed with? 'You've been withholding truffles from me.'

For one moment she looked at him as though he were raving, but then her eyes narrowed and a cynical smile appeared on her lips.

'We had truffles only last week.'

'Yes ... but not of the Périgord variety.'

She obviously wasn't going to make it easy for him.

'Shall I have a word with Mrs Proops? Perhaps she can provide the truffles you want.'

He shuddered inwardly. 'I was thinking that you, specifically, could help me. Truffles are what I'm after. Not trout.'

'Well, I don't know. Truffles are rather rich, aren't they? You might gorge yourself on them and then need to take a cure.'

He glanced over at Alfred to see a slight frown traversing the normally implacable features. 'One minute they're having a regular conversation', he imagined the footman telling the rest of the staff. 'Next they're going on about blooming truffles.'

'Yes, please,' he said.

The cynical smile returned. 'Well, I must confess you've been very good, waiting all this time. But I don't think we should talk about it, not right now. Really, affairs of that sort should just happen naturally, shouldn't they?'

George drained his glass of wine. The knowledge of what they were really talking about was making him feel a little light-headed.

'I ought to pick my own, you mean?' he queried, keeping to the truffle motif for Alfred's benefit but also because it suited his purposes. 'Tonight, say?'

He was hardly breathing, his heart making lurching movements inside his chest. She threw up her hands in a despairing gesture.

'Yes, tonight! Go out searching for French truffles tonight! Do whatever you please, you mad boy! Anything to drop the subject!'

She returned to her meal with a friendly smile, and so too did he, but found he could scarcely hold his knife and fork, feeling the colour flow to his face. What clearer sign could she have given? Saying the need for talk was over! The conversation moved on to other, more prosaic topics, but an atmosphere had invaded proceedings.

Everything he touched had a richer texture and all his senses were operating at greater efficiency. Ah, such exquisite embarrassment! He hardly dared look at Emily, but then the fever appeared to have affected her too. As the meal progressed she seemed to retreat into herself, perhaps suffering from nerves at the step she had taken in their relationship. They were halfway through dessert when she rose from the table.

'Night, then, George. Time for bed.'

His eyes, tinged with disappointment, followed her to the door, and he listened to her footsteps on the stairs as they faded away. Had she forgotten? Had she thought his sexual itch had suddenly been cured and didn't need scratching? He ran over in his mind not just the substance of her final words but her manner. That saucy smile. Yes, the message was only too plain. Slowly he mounted the stairs – drunk, quite willingly, on a flyblown hope. Stopping to think about what he was doing would only dissolve the dream. And now – deep breath – he was on the landing. He tucked his hand inside his waistcoat in the manner of Napoleon before, a moment later, pulling it back out and straightening his clothing. Perhaps the Austrian Army could be called to account on another day. As he opened her door, wearing the broadest of grins, he pictured the love the two of them would share ...

In point of fact, it was so long since he'd stood on the threshold he wasn't even aware that the bed had been moved to the top right-hand corner of the room; unmolested, for the time being, from human invasion. (He had vaguely expected to see Emily, propped up on a tidal wave of pillows, wearing that same suggestive smile on her face.) In certain respects this was a bluestocking's room, confirmed by the massed battalions of books residing in an old mahogany bookcase next to the window. In other respects it belonged to a society beauty, a jumble of fans, shoes, ribbons and gloves obscuring much of the carpet.

Emily was seated with her back to him at her writing table and was apparently so absorbed in her labours that she hadn't noticed him enter. He knocked on the open door.

'George!'

Her hair flounced round and it was difficult to tell whether her face registered mainly surprise, embarrassment or anger.

'George. Don't come in here.'

'I'm sorry to disturb you. I was hoping to talk to you on a rather delicate matter.'

He said his prepared line anyhow and, still smiling, started to advance, increasing her discomfort.

'George. Please!'

He stopped a few feet from where she was sitting.

'Not now. Tomorrow. I'm busy now.'

He gazed into her eyes, hoping for some sign of reassurance, but had to look away, his attention falling on the note in front of her.

Dear Teddy
I need to talk to you about our arrangement

He glanced back at Emily to see that same look of forbearance on her face. She hadn't been thinking about their dinnertime conversation at all.

'I thought,' he went on in spite of himself, 'that since it was our anniversary and you said you didn't wish to talk about – you know – the understanding we came to. At least not at the dinner table ...'

She was shaking her head, regarding him with a certain sadness.

'Obviously I made a mistake,' he added.

He stared at her for another second, unable to think of anything further to say ... and left, not even closing the door.

Back in his bedroom he stood, very tense, at the open window.

That face, that innocent face! Frowning at him as though he'd committed some crime! God, how he hated that look! How he wanted to grab her hair and force her to read that note aloud. 'What's this? What's this, eh?' And she'd have nothing to say. There'd just be the abject sound of her tears.

Dear Teddy ... our arrangement.

Some intruder seemed to be screaming the words in his ear in case he'd forgotten them. Dear 'anyone else' wouldn't have mattered. But that name – that innocuous little name – brought phantoms of fear and uncertainty to the surface of his mind. Something was – had to be – going on between them. His wife and ...

Outside, the placid summer evening seemed only to mock his

predicament. He was dimly aware of the outline of trees, the fresh country tang which hung in the air, but shut in his poisoned, Emily-saturated, world it all seemed to pall. The vaulted ceiling of stars glittered as a hundred thousand points of light, boring him to tears. Overseeing everything, hovering like a mist, was Emily's beauty: Emily in love. Could it be that her face, a little more flushed than usual at dinner, was subtly betraying an emotion that hitherto she'd managed to resist? It was incredibly tragic: he loved her so much and she loved another. Perhaps she and Pilling were the human equivalent of swans and he, a far more common sparrow, was tampering with the laws of nature. There was no sign of encouragement in the depths of the night, no response to his heartfelt yearning – just mute confirmation of his profound depression.

He retired to bed, but at twenty minutes to one, finding no respite from his worries, took up his post at the window, remaining there for over two hours. Then, feeling no better for his vigil, he crept back under the sheets. To his fevered imagination it sounded as if gravel was being thrown against the window he'd just closed. But tired and past caring – especially with the antics of children – he fell asleep, oblivious to the sun gently spreading its rays on a foreign land.

10

A Religious Affair

The postbox was empty. George gazed through the glass pane and then opened the door. Perhaps it possessed a false panel. No. Of course it didn't.

For a second or two he continued to stare inside the box before sensing someone standing nearby. He jerked his head to find Mrs Proops, the housekeeper, peering down at him. As usual she was dressed all in black, her rather masculine features accentuated by her severe hairstyle.

'Mrs Proops! I didn't see you there.'

He closed the box and drew himself up to face her. Mrs Proops had never been his favourite servant – in fact, he actually liked all the others – and in spite of valiant attempts to obtain her support she'd always remained unremittingly hostile. There was something both resentful and proprietary in her attitude, and the death of Lord Delsey had apparently only served to increase her petulance. Certainly not lacking in efficiency – she was a kind of starchy Torquemada – he'd always suspected her of being unduly harsh with the younger servants and was left with the impression that, as the oldest denizen at Stockley Hall, she attended to recent usurpers like himself on sufferance only.

'The next post is at half past five,' she said.

'Yes, I know. I was just wondering if a letter of mine had gone out.'

'The postman comes at midday. The time now is nearly two o'clock.'

'Really? Late as that, is it?'

He was quite aware of the hour but wished to justify his examination of the postbox. She arched her eyebrows, adopting her customary sneer. Her conduct towards him was wholly unacceptable, of course, but Emily had opposed any suggestion of letting her go on the grounds that her father had been a friend of Lord Delsey's, only sending his daughter into service after squandering away his money. Another point in her favour, albeit rather negative, was that if housekeepers were meant to be fierce, dragon-like creatures, a certain pride could be taken in acquiring such a fine example of the breed. A house had a greater sense of itself somehow with Death stalking the corridors.

'Would it be convenient for Mary to attend to your room now?' she enquired.

'Yes, that would be fine. I – er – wasn't feeling quite myself this morning. Bad headache.'

'I could send for Doctor Wetherington if—'

'Oh, no, no. It's over now. Just need to find your mistress ...'

'I believe Mrs Erskine is outside in the rose garden, enjoying the sun.'

He wandered off. There was a hint of mischief in her last remark as well, but he kept his own counsel. The conversation hadn't seen him at his best, but it was just too early in the day.

Over the next week or so he was especially vigilant of correspondence entering or leaving the house. The 'Dear Teddy' letter may have escaped his clutches, but thenceforward he was thoroughly unscrupulous. Letter-racks were raided, postmen cross-examined, servants scrutinized for hidden pouches. (The tactic of examining Emily's room was naturally never considered.)

The result of all this detective work? Nothing. But there were, in any case, other ways of communicating. Indeed, a single note could stipulate that they should meet every day from then on, removing the need for further dispatches. It was evident, too, that Emily couldn't conduct an affair without meeting her lover from time to time, and to do so she'd need to disappear once in a while. George racked his brains to think of all the times when they'd been apart. There were long afternoons with friends to account for, daylong shopping expeditions to Southampton, games of hide-and-seek in the woods. The number of opportunities seemed endless ...

And yet, in all honesty, would such random encounters suffice in a steady relationship? The two of them would need to organize some sort of system, and apparently, discounting church, there were no other regular times when he and Emily were separated.

And he could not believe ...

Well, the advantages of having an incisive mind! Cutting out all the chaff and leaving just two despicable pieces of wheat! Only once in recent memory, on the occasion of their anniversary, had Emily forsaken church. But the likelihood of her, or Pilling, being devoutly religious! It was a wonder he hadn't suspected anything before!

And yet ... Well! It still seemed unlikely somehow.

Certainly, as the week dragged on, Emily provided no further reasons to doubt her fidelity. In fact, she seemed increasingly introspective, spending large amounts of time locked in her room. It became quite tiresome monitoring her movements, and on the Thursday afternoon, having ascertained from Mary that Mrs Erskine was resting and didn't wish to be disturbed, he decided to go for a bicycle ride.

Without really thinking about where he was going, he headed in the direction of Tapser's Ruin, following the route of the previous Saturday. Turning the corner to face the opening – where he'd overheard Emily and Constance – he stopped still in amazement. There was Constance, unmistakably Constance, standing with her back to him, wearing the same clothes, adopting *exactly the same pose he'd assumed* on the day of the picnic. Even her hand was tapping against the wall in the same casual manner. Not wanting to embarrass her by calling attention to himself, and unable to assign a reason for her behaviour, he turned on his heel and left the scene as quietly as possible.

Saturday had arrived. The gong for breakfast had been sounded. On the sideboard in the dining-room rows of little spirit lamps warmed large silver dishes, and tables were allocated with their various themes. Fruit was on one, porridge on another, the main table showing off a selection of hams and small game birds. Breakfast was George's favourite meal of the day, and though silence had been the rule which operated at Sandhurst (to allow time to adjust oneself to waking up), he generally felt inclined to chatter away.

'I've been talking to Hayes about Stockley Woods. He's been working hard lately, clearing out wide pathways at various points. I thought we might stroll over there this afternoon and view his handiwork.'

Emily stifled a yawn. 'If you like.'

'Hayes thinks the woods have never looked more splendid. We've never been blessed with so many pheasants. Perhaps ... I was wondering if we might arrange a shooting party this autumn. Hayes could round up some beaters from the village and ... You don't approve ...'

Emily was frowning; looking slightly pale.

'George – no, I really won't tolerate it. Such cruel behaviour. There's no necessity for it – and turning it into a sport is even more appalling. Aren't you familiar with the concept of universal kinship? We're all part of God's kingdom, you know.'

She was quite earnest, that was apparent. But though he was in no mood for an argument, especially since Mrs Proops had now joined Alfred next to the service screen, he wasn't yet prepared to see all of Hayes's work go unrewarded.

'Emily, dear. Look at this table. What are we eating?'

She gave him a withering look. 'What are *you* eating, you mean. I'm strongly considering becoming a vegetarian.'

The slice of ptarmigan which was dutifully heading towards his mouth hovered dramatically in front of its target.

'Thou shalt not kill,' she added.

'Ah, yes.'

This subject could be broached another time. It was beginning to make him feel uncomfortable in any case. He was suddenly reminded of another matter.

'I was planning to tell you: I've decided to go to church with you tomorrow.'

His tone was deliberately offhand, but it was clear his announcement had made quite an impact. Emily gazed at him in wonder before resuming her breakfast, apparently too shocked even to pass comment. When she finally spoke, after another few seconds had elapsed, her words took him completely by surprise.

'You must excuse me. I'm not feeling very well.'

She stood up from the breakfast-table, smiling weakly, and made her way out. The shock; the suddenness! His instinct was to dash after her and offer some comfort, but an overriding suspicion kept him pinned in his chair. Amazement, yes, he'd expected, but this unnatural whitening of the gills, the fearful look in the eyes. All the hallmarks of guilt were imprinted on that face.

Needing some air, he quickly exited the house. The reason for her abrupt departure had to involve Pilling and their arrangement. A hollow ache settled inside his chest. But how exactly? And to what extent? Undoubtedly the most straightforward course of action was to confront her at once. But then how would she react? Were they already on the verge of a permanent breach? Her behaviour over the last week – shutting herself away – had certainly been odd. Was she pining for her lover? Was the suggestion to go to America a last, guilt-ridden attempt to escape her addiction to the man? Was it too late to hold her to that even now? Was it? Oh, God, he was desperate …

'Looks as if a squall's blowing up, sir.'

Someone was talking to him – the subject, in fact, of their recent conversation.

'What? Oh, yes, indeed, Hayes. Best be getting in.'

The gamekeeper passed on his way, but George remained where he was for a while longer. A brisk wind ruffled his hair and little points of rain jabbed at his face. Think – think … He must think. It was clear that Emily and her fellow conspirator were due to meet tomorrow at the usual time and place. But on this occasion she wouldn't be there. So Pilling would wait and wait – and then worry. Perhaps she'd been disturbed by the thought of him doing something rash, such as marching up to the house and creating a scene. Or, less conceivably, something really ghastly might be on the agenda. An elopement, for example. If so, that would certainly explain her behaviour.

Except that nothing had really happened over breakfast. She had simply *feigned* sickness. Meaning she was going to escape while he was in church. So … he would stay at home. No! He would tell one of the servants to watch over her for signs of a miraculous revival – though they would consider him either callous or deranged. Ah, but better still – what if he were to examine *Pilling's* movements! Spying on

Emily had provided no clues to the mystery, but trailing that scoundrel should instantly improve his chances of determining the truth. At least he would be following an active course.

11

Church

For the remainder of the day he fine-tuned his plans, but the sharp downpour which fell overnight, bringing with it a sparkling dew, seemed to throw everything into a clearer light, including his own thoughts.

Of course he couldn't follow Pilling. He might be waiting outside his house all day. And even if Pilling *did* go out, his weak knee restrained him from serious pursuit – assuming Pilling didn't notice him at any point. The only option left was to traipse over to church, ascertain the other's non-appearance, and pay a call on his residence. Then, the probability being that Pilling had absented himself, question one of the servants as to his whereabouts.

Yes, that was what he had to do.

He was up before most of the servants and was sorely tempted, purely through frustration, to start preparing breakfast himself. But, to his credit, he managed to suppress this outbreak of enterprise, which would only have offended the older members of staff, just as he resisted making enquiries after Emily's condition, which he rather assumed to be bad. Long as the morning might be, he was not going to be diverted from his mission.

Church!

It sounded ridiculous and yet there he was, when the time came, in one of the more humble pews at the back, listening to the five-minutes bell waking up every remote corner of the British empire. His presence had drawn some attention already – as a well-known non-churchgoer – and he wasn't sure if, as a prominent figure in the village, he was entitled to a position at the front and was embarrassing everyone by his lack of protocol.

Pilling had not arrived and he could see several excellent reasons why. Hopley, George's butler, was glowering at the back of the choir, his thinning hair greasing the dome of his enormous head. A couple of the maids, all feathers and preening, were whispering frantically to each other over to the centre-right. And a few rows in front of him the magisterial presence of Mrs Hedges, the cook, sat in unflinching obeisance, her ample figure decked out in black frills like a pot-bellied but generous-natured poodle. Fortunately, Mrs Proops didn't seem to be in the vicinity, but this was no doubt because she was taking care of the invalid at home. Otherwise, there were numerous witnesses here who would have noticed surreptitious glances and their ilk – which is why, of course, Emily and Pilling met elsewhere.

Thus it was quite a blow to George's conspiracy theories when Pilling strutted in, apparently on his own, and removed his top hat. Exchanging a few words with the verger, who handed him a prayer book and a hymn book, he clattered up the aisle with his malacca cane, kneeling down on a hassock in one of the front rows. George had always regarded Pilling as a fop, but now, with heart pumping with extra urgency and fingers pressed hard into his palms, he viewed with revulsion the high line of his head and shoulders and the peculiar sheen of his hair. Was this really the man to whom Emily had entrusted her affections? How utterly, utterly sickening if true. Anyone acquiring the right to be called her lover would have gained his disapproval, but for Pilling – Pilling for God's sake – to be the one she'd finally chosen! The man was nothing more than a conceited blackguard who'd hopefully return one day to the snake pit he'd originally deserted.

As these Christian-like thoughts passed through his mind, the white-surpliced rector entered from the vestry, and the congregation climbed to their feet.

What then transpired, in the way of psalms and lessons, George found quite tedious, and it wasn't until the sermon that his interest was moderately aroused. It was on the subject of forgiveness: God forgives those who truly repent. The rector was discoursing about Biblical misconduct.

'Noah was drunk on one occasion. David's son, Amnon, violated Tamar, his half-sister. Moses killed an Egyptian who was attacking a

Hebrew. We are, all of us, capable of committing evil. The human condition is one of weakness and temptation.'

George nodded in cynical recognition. Members of the clergy were either, from his experience of the matter, advocates of hope and salvation or, in the present case, death and damnation. He was mildly surprised, then, when the speaker continued:

'And yet how can we ask for God's forgiveness when we don't forgive others? When the scribes and the Pharisees brought Jesus an adulterous woman he stopped them from casting stones, saying to her, "Go, and sin no more." Indeed, when Peter asked, "Lord, how oft shall my brother sin against me, and I forgive him? Till seven times?" Jesus replied, "I say not unto thee until seven times: but until seventy times seven." God, then, could forgive this woman innumerable times and we should try our utmost to follow that philosophy.'

The dowagers in the congregation sniffed as one, affronted by a God who could lower His standards to the extent where such fast behaviour was actually tolerated.

'We are all part of the same body, all God's children, all sinners unable to judge others. I trust there is no one here today who allows a grievance to dominate their thoughts. Forgive your enemies fully in your heart, and God forgives you.'

The service concluded noisily – the congregation were obviously in high spirits after their ordeal had ended – and plainly the moment had come to escape. George glanced over in Pilling's direction, but to his dismay the lady beside him returned his gaze. Moreover, though he didn't recognize her at first, this was no stranger, either. It was Constance Appleby, the ubiquitous Constance!

There was no doubt her appearance had altered. The cycling clothes had been discarded and in their place a clingy frock displayed a very rounded figure. Her face, too, which before had been flushed and puffed out, now looked less under attack, almost demure. But in any case the game was up. She advanced towards him, bringing the Malacca Cane along too.

'Where's Emily?' demanded Pilling.

'Ill.'

There was a slightly embarrassing pause.

'What's the matter with her, George?' This was Constance.

'Oh, some sort of stomach complaint. Mrs Proops is looking after her so she's bound to die before long.'

Constance's jaw dropped in exaggerated fashion. 'Oh, George!'

'Must be serious,' observed Pilling, 'if she's not in church this morning. Unusual to see you here as well.'

'I've come to pray for her.'

'Oh, George!'

Pilling still looked very grave. 'Well, I'm busy today, but I'll drop by and see you both tomorrow. Tell the little goose I'll check up on her then.'

George's face coloured, his mouth forming the 'goo' shape he'd recently witnessed (the full word imprinted on his brain). The crowning audacity! Being ordered to hold the day open so that Pilling could call on his wife!

He watched as his two companions exchanged polite greetings with the rector, and then they filed outside. It already looked as if a blazing hot day was in prospect and the frock coats and white dresses glittered in the sun.

There was a lull in the conversation; then, to George's further disbelief, Pilling leant across to Constance, half-whispering, 'I'd consider it an honour if you'd allow me to walk you home.'

The recipient of this request appeared a little nonplussed but managed, 'Thank you, I'm sure, but if you don't mind I'd like a few words in private with George. Good morning.'

Pilling stared at her for a second, turning a bilious colour; then, replacing his top hat, spun on his heels and strode briskly away, removing his gloves as a signal of defeat.

12

Constance

They began walking towards Constance's house, Eveley Manor, at the opposite end of the village to Stockley Hall. George's mood had lifted considerably and he soon became even more impressed with his new-found friend's perception of human nature.

'Ugh! Do you know, George, I really find that man's manners ingratiating. Even when he's telling me the weather's charming he manages to sound furtive. I'm so glad you rescued me from him.'

George motioned self-deprecatingly with his hand. 'Think nothing of it. In future I shall consider it a duty.'

'Yes – do. He's always so pompous. I thought the way he spoke to you at the picnic was a – was a disgrace.'

He gave a little chuckle. It was impossible not to like her. They turned a corner and, to shield herself from the sun, she moved her parasol from one hand to the other. Feeling that they'd suitably disposed of the character of Pilling, he ventured to enquire why she had moved to Eveley.

'Oh, you have to go back to when I was fourteen. I stayed with Emily the whole of the summer.'

'Up at the Hall?'

'Yes, it was wonderful. I remember us trooping off to church, just like today. I could never get over Mrs Hedges' singing. Did you hear her?'

'I'm not sure. She was facing the other way.'

'She was the flat, discordant foghorn drowning out the choir. Heavens, I daresay I know more about your servants than you. Mrs Proops, for instance. Now she's changed awfully. Quite a jolly soul she was in those days.'

George shook his head. 'Not *my* Mrs Proops. The one I know is a professional misery-maker who wears a shroud.'

'Oh, no, she was different then. I think she was quite close to Lord Delsey. I once went into his study and saw her with her hand resting on his shoulder.'

'About to sink her fangs into his neck, you mean?' She was obviously jesting.

'I was a bit surprised myself. But then, you know, he was very sad and lonely after his wife left. Why shouldn't he find some amusement in life?'

George blew out his cheeks, recalling the stern look invariably worn by the noble lord. In the light of his opposition to his and Emily's marriage, how ironic would it be if he'd once had an affair with his housekeeper?

But Mrs Proops of all people!

Constance went on to talk about the other servants, saying she remembered Hopley when he had a full head of hair – possibly the most incredible remark she'd made thus far. Then she grabbed him by the arm – they were strolling along the High Street – and gushed, 'George, do tell me about the war. I feel so sorry for the young soldiers who died and those who were injured like you. Was it really quite beastly?'

'Yes, quite.'

The grip she was maintaining on his arm was perhaps overstepping the bounds a little, but at least she was striving to be friendly – a not unwelcome development in his present frame of mind. They arrived at Eveley Manor and she took him around to the east wing by the stables.

'You can't possibly walk all the way back again!' she exclaimed. 'Peters! Prepare a carriage. You can take Mr Erskine and myself to Stockley Hall – following the country route.' She whispered to George conspiratorially, 'We don't want to drive through the village again. You know how people gossip.'

He nodded, thinking that people might already have their suspicions since they'd left church together and made rather a public display of themselves walking back to the manor house. Yet there was no point in making things worse and, in any case, he was still gloating over the prize snub dealt to Pilling.

'I want to show you something,' she said, as they started moving. 'This needn't take long, so don't worry.'

'You sound exactly like my dentist.'

'Oh, George!'

He leant back into the comfortable leather, burnished by the soothing heat. What could she possibly have in store for him? Perhaps something involving Tapser's Ruin and an explanation of what she'd been doing there recently. All very mysterious and exhilarating!

'So you and my wife are old schoolfriends?' he asked, hoping for more information about Emily.

Strangely, for the first time, Constance seemed to check herself. 'Yes, we knew each other very well. She was "Little Miss Perfect" of course. Left here, Peters!'

The coachman glanced over his shoulder with a hint of irritation.

'Perfect?' George queried. 'Surely you must have outshone her in some respects?'

She appeared to be lacking in confidence and he wanted her to admit to one past triumph at least. Since the mention of his wife the conversation had definitely taken on a more sombre tone.

'Only stupid things,' she said, frowning. 'Like mirror writing. Where you write squiggles and they make sense in a mirror.'

There was a gap in the conversation while he absorbed this piece of news. Such a skill was not altogether redundant, proving useful when it came to hiding information from servants in postcards, but had little else to commend it.

'Oh, and palm reading,' she added. 'Goodness, I nearly forgot. A gypsy passed the knowledge to an aunt of mine and she passed it on to me. Here, give me your hand.'

She cupped his right hand in her own and began prodding it in various places, pinching and examining each finger in turn.

'Now, let me see. Yes ... yes ... I can see you're a compulsive nail-biter.'

'You have a real gift.'

'And you're a ditherer, someone who can't make up his mind. Yet when you do – yes, yes! – you act decisively. Ah, what have we here?' She stopped talking for a while, deep in concentration. 'H'm, this is interesting, most interesting. I see another ...' She carefully placed his hand back on his lap.

'Another?'

'Sorry. I don't think you're quite ready for my prophesies.'

'Another death in the family?'

'Oh, no, nothing like that. Another person in your life. There, I've said too much already.'

The woman was mad, quite mad. 'Well ... thank you, anyhow. 'Long as it's not someone chasing me for money.'

'You know, George,' she continued, abruptly changing the subject, 'we've actually met before, you and I. When we were both living in London. Do you remember?'

'Um-m. You have the advantage of me, I'm afraid.'

'Oh, George! I remember you looking so dashing in your uniform.'

'I had a bit more hair in those days.'

'No, no. I think you look very distinguished now.'

Her gloved fingers made a pass through his locks in apparently frank appreciation while he pondered something to say to defuse the situation.

'Perhaps I ought to wear a wig. Something baroque, in the style of Charles II.'

The shriek of laughter which greeted this remark took him aback somewhat, but perhaps the image of his face looking out morosely from underneath a mass of black curls appealed to her for some reason.

'I thought you were awfully amusing at the picnic,' she remarked, when she'd sufficiently recovered. 'We'll have to arrange another one, perhaps on the roof of my house.' She looked at him intensely. 'I must confess I've been cycling to keep fit, every day virtually, since the day of our outing.'

'That's very worthy of you.'

He remembered Emily had once remarked to him, a little unchari-tably, that Constance, while being 'normal' in other respects, was slightly unbalanced on the subject of her *embonpoint*, making frequent envious comments about Emily's figure.

She leant forward, tapping the coachman on the shoulder for a whispered conference, before returning to him and saying, 'Climb down, George. We're going for a little walk.'

This whole episode was developing almost dreamlike qualities!

They were in a beautiful patch of countryside, not anywhere he recognized, next to a gate leading to a cornfield. Constance was quiet now, simply linking her arm in his and steering him along a dirt path splitting the yellow. The mood had dramatically altered; the closeness in the air transferring itself to them. Now and then her hand would brush against his or she would press her body a little closer to negotiate an obtrusive reed, all of which added to his excitement. After a while of this silent titillation he started to sweat quite profusely, as if the thousands of crickets were spitting at him in the sticky heat. Worse still, unhelpful thoughts began to circulate in his mind, not placated by the fact that she was always fully dressed every time he glanced in her direction.

It was incredible. Here he was, a married man, barely forty minutes after leaving church, in the middle of nowhere, with a friend of his wife's, whom he was lustfully surveying. Even her rather full lips and puffy cheeks had a primitive eroticism and he was torn between a desire to grab her shoulders and wrest her round, or escape, cowardly running away.

It was odd that he hadn't felt the same way at the picnic – perhaps Emily's icy presence had doused her friend's sexuality – but the thought now of gripping her thighs and burying his face in the ample folds of her muslin dress was one that would not leave him.

'Help me over the stile, George.'

This was ridiculous. Either he was going mad, or her voice, soft-spoken but insistent, had taken on a new carnality.

He clambered over to the grass field beyond and lifted her down, hands posted under her rib cage, enjoying the waft of her breath on his collar. It was unbelievably tempting to 'accidentally' fall on top of her.

This was a real woman, earthy and deeply satisfying. He put his arm around her waist, savouring the curve tapering in from her buttocks. She gave a slight demurring sound but seemed to accept it. Spiritually they were already making love, every sway of her breasts increasing his ardour.

'You know we're actually trespassing?' she murmured. They stopped walking. 'Here we are. This is what I wanted to show you.'

They were opposite a large barn, long since fallen into disuse, with

rotten wood shakily keeping its mouldy shell together. A couple of
mangy cows were lazily munching away to one side.

Constance stood facing him, in front of the barn door, her arms
akimbo.

'This is where I spent a lot of my childhood. Where I used to go
when running away from home. Or when I wanted some boy to kiss
me.'

His breathing grew shallow and a wave of longing stirred inside
him.

'They were all willing,' she pointed out calmly. 'In fact, they all
seemed to be obsessed with my body, staring at it as if I had some
strange disease.'

Slowly, slowly, she let her hands rise up the contours of her torso
until they propped up her breasts, all the time eyeing him invitingly.

Then, swivelling on her hips, she opened the barn door and
stepped in.

His mind, what was left of it, was in complete disarray, drugged by
the tantalizing prospect on offer. He couldn't follow her in, just
couldn't. It would be akin to entering the gates of hell. And yet – God
help him – he wanted so much to plunge into the furnace and indulge
himself utterly. With her, no one else but her. His heart was pounding
in little wild jerks and his legs were so weak they could scarcely
support him. It was obvious she'd do anything, *anything* – a
bewitching, beguiling prospect. There was really no other choice.

Light filtered in through the chewed wood boarding the sides of
the barn, throwing half of her into shadow. Her hair, surprisingly
long, rolled pell-mell down her bare back and, as he approached, she
lifted it up with her hands. His fingers closed round her heavy bust
and he kissed the downy hairs on her neck to her sighs. She said something commonplace about his future being in his hands and then their
tongues entwined: their love sealed.

She was very passionate, hopefully making up for his lack of experience. But when the critical moment in their lovemaking came,
Constance sitting astride him, George could not help closing his eyes
and thinking of Emily – sweet, wasp-waisted Emily.

The moment was over.

He felt sick.

From being Mr Hyde he had reverted to Doctor Jekyll with all the attendant guilt. This was adultery, what he dreaded most from his wife. Moreover, to add indignity to his sin, this woman was huge. Her rounded body, plagued by puppy fat, now seemed enormous, her stupendous thighs pinning him to the ground. Her red face, buoyed up by a reckless passion, was beginning to look a little moonstruck, while the groans which before had made him feel like a towering (albeit balding) Adonis, now sounded akin to some sort of wounded animal, her squawks increasingly reminding him of the incident on the way to the picnic-site when she'd fallen off her bicycle. He had partaken of the fruit all right. And yes, he had found it decidedly bitter.

Constance, perhaps sensing that the moment had passed too, squelched herself off him and lay on her back, eyes closed, apparently satisfied. The fire in her face had fizzled out a little and she looked almost radiant; one could say maternal.

Belatedly – very belatedly – thoughts of babies screamed their way through his head. He had been stupid, unbelievably stupid. Lust had ruled his mind – a lust which, passion spent, seemed vile and distasteful – and now it seemed as if a ring of devils were dancing around him, pointing and guffawing hysterically. He climbed to his feet and dressed quickly, feeling and looking a mess. Her stomach already seemed to be exhibiting the early stages of pregnancy, bearing the child that no doubt filled up her prayers. Yet it was useless pursuing this line of thought and, not knowing what else to do, he sat down next to her naked body and stared balefully at her conscience-free face. This woman had the potential to ruin him and he could do nothing about it. She curled up contentedly, rubbing her feet together and indulging in the most luxurious yawn. Her complacency was appalling.

'Say something nice to me,' she crooned, eyes still closed, 'something really lovely.'

For the moment, however, he couldn't bring himself to speak. She gazed at him with the puzzled look of a child, unsure of itself. The silence resounded.

'George.' There was a little catch in her voice. 'Is anything wrong?'

'Wrong?' he echoed, awed by her innocence. 'My marriage is wrong.'

There was no point in hurting her feelings unnecessarily. Any blame for what had happened he attributed entirely to himself.

'I understand.' She sat up and slung a friendly paw around him, allowing the rest of her body to rearrange itself. Before he could intimate that perhaps they'd made a mistake, she added, 'Emily's told me about the way things are between you.'

His ignorance returned to slap him in the face. The phrase 'the way things are' gave him a creeping sensation.

'What d'you mean?'

Constance blushed. 'Well, dear.' She shifted her naked mass about uncomfortably. 'You understand your marriage better than I do. You and Emily are obviously good friends. But – well,' she giggled nervously – 'why did you come here with me, in the first place? You must have been unhappy.'

'I was confused,' he said at length. 'Emily's not a very loving person.'

There was nothing to add to this sad admission and part of him wanted to burst into tears. Constance tightened her grip on his shoulder and neither of them said anything for the next couple of minutes. Was this, then, the end of his marriage? Had he finally given up hope? The evening of his wedding anniversary – the agonizing moments he and Emily had spent staring at each other in her room when the smallest token of affection would have sufficed to save him from humiliation – had brought everything to a head. Whatever her reason for marrying him the physical side of their relationship obviously hadn't counted in the least. She had strung him along with a promise of reviewing matters, but when the time had come she hadn't even shown the courtesy of discussing the issue.

And now it would never be discussed. Never. He was a reasonable man. He could have accepted another postponement. In a way he wouldn't have minded so much if the answer had been negative, but she had broken her promise, shown him an utter lack of respect. At least Constance had displayed an honesty in her feelings, acted in a manner he'd always dreamt Emily would act, allowing him to live out a fantasy.

'George, why do you suppose I brought you here?' she said, breaking the silence.

'You wished to show me where you'd spent your childhood.'

She found this highly amusing.

'You know the real reason, don't you?'

She smiled; then looked away distractedly. She seemed to be measuring her words carefully.

'Emily's a friend of mine, but I was wrong about what I said earlier. She isn't perfect, not by any means. She has a tendency to dominate people.'

He opened his mouth as if about to speak, but then shut it again.

'I always thought it would take a special man to put up with her behaviour. And I could see, at the picnic, you really were remarkably patient and understanding. But George,' she continued, now talking very excitedly, 'it doesn't have to be that way. You *could* enjoy an equal relationship with a woman. You and I are the same.' She grasped both his hands, gazing at him intensely. 'We've just made love and it was wonderful. Both of us are kind, gentle people who could be happy together. I know it, George. I feel it so strongly.'

Her face was alive with hope and joy, magnifying the sin a hundredfold, and making him feel a sort of inner despair. Modern society, of course, took a very lenient view towards infidelity – following the lead set by Edward VII and Mrs Alice Keppel – and it was considered extremely bad manners not to invite a man's mistress as well as his wife along to weekend house parties. Yet George had always abhorred that sort of licentious behaviour and, in any case, was petrified of being cuckolded himself. She – Constance – had seemed so quiet and unassuming, but ... well, perhaps she was right. They *were* quite similar and she'd somehow developed a hopeless infatuation. Oh, God, what a mess. What a hell of a mess.

She lowered her voice. 'Perhaps I could talk to Emily. Explain the way we feel about each other. It'll be hard on her, but maybe I could persuade her to understand.'

'No! Don't do that!'

She wedged his face between her hands and fixed him with her sad-looking eyes. 'I think there's a special person for everyone in this world.'

He almost wanted to laugh: this was his view as well. 'Who's the man for Emily then?' he asked sarcastically.

To his consternation she seemed to take this seriously. She looked down and, frowning a little, said under her breath, 'I have my suspicions.'

He threw her hands away from him – unable to spare her feelings any longer – and stood up. 'Who! Who d'you mean?'

She blushed fiercely. 'Who do you think? Does it matter?'

They glared at each other and, for a second, he still hoped she was making some cruel joke which her resentful face would soon confess to. But no. She remained indignant, confirming all the hints and nuances he'd tried so hard to ignore. This, then, was the last piece of evidence he needed to verify his worst thoughts. He closed his eyes, the tears running freely down his cheeks. Emily didn't care for him. She couldn't. And secretly he'd known it all along, right from the beginning. A picture came into his head, jiggling about in uproarious colour, of her and Pilling engaged in a similar activity to himself and Constance a few minutes before – except, of course, having more fun.

And even when they weren't making love he imagined them laughing at the way they'd fooled him, made him look – what was Emily's word? – like a chucklehead. It all seemed ridiculously clear now. Pilling, replete with overweening pride and triumphant sneers, was the only man who could truly satisfy her fastidious cravings, while she, the beautiful wife of a pathetic, balding, trumped-up war hero, obviously took his fancy as well. Lord Delsey had been right all along in saying that she'd leave one day – following the lead set by her mother. His stupidity, it seemed, was boundless, compounding the shame he felt through his own feebly adulterous response. 'No understanding of people' she'd said to Constance at Tapser's Ruin. It was such a damning indictment – undeniably true. And Constance, thinking that the signs were so evident he must be colluding in his wife's affair, had thrown herself at him for that very reason.

He looked over to find her quietly sobbing – dishevelled face buried in plump little hands – fully dressed now and respectable. They'd both been rejected at the same time, but in his case he'd been deceived by his spouse, the person who'd pledged herself to him and to whom he'd devoted the last three years of his life.

'I'm sorry,' he said, aware of the inadequacy of his words.

The journey back, not surprisingly, was subdued and, no doubt, the patient coachman had a strange tale to relate to his family that evening. Both of them, though quite courteous still, were indulging in their own private thoughts, making conversation impossible. For George it was more than ever apparent that Emily – sweet, cruel Emily – wasn't just an important facet of his life. She was, inextricably, his *raison d'être*: bright-eyed, ravishing; not least, somebody else's. There'd been a time when there was nothing he thought he didn't know about her: her way of dressing, her mannerisms, her points of view. It felt as if his brain was uniquely designed to index her lifestyle and movements, recording each and every aspect. Even a change of shoes – which occurred with alarming regularity – simply replaced one form of sublimity with another.

And yet, save for these facts gleaned over the years, what did he really know about his wife, if anything?

13

James

He was dropped at the end of the drive. It seemed that Constance had decided she wasn't going to be bitter towards him – that would give him a sense of worth. Instead, she was going to ignore him whenever possible. So with the coachman turning a deferential cheek in his direction and Constance a disdainful one, he said his goodbyes to a couple of profiles and limped wearily up the drive.

Would Constance keep her mouth shut?

The front door opened as he approached the house and a well-groomed doctor emerged, his black frock coat just about covering his portly frame and an Albert watch chain draped across his corporation.

'Ah, George, found you at last. Just called on your dear wife. She was asking after you. Wants you to go up and see her.'

'Yes ... yes, of course.'

'Perfectly safe, old chap. No need to look so worried. Touch of food poisoning, that's all.'

'Oh, good.'

'Yes, she's much better now. The colour's come back to her cheeks. She's a grand lass, your wife.'

He forced a smile. The old Gladstone bag-swinging buffer had no doubt doted at some length on this particular patient.

They chatted for another five minutes before Wetherington departed, but his mind was on other matters. Should he see Emily straight away? He wasn't sure he could face her at the moment, not after recent events. She'd requested his presence, but that was no reason why he should automatically fall into line. The 'touch of food poisoning' had doubtless been suggested to Wetherington and the latter had picked up on it eagerly.

And yet he knew all along he was going to see her – of course he was. It was hardly a point of consolation but at least he too had a secret to withhold. They could both lead duplicitous lives – even if he was probably going to be miserable as a result.

He rapped on Emily's bedroom door, receiving a croaky 'Come in'. She was lying on what seemed about ten plumped-up pillows looking, admittedly, quite pale and dishevelled. As soon as she glanced up and saw him, however, she brightened.

'Dearest, where have you been? Come and sit here.'

He sat halfway up the bed, further away than directed, quickly taking in the rest of the room. Gone were the papers previously littering the desk, not least that letter to Pilling which had so upset him on his last visit.

'Did you enjoy church?' she asked, managing a smile.

'It was deevy,' he replied, adopting one of her favourite words. 'I think I'll be going every week from now on. It's a great place to meet people with similar interests.'

She looked at him quizzically, perhaps wishing she had another ten pillows to ease her discomfort. In spite of his guilt over Constance, he'd instantly felt a dull ache in his chest upon entering the room, seeing Pilling with his arms around her, their lips meeting ...

'Who did you see, then?'

'Teddy.' He gazed directly into her eyes. 'I met up with Teddy, but I think he was more interested in making friends with Constance.'

This was deliberately aimed at hurting her – and, in the process, himself – but, if anything, she seemed more pleased than distressed.

'He said he'd call round to see us tomorrow.'

'He said he wanted to see *you* as well?' She blanched.

'That's right. He specifically mentioned seeing both of us.' Did she think Pilling was exclusively hers? He'd been asked to pass on the 'little goose' remark, but such a friendly overture stuck in his throat.

'So how are you feeling?' he asked after a slight pause, unable to avoid the obvious question.

'Much better now that you've arrived.' Her eyes renewed their sparkle. 'I think I might try and go for a stroll this evening. Get some fresh air.'

Evidently he looked quite hopeful at this point.

'On my own.' She reached out to squeeze his hand. 'I don't want you catching any more of my germs than necessary.'

'Fine,' he muttered, baffled by her reasoning and already intending to follow her.

'George.' Her mood perceptibly changed. 'You don't seem as cheerful as usual. You seem more serious.'

He regarded her cynically. An evil voice was telling him to make love to her there and then, regardless of her feelings. All she was wearing was a flimsy peignoir which he could easily grab by the lapels and force open. She was his wife after all. Not a stranger in a dirty old barn ...

'Nothing's changed, has it? We're still the same.'

He found he wanted some air himself. In the last few hours he'd turned into a person he hardly recognized and didn't particularly like. He'd behaved exactly in the same manner as Emily, committing adultery, but, unlike her, couldn't so easily control his feelings, acting innocent of deceit.

'Nothing's changed,' he reiterated, producing a tight-lipped smile.

That seemed to reassure her somewhat for she then gave him his instructions for the day, a series of errands and reminders. His mind, though, was wandering. The day before, his mood surprisingly optimistic (perhaps swayed by the knowledge that Emily and Pilling couldn't have met up all week), he'd written a little poem, dedicated, of course, 'To my wife'. The question remained, however, whether to present it to her or not. His latest offering was as follows:

> *Her face is kindness, and her eyes*
> *Shine brightly with such calm intent*
> *That thoughts too perfect to surmise*
> *Find sanctuary as Nature meant,*
> *In Beauty and a truth that lies*
> *In her sweet heart, so innocent.*

She finished giving him her shopping list of duties and he handed her his billet-doux.

'Very good.' She smiled obligingly.

Somehow he'd expected more. It had been a mistake. Feeling the colour rush to his cheeks – his dignity plainly teetering – he left shortly after, still trying to appear reasonably unruffled, while vowing to himself never to write any more poetry.

But attempting to hide the misery within was doomed the moment the misery without, in the person of Mrs Proops, appeared on the scene, bustling towards him from the end of the corridor, keys jangling from the chatelaine round her waist. Their last conversation had not been a success and he was in no mood to repeat the experience.

'Ah, Proopsy. How's the patient been behaving?'

Two dots of black peered suspiciously back at him out of two narrow slits. Although she was really a spinster and there was no legitimate reason for adding the married title to her name beyond that of courtesy, she was doubtless unimpressed by his form of address.

'*Mrs* Erskine hasn't been at all well.'

The stress on the first word was almost imperceptible.

'H'm,' he said dubiously. 'Touch of food poisoning apparently. And yet we both ate the same things. Odd, don't you think? I suppose that's why I find it difficult to believe it could be all that serious.'

She frowned. It was almost as though she were looking down on him despite the fact that he was at least a foot taller.

'In any case,' he continued, 'she's obviously been in the best possible hands.'

He searched her face in the hope of seeing a softening of her features but, if anything, the smell which she carried around under her nose, profoundly affecting her expression, seemed to take on a more pungent odour. Whatever happened to the word 'sir'? 'Very kind of you to say so, sir', with a dab of crimson on the cheeks and maybe a polite curtsy. Then he could have said, 'Carry on, Proopsy', and dismissed her. Instead, he had to endure those surly eyes, that defiant jaw, the whole disdainful facial façade.

'Well, carry on, Proopsy,' he said all the same.

She walked off silently, not letting good manners disturb her mission. But as she hovered outside her mistress's room, preparing to go in, an idea struck him and he burst out laughing, maniacally, hysterically. She looked round, shocked, and perhaps for the first time in her life, blushed the purest vermilion. Then, fiddling with the door, she escaped.

He was going mad, quite mad. Such an outburst could only come from someone under a great deal of stress, far more than he imagined. Somehow he had to calm down. Take deep breaths, deep, deep breaths. At least his next course of action was clear. If Emily *did* decide to go for a stroll in the evening, he had to follow her, experience the grim pleasure of witnessing her treachery at first hand. Then he could judge – once and for all – if there was any hope left for the two of them.

For the remainder of the afternoon he stayed in the library, with its smell of fine wood and old vellum. (The scene of Emily's most painful memory, it had been largely redesigned since her childhood.) Here he was interrupted only once – by Hopley's son, James – who froze when he saw him, his guilty-looking face suspended in fear.

'Come in, James.' George extended his arm in a welcoming gesture. 'What brings you here?'

The boy squirmed in embarrassment. 'Nothin', master. Jus' thought I'd do some readin'.'

'Highly commendable, too. You need a break, I'm sure, from all your duties.'

Hoping to place the other at his ease, he went back to reading a medical tome – he had an interest in the subject and wanted to take his mind off Emily – while James remained stranded in the middle of the room. The boy's presence in the library, in any case, was highly questionable – certainly his father would never have approved – and the excuse that he wanted to peruse the master's collection was a trifle impertinent to say the least. But escaping a reprimand, and anxious to leave, he was clearly unsure what to do next. Points of red appeared on his cheeks, forming a contrast with his pristine white collar.

Presently George laid aside his book and looked up. His concentration had been disturbed and his thoughts had turned to other matters.

'Ah, deary me! The trouble with all these books, James – the trouble is knowing where to start, don't you agree? I tell you what! If you're looking for something to do – only if you've nowhere else to go, mind – I've got a job that might just interest you. Care to take part in a competition? It involves detective work.'

The boy's jaw perceptibly dropped but he managed, 'You mean like Sherlock Holmes, master?'

'Precisely. But it shall have to be carried out in complete secrecy. No telling your good father.'

The hint of a frown invaded his open features as he grappled with this concept. 'You want me to spy on him?'

'No, no, old fellow. This has got nothing to do with him. It's simply better that as few people know as possible. Just you and me, for instance.'

He now looked totally confused.

'In fact,' George added, 'that's where the competitive element comes in. I don't believe you can keep your mouth tight shut about our little secret.' James automatically pressed his lips together. 'And what's more, I've got a sovereign which says you can't.'

He took out the coin in question and laid it on the table.

James's mouth gaped open again and he gazed at the gleaming metal object as if he'd just discovered the lost treasure of the Incas. Apart from his collar, the rest of his apparel – jacket, waistcoat, breeches and boots – had evidently been worn a great number of times, and it was clear that Hopley didn't spoil his son.

'I wish to surprise my wife,' George explained, leaning forward and muting his voice. 'There's a chance she might go out tonight and, if she does, I need time to prepare her present.' He looked round shiftily. 'I daresay she'll be going on foot, so all you have to do is follow her, then warn me in advance when she comes back. I'll make up some excuse for not accompanying her.'

James's face at this point was entering advanced stages of stupefaction.

'Now I know all this is fairly unorthodox. I know you think I'm incapable of lying to my wife. But believe me, James, you'll be doing us all a big favour by carrying this out. Now it's very important' – he gave the library door another furtive look – 'that you pay close attention to where the mistress goes, who she meets, if anyone, and what they say. It's possible, you see, that people more unscrupulous than you or me might have got wind of what I've been planning and give the game away. I want you to report back everything you see and hear as my only witness. What d'you say?'

The boy gazed wonderingly at the money on the table and nodded his assent.

'I know you'd do it for nothing, James, but this is my present for your services and your discretion.' George rescued the subject of James's devotion, tucking it back into his pocket. 'Now run along – and be sure your father can tell me where you are if I ask him tonight.'

Almost taking George literally when he said 'run', James hastily made his exit. It hadn't occurred to George, before the boy appeared, to use an accomplice, but all in all it seemed to be the perfect solution.

However, as the rest of the day dragged on and he ate his dinner alone, the feebleness of his idea – comparable to his earlier plan of following Pilling – struck him with a depressing forcefulness. How could he be so stupid? Even if he spotted Emily walking out of the house, he still needed to alert James. And even if his father knew where the boy was – say, in his room above one of the coach-houses – he still needed to fetch him.

After the meal he spent another hour ruminating over his lost intelligence; then went to bed early with a splitting headache.

He awoke at about half past eleven.

Surely Emily had left and come back by now? If she'd returned, or if she'd decided to stay in her room, she would certainly have locked the door – a chore which she undertook with superstitious regularity. But if she was out – at this ungodly hour – her door would presumably still be open.

Brushing aside his eiderdown and donning his dressing-robe, he stepped out onto the landing. All was quiet. What he was doing was awful, it really was, but there was no turning back now. He gritted his teeth – as if that would help – and gripped the cold metal door handle to her room, holding it down and then pushing ...

Heavens, it had given way! He really hadn't expected ...

He stood motionless for a few seconds, the door remaining ajar in his hand. Did that really mean she wasn't there? Even though he'd concluded as such a moment ago, it seemed unlikely somehow. Far more probable that she'd gone to sleep and simply forgotten to lock her door. Hence it was not in his interests to be caught creeping into her bedroom.

A sound behind him, muffled but distinct, sent an electric shock through his body, and he whirled round. Mrs Proops, replete in her nightclothes and slippers, her hair still looking remarkably austere, was descending the red pile staircase, standing at the bend between the first and second floor, staring directly at him. There was nothing to do. He closed Emily's door and, conscious of the housekeeper's withering gaze, retreated to his bedroom, sweating profusely.

14

James's Story

The tap-tap-tap which was beating out sounded like an ancient door being knocked in a far-off land.

Tap, tap, tap ... Tap, tap, tap.

Strange. It was more distinct now. Closer. Yes, much closer. Almost as if ...

Lord ...

He struggled out of bed – feeling the blood draining from his face – and fumbled for his dressing-robe in the available light. Who on earth could it be, calling at this hour? He opened the door to reveal two excited coal-black eyes, set in a pink and frozen landscape, the tousled hair of the boy bunched into the shape of the cap he'd been wearing.

'James! What are you...? Come in. Come in, my boy.'

He scuttled off to light the bedside lamp leaving James hovering on the brink, obviously unsure whether he was allowed to enter in spite of his entreaty.

'Step lively, man,' said George, losing his sleep-induced croak and opening the chest at the foot of the bed to reveal a healthy supply of medicinal beverages. 'You've already woken me up. How much worse can things get?'

He poured out a well-upholstered whisky and James sat down on the chair nearest the door, tucking his mud-splattered boots underneath. The glow from the lamp seemed to bounce off his face and his eyes registered an intensity which made George's stomach perform a little flutter.

'Drink,' he urged him. 'It'll do you good.'

James sipped from the glass, subduing a cough into a more manly wheeze.

'Thank you, master. It's a wicked night, to be sure.'

He took another sip, controlling his reaction to it more efficiently.

'What happened? Did you follow her?'

James nodded.

'When did she return?'

'Jus' now. A few minutes ago.'

George glanced at the clock on the mantelpiece. 'But it's a quarter after twelve.'

'Aye, master. I know you said to warn you when the mistress were comin' back. But she were goin' so quick, I couldn't get past her.'

'Yes, yes, never mind about that. I'll surprise her with her present tomorrow. Now, tell me everything that's happened.'

James cradled the glass in his lap, staring at it like a crystal ball.

'Well, for a long while she stayed in her room. I tried to keep a lookout but everyone kept movin' me on. By half nine or so I were famished, so I went down to the kitchen for a bite to eat. Mrs Hedges doesn't mind – well, not much – an' I were all on my own when I seed the mistress in the passage, all dressed to go out. She smiled an' said sorry for disturbin' me, sayin' she jus' fancied a walk. "Don't tell anyone", she says. "Mr Erskine wouldn't agree to it so soon after my illness."

'Well, I were in a fix, thinkin' of what she'd do if she caught me followin'. Then I thought of how you'd feel if I stayed in the house. So I waited till she'd gone, then took after her.'

'You did absolutely right,' George assured him to his obvious satisfaction.

'She didn't run to the back door, but she were fair skippin' down the drive. I might've lost her if it hadn't been for 'em white gloves she were wearin'. Took on a life of their own, they did. She turned right at the end of the drive, behind the hedgerow, an' I ran down after her. She'd vanished.'

George frowned.

'She'd gone, vanished. I started up the road, thinkin' she'd turned the corner. Then I seed her, goin' across the field. It were all open there an' I thought, if she looks round, I'll fall to the ground. But she kept goin', into the wood.'

George's hands clenched and the line of his mouth tightened. Didn't want him catching her germs, was that the story...?

'It were grim in there, master. The light were poor an' the trees covered you up. I got to thinkin' all sorts might be lyin' in wait.'

He took a sip of his drink in recollection.

'After a while I seed the mistress at the edge of the pond. I was worried that if she got to the gate, I'd lose her again. But in my hurry I stepped in a ditch. I lay on the ground, hopin' she'd think it were a frog. It were a nasty moment, though – maybe for both of us. When I looked up she'd passed through the gate. I went after her, not carin' where I trod. I could jus' see her hat an' gloves halfway down to Potterslake Farm.'

George took a draught of his whisky and soda. He'd known for the last half-minute or so she was visiting Pilling, but now there was absolutely no doubt.

'Afore long she reached the yard. I hid behind the wall an' seed her go to the front door. She knocked, fiddled with her hat a bit, an' Mr Pillin' let her in.'

'Not one of the servants?'

James coughed, raising his hand to his mouth. 'I heard, master, that Mr Pillin' discharged his staff a few days ago.'

'He did what?'

'Told 'em to go. My cousin worked under Mr Pillin' an' he were very upset. Mr Pillin' said he'd debts to pay, an' all he could do were ask round an' see if other work were goin'.'

'Well, he didn't come to me,' George said, realizing that Emily must have known all the details. 'Besides, he can't have money worries, I don't believe it. He must have inherited a fortune from his late wife.'

James was silent, but another thought struck George. Pilling could have dismissed his staff to avoid suspicion over visits from Emily. It scarcely seemed possible he'd go to such lengths to preserve their secret. And yet ...

'Carry on, James.'

'After she'd gone in I creeped up to a bush near the door. Perishin' cold it were, an' two hours passed, I'd say, afore anythin' happened.'

He paused again, perhaps waiting for a commendation, but George was too busy imagining the terrible goings-on *inside* the house, chewing away at what remained of his nails.

'Then the door opens. I couldn't hear the mistress, but he says, "Goodbye, my dear, sweet sister. I'm sure you won't let me down."'

'Hold on. He said what?'

The boy faithfully reproduced his last sentence.

'Sister? Emily doesn't have any brothers or sisters.'

'Mr Pillin' did say it in a funny way, as if he were makin' mischief.'

'How did the mistress reply?'

'I don't think she said anythin'.' James hesitated for a moment. 'I thought they might be related, master. My cousin heard some such—'

'No, no. Quite untrue.'

Of course, he saw it now. It would be in the interest of the young lovers to encourage rumours of a sibling relationship. That would be an astute way of offsetting the gossip surrounding the frequency of their meetings. Very clever. And calling Emily 'sister' was a sarcastic reminder of this.

'A joke in poor taste,' he added to James.

'I think she thought so too, master. She set off again in the same way she left here. Brisk, you might say. I wanted to follow, but Mr Pillin' jus' stood in the doorway, lookin' at her till she'd gone. Smilin' to himself.'

A muscle twitched in George's cheek. 'Did anything else happen?'

'No, she came straight back here. But it were bitter cold. I think if she were feelin' unwell ... that sort of walk ...'

'Quite. But she's back in her bedroom now?'

'I think so. Did you prepare her present?'

'Oh, yes, that's all settled. Don't worry about that. And you've certainly played your part, James, a quite magnificent effort. About time now, though, you went to bed. Good night, little chap.'

The boy set his glass on the chest of drawers and, looking slightly glum, shut the door behind him.

George made preparations for bed again, trying to force his unbending mind on to some other topic. Damn the man, damn him! Having the nerve to grin at the sight of his wife stealing guiltily away into the darkness. He reached for the whisky bottle and took a hefty gulp. If Pilling was standing before him now, he'd wipe that smirk off his face, by God he would! *So you think it's amusing to break up a marriage, do you? Not so funny now, eh?* Breathing heavily, his heart hammering against his chest, he took another swig from the bottle. Damn him! And damn her as well! If anything, she had even less excuse for her behaviour. She knew how he felt. She *knew* and yet she'd still fallen into the arms of that popinjay who probably didn't care for her a fraction as much as he did. His eyes filled with tears. How could she take his deepest, most precious, feelings and tear them into little pieces? How could she?

Half an hour passed and he lay absolutely rigid in bed, staring into darkness. The rest of the whisky bottle had gone and the line between wakefulness and unconsciousness was beginning to blur. She didn't love him. Couldn't, just couldn't. Simply taken pity on him, that's all. It was all over and, though it was death to contemplate, he'd relinquish all rights over her, let her have her freedom. Oh, God, he could hardly breathe. But it was better – for his sake as well as hers. Somewhere, a long way away, people were talking, Emily certainly, but he was no longer interested. Time to sleep … sleep …

He awoke with a start as though someone had cried out loud into his ear. *What on earth was that!* He'd definitely heard a little shriek. A cat perhaps? He sat upright in bed, trying to recognize any other sounds. A minute elapsed and then a door creaked before gently being closed.

Emily's door!

He grabbed his dressing-robe and rushed out onto the landing. No one was there. But wait! He could hear footfalls on the staircase. He dashed over to the banister, glimpsing the trail of a dark overcoat whisking round the curve to the ground floor.

'Hi! Hi, you there!'

There was no response. He waited another second, swaying backwards a step. Oh, hell, he'd had too much to drink, his head was pounding. Whatever he saw, or thought he'd seen, would just have to be forgotten. The memory of James's visit earlier in the evening surfaced in his mind and he groaned inwardly. He'd sent that small boy out to spy on the cruel intrigues of adults and he'd reported back everything in his pure, innocent fashion. Nausea rose in his throat and it was all he could do to return to his room and climb back into bed.

No sooner had he laid his head upon the pillow than he was

confronted with the most arresting image – vivid and disturbing. Tapser's Ruin loomed up before him, a black crenellated spider's crown, drawing him, magnetically, into its clutches. But what treasures were inside! The rooms were decorated in the most ornate fashion, with dazzling candelabra, rugs of the deepest wool, silk draperies and the most recherché plant life abounding in nooks and crannies.

But where was everyone? There was absolute silence.

The doors to the outside world were locked, leaving him trapped inside his gorgeous prison, lungs tightening in the squandered air. He started to panic, moving bookcases in a desperate bid to find hidden passages. Then he heard them, *sotto voce* at first, building up into an unmistakable sound. Voices, familiar voices. He half-ran, half-hobbled, up several flights of stairs, cowering next to the last twist in the banister. Emily had her arm around Constance's neck and was leading her into the bedroom. 'Come, my dear child …'

The picture faded and another one hove into view. Doctor Wetherington had arrived. Emily was unwell. George was standing outside her bedroom listening to her groans. But what sort of groans! Tears welling up, he rushed in to discover the doctor treating her leg for the most horrible-looking port wine stain, evilly swelling and strewn with tiny white spots. She was screaming, dementedly, at George to get out.

Yet another scene. The idea occurred to his lust-addled mind, to steal into Emily's room, make sure she was asleep, and crawl under the covers for a few minutes. Such joy and pleasantness! Knowing that she was there, lying beside him in the dark, dreaming, breathing … But hold on a moment. She wasn't there at all. A light was on somewhere, showing that the other half of the bed was empty. He turned to his side, looking up … to be confronted with this wild staring woman wielding a carving knife …

He was awake.

Really awake. These were his blankets, his bed. Thank God the nightmares had ended, everything back to normal. But … what was that? A man was shouting. Something about the mistress. Oh, Lord. A woman's scream. The house seemed to be in the throes of hysteria, people stampeding along corridors, crying out for help. The door was suddenly thrust open and Hopley, James's father, appeared in the room, his few hairs dishevelled and a wild look upon his face.

'Sir, come quickly! It's Mrs Erskine!'

'Wha— What's happened?'

'There's been some sort of accident. Please! Come quickly!'

Part Two

15

The Morning After

Doctor Wetherington repeated himself, obviously under the impression that George was not in a fit state to comprehend his words.

'Emily passed away during the night. I'm so sorry, old chap.' He rested his hand on George's shoulder. 'If you need any help, then Norah and I – well, you only have to ask. It's a frightful shock, I know.' He let out a sigh and then, with evident regret, broached the subject of his professional responsibility. 'Look, I don't expect you to take this in but, having made a preliminary examination, I find it impossible to determine the cause of death. Emily seemed to be making a full recovery yesterday from that stomach upset and was in the best of spirits. I simply don't understand it.' He scratched his grizzled head. 'I don't suspect foul play, of course, but I've sent for the police surgeon in order to get a second opinion. In the meantime I'd better stand guard. There's a key in the door on the inside, but I think it's best if everything's left exactly as it is. Have courage, old chap.' He patted George on the shoulder again and withdrew.

A few moments later Hopley appeared at George's side. 'There's a Constable Tulley to see you, sir.'

A young man in a uniform was standing nervously in the hall, pretending to admire a large tapestry pinned against the wall. 'I'm very sorry—' he started, and broke off. 'Inspector Gwynne should be here shortly, with Doctor Feltham. I'll – er – just go upstairs then.'

Without really knowing where he was going, George made his way to the study. The room was unoccupied and he shut himself in, leaning back on the door and closing his eyes.

For Emily not to be alive …

Her face appeared before him, eyes sparkling like emeralds. She was so vital and brimming with life. He'd never suspected for a moment when she'd left the breakfast-table in a rush ...

Oh, God, what had he done? She'd been ill – really ill – and he'd watched her so closely that she'd been forced to escape late at night in the cold. He'd as good as killed her. Killed Emily. He sank to his knees, rocking back and forth, face buried in his hands, sobbing. Far better that she'd gone to live with Pilling and their marriage had broken up than—

Somebody was knocking at the door – knocking quite loudly. How long had they been there? Oh, please let it be her! After all, this night-marish existence couldn't be real. If anyone was dead it was him. He rose to his feet and—

No, don't open it! Don't open it in case the nightmare was real.

He took a step backwards, but the caller, Hopley, was already entering. Perhaps even now if he spoke about other matters ... didn't look quite so grave.

'Inspector Gwynne and Doctor Feltham have arrived, sir. I believe Doctor Feltham has already gone upstairs, but the inspector is waiting for you in the morning-room.'

The butler withdrew and George, suddenly finding his breath again, somehow managed to pull himself together sufficiently to follow him, wiping a tear from his cheek. All that mattered was lost. Gone forever.

They arrived at their destination to find that the embarrassed constable had come downstairs to join the inspector.

'Mr Erskine?' said the inspector, extricating himself from the sofa. 'You must be extremely upset and in a state of shock.'

George nodded.

'We'll try not to stay too long, but Doctor Wetherington has confessed to being somewhat vexed by your wife's sudden death. If you wouldn't mind answering just one or two questions, then we'll be off.'

'Fine ... fine,' he murmured, dropping into an armchair. His voice sounded disjointed; he was not fully in his right senses.

The two policemen sat down as well and the inspector smiled weakly. He was a rather sad-looking man, with limpid eyes and a scimitar of magenta carved out under each eye. His bulbous nose was extraordinarily large, a facial landmark which he'd tried to mask by growing the thickest of moustaches. The main problem, though, lay in co-ordinating his lumbering features – his mouth might gape open like a rusty drawbridge or his spade-like hand might hang in the air as his mind adjusted itself to an original thought. In fact, brain and body were in a perpetual *pas de deux* which lent the impression of quite clever idiocy.

'May I ask you first if you heard anything suspicious this morning?' he began. 'Out of the ordinary so to speak.'

George hesitated for a second, but there was really no choice.

'Yes. Yes, I did hear something, as a matter of fact.'

Stutteringly, he recounted for them the small cry he'd heard (making the scribbling constable shudder) and the sound of Emily's door opening and closing. Only when he was disclosing these particulars did he realize that there was a strong chance he'd listened to his wife's murder. *While doing absolutely nothing.* The real talking point, however, was the vague figure he'd seen at the bottom of the staircase. Much as the inspector tried, he could not extract a more extensive description of the intruder. In the end he turned to the constable and said, 'Tulley, go back to the station. Send word to neighbouring constabularies to be on the lookout for a man or woman wearing a long, dark overcoat, possibly out of breath. Tell Sims to go to the railway station. Gray and Wilson can go to The Three Bells and The Journeyman, making discreet enquiries. It's probably too late for the bloodhounds, sir,' he said, turning to George as the constable lingered by the door. 'There's been a light drizzle this morning.'

George stood up, hoping the inspector would follow suit, but the latter settled back into the sofa and took a pipe out of his waistcoat. Members of the police would normally have been shown out through the tradesman's entrance, but George accompanied the constable to the front door before retiring to the study. He wanted to sleep – waking up in a world in which Emily was alive – but his mind would not rest. The noises he'd heard which he'd attempted to describe to the police: did they have any meaning? Why in heaven's name had he had so much to drink when he might have been able to save her?

And now, how could he possibly live with that knowledge?

After twenty minutes or so he was disturbed by the faithful Hopley, passing on the message from the police that he could view his wife's body if he wished to do so. It was odd how it seemed an infringement of Emily's privacy, so jealously guarded during her lifetime, to undergo such a procedure. Very shortly her concealed form would be borne away on a stretcher. No, he could not witness even that ...

Another hour elapsed before Hopley once more appeared at the study door.

'I beg your pardon, sir. The inspector would like to talk to you again – in the library.'

George passed a hand over his face. God, he was tired. So awfully tired.

'I think perhaps it would be more appropriate, Hopley, if in future you showed the policemen to the drawing-room – rather than the library or the morning-room.'

'Very good, sir. But on this occasion I discovered them in the library.'

'Oh! Well, I suppose under the circumstances it's fine for them to have the run of the place.'

Hopley bowed, emitting an almost imperceptible snorting sound. 'If you'd care to follow me, sir.'

A couple of minutes later George was facing Gwynne across the oak table in the library. The constable stood towards the back of the room, the eight silver buttons on his tunic proclaiming their highly polished state. The inspector was very polite.

'Sorry to disturb you again, sir. I thought you'd like to know the arrangements we've made with your wife. She's been taken to the mortuary for a full post-mortem examination. We'd just like to ask you a couple of further questions, if you don't mind.'

'Go ahead.'

'Well, you wouldn't happen to know whether your wife slept on her side or her back?'

George stared at the inspector incredulously. 'Um, her back,' he decided.

'All the time?'

'I daresay.' The subject of Emily's sleeping habits was a painful reminder of the gulf which existed between them in certain respects. 'What does it matter?'

'Well, we've found traces of make-up on her pillow.'

'So perhaps she turned over during the night.'

'The make-up was found on the *other* side of the pillow. In other words, she'd have to be sleeping on her side – with the pillow turned the other way round. Or she could have been sleeping on her back – which you say she does most of the time – with the pillow placed over her face.'

George frowned, not quite sure how to respond. The image of a pillow being placed over Emily's lovely face was horrible and he could feel his stomach muscles tighten. 'Is that your view, then, Inspector?' he asked after a few moments.

'Well, it does seem a bit strange that the murderer, having suffocated your wife with a pillow, should replace it under her head – assuming it is murder, of course. Does your wife normally lock her door at night, may I ask?'

'Always.'

'And how many people possessed a key to her room?'

'Only Mrs Proops.'

'Ah … H'm. There are no other keys available to members of the household?'

'That's right,' George said, feeling increasingly uncomfortable. 'Mrs Proops is the only person Emily allowed into her room. What of it?'

'Well – if you'll excuse my impertinence – how do you know which way she sleeps?'

George pursed his lips. 'Because I'm her husband.'

'Quite, quite!' The inspector responded in the same offhand manner. 'I wasn't trying to suggest anything, sir. Please forgive any unintended inference. I must just ask you, though: is there anyone you know who might want to kill your wife?'

'No.'

The inspector seemed satisfied with this for he then proceeded to talk about *other* murder cases before, lightning-quick, picking up a book on the table and saying, 'Been reading this, sir?' He thrust it towards George, allowing him to barely glance at it.

'Yes, I believe so ...'

'*The Student's Handbook of Forensic Medicine*, dated 1895. I have a copy myself as a matter of fact. Very informative on the subject of arsenic. Look, you can see if I relax my grip – there – it falls open just at the start of that section.'

George regarded Gwynne in astonishment as he gave a demonstration. Of course he remembered browsing through the book, desperately trying to forget about Emily and Pilling. And yes, he had noticed the spine was slightly damaged – but not by him. He tried to retrieve the situation.

'I was studying that section in particular, Inspector.'

'Oh, yes?' Gwynne raised his eyebrows.

'A friend of mine during the war was addicted to the stuff. It was the anniversary of his death not so long ago and, on a whim, I decided to investigate the matter.'

The inspector smiled but his dead eyes looked more inscrutable than ever. George had the overriding feeling that he did not believe him.

16

Inspector Gwynne

The inquest was held the following afternoon, a small affair, hastily cobbled together, in the drawing-room at Stockley Hall. Since George was dreading a drawn-out enquiry, this particular arrangement was ideal – not least because the press hadn't been informed – but the exercise was a distressing one nonetheless. Indeed, the exchange between the coroner and Doctor Feltham was so vulgar in its attention to physical detail that he walked out of the room after a couple of minutes, nearly followed by one of the jurymen, who was ordered back.

The following morning he cycled to Tapser's Ruin and stood at the open window where he'd overheard Emily talking to Constance. It was probably that occasion which had made him realize she'd never feel the same way about him as he felt about her. He'd fervently hoped that their marriage would make a difference – and never quite given up hope that one day he might win her over – but eventually she'd sought recourse in another man, one whom she was prepared to go to any lengths to see. Perhaps it would have been better if she and Pilling had met three years ago and he hadn't entered her life at all. Certainly if she could choose Pilling as her sweetheart, then it was true about his lack of understanding.

And now she was dead, placing a seal forever on all those wasted whimsical thoughts. He imagined her last few breaths, her final gasp, before that awful coldness enveloped her body, extinguishing that vibrant life. This, then, was the tragic conclusion that she was hurtling towards, the final twist in the story. And his life – which he'd endeavoured to document so wittily for her exclusive entertainment – now seemed shallow and insignificant.

Back at Stockley Hall he felt more charitable towards Inspector Gwynne when they discovered each other in the drawing-room. They even spent a few jovial minutes talking about Gwynne's four-year-old granddaughter, who was temporarily staying at the inspector's house and preventing her grandfather from obtaining any sleep. It was evident that the policeman was deliberately steering the subject away from the main area of interest, but George nonetheless appreciated the thought behind the gesture. Gwynne really was a capital fellow in many ways. Society might draw attention to their differing status, but perhaps under different circumstances they could even have been friends.

'Sherry, Inspector?'

'Oh, that's very kind. Normally I'd say I was on duty, but it's been a long day.'

George trundled off to the drinks cabinet. 'Tell me about the investigation,' he said over his shoulder.

'Well, I know this is painful for you to hear, sir. I noticed you left the room during Doctor Feltham's testimony. But I think it's important to give you the gist of his evidence, as well as the findings of the Home Office pathologist, Sir James Fletcher. In the opinion of the doctors your wife was almost certainly murdered.'

George stopped pouring drinks. He'd already been informed of the verdict of the inquest of course – 'wilful murder' by some 'person or persons unknown'. His reaction was purely distaste at the thought of Feltham's thoroughly lewd post-mortem examination.

'How?'

'Well, it appears that she was strangled. There were bruises around her neck and a certain bone was broken. It's possible the murderer started by using his bare hands but then decided to use one of the pillows.'

This was horrible, *horrible*. George tightened his fists in anger.

'Her lungs were slightly congested and there were bubbles of saliva flecked with blood around her nose and mouth. She probably didn't put up much of a struggle, but that might be because there was a smell of alcohol.'

'Alcohol? Are you sure?'

'I'm afraid I don't know the full medical details. I do know we didn't find any trace of alcohol in her room. In fact, I was hoping, sir, you might be able to shed some light on the matter.'

'Um, no ... no.'

George handed him his sherry. Goodness knows he'd had a fair amount to drink himself that evening. The interview had become ominous somehow, underlying the friendliness. Perhaps with murder established he ought to be more careful in his remarks. If it was known, for instance, that he'd sent James to follow Emily to the house of her lover ... well, the consequences for him could be serious indeed.

'Cigar, Inspector?'

'Oh! Yes, thank you.'

George reached for the finely carved cigar case but hesitated at the last moment, his hand shaking. The case had been Emily's present to him on their recent anniversary. *My darling, you are the next Wordsworth!* He found the armchair and slumped down.

'Sorry, Gwynne. Just need a moment.'

'I quite understand, sir.' The inspector's voice sounded a little strained as well. 'We'll do everything we can to catch your wife's killer.'

George nodded, still struggling to compose himself. 'Have you made any progress?'

'A little, yes. We've been working on your suspicion that an intruder broke into the house. I've had my men check all the windows and doors and there doesn't appear to be any sign of a forced entry. But since the back door was open, he might well have come in that way.'

But you don't believe that, do you, Inspector?

'And then there's your wife's room. I know you told us she always locked her door at night. But are you absolutely sure?'

'I suppose she might have forgotten. Mrs Proops woke her up each morning so she would know.'

'Ah, yes, Mrs Proops. Your housekeeper has told us she saw you at eleven thirty leaving your wife's room.'

'Yes?'

'*Were* you leaving your wife's room?'

'Um, yes.'

'Did you see your wife?'

'Um, yes.' The words were out before he could check their progress. 'I was just saying good night.'

'Just saying good night?'

'Well, we talked for about five minutes.'

Silence. Then something rather crafty occurred to him.

'Fact is, Inspector, we were discussing the position of Mrs Proops. Whether we could afford her or not.'

'Ah, hence the unusual hour. To ensure privacy.'

'Exactly.'

'So it must have been quite a shock to see her on the stairs.'

'Precisely.'

'This is interesting, very interesting,' murmured the inspector. 'If Mrs Proops knew her position was in jeopardy … H'm! This is something we need to look into. She certainly had the opportunity—'

'Well, I don't see how she could have known anything,' said George, in some alarm at the impression he'd given.

'Nevertheless,' insisted the inspector, 'she's somewhat of a character, isn't she, your housekeeper? Doesn't show a deal of emotion. When we questioned her about seeing you on the stairs she said she was in the process of turning down the lights. I suppose if she'd carried out the murder she'd be more likely to head back to her room rather than go downstairs – assuming you saw the killer escaping, of course, sir.'

'H'm,' agreed George without conviction.

'In any case there's the key that was left in your wife's door to account for. You'd expect Mrs Proops to use her own key to gain entry, to avoid waking her mistress. The key left in the door was definitely your wife's. We checked. And even if Mrs Proops was cunning enough to let herself in and then place your wife's key in the lock, we should still be able to catch her out with fingerprints.'

'Fingerprints?'

'Every fingerprint shows markings that are unique. There was a case last year where a man was charged with burglary on such evidence. All clever stuff, I assure you.'

George smiled vaguely. Was he meant to think the police were bound to catch the murderer eventually?

'The other thing to be said for Mrs Proops is she did seem very concerned to help us. She told us that Mrs Erskine seemed troubled in the last days of her life. Not just laid low by her illness but very much absorbed in her thoughts.'

'Yes, I noticed that.'

'Then, of course, Mrs Proops was implicitly trusted by Mrs Erskine, wasn't she? Forgive me for asking, sir, but do you know why your wife should lock her door at night? Was she frightened of anything?'

George swallowed, playing for time. 'Oh, yes. Yes, she was. Dating back to her childhood. She was plagued by a fear of – well, I suppose you could call it the demons of the night. Phantoms. She thought she could lock them out.'

Considering his mental state, he was quite pleased with this response as well. There was no point in taking exception to the man's intrusive curiosity – he was only doing his job after all – and the situation had been retrieved with another white lie.

'Oh, I see,' said Gwynne. 'Yes, that would explain it. Well, I think that leaves us with only two possibilities. On the night of her murder she either forgot to lock her door or she knew her attacker and let him in willingly.'

'H'm.' Another blind alley statement.

'Well, that's about as far as we've got.' The inspector placed his empty sherry glass back down on the table and rose to his feet. 'Oh, yes, one last thing. We came across a pair of your wife's shoes. They were absolutely filthy. You wouldn't know if your wife went for any long walks on the night of her death?'

'Sorry, Inspector,' he said instinctively.

Gwynne jotted something in his notebook and, on this rather sour note, left the room.

Scarcely had he gone before his presence was replaced by Constance. The last time George had seen her, fiery-faced and watery-eyed, she'd been twittering 'Oh, George!' to the point where he'd thought his name might actually begin with an 'O'.

'Oh, George!'

He stood up obediently and she threw herself into his arms, blubbering.

'I'm sorry. I'm so awfully sorry.'

He gripped her shoulders and pushed her gently, but firmly, backwards. It was unfortunate, since she must care about Emily as well, but her presence was just too painful a reminder of his infidelity. Even in the light of his wife's deception.

'I know how you felt about Emily, George. She was a dear, dear friend to me too. I can't believe she's gone.'

She let out another volley of sobs while he regarded her despondently. It was not that he didn't have any respect for her feelings, but the way she was making a spectacle of herself was appalling. To burst into somebody's house and start wailing like that! It seemed an age before she composed herself and began talking normally – normally for her at any rate. Over the next couple of hours he discovered, among other things, that they'd suffered a terrible misunderstanding. Everything had happened 'too soon' and he had been overwhelmed by a sense of guilt which she could fully appreciate. But now 'we' could put that behind 'us'. She was here to help. To look after him.

At this point that familiar maternal expression was beginning to transform her face and he found himself grimly contemplating the possible consequences of that mad afternoon in the barn. No, he dared not risk offending her; not yet at any rate. But then again, he could not be too friendly, if that was conceivable, because, looking at it from the inspector's point of view, she represented a possible motive. The fact that she was half-cracked in her feelings towards him was probably of small consequence to the police.

On the other hand she *was* quite helpful. Over the next couple of days, desperate to be of use, she largely took over the funeral arrangements, and her protective attitude was valuable in keeping the neighbours at bay. Typically, she wanted to offer a large reward for information leading to an arrest – a not very publicity-shy idea which he vetoed on the advice of Inspector Gwynne. In fact, she treated the police as if they were part of her extended family, scolding them for taking up too much of his time, a stance which, while being petty, was also in tune with her obvious conviction of his innocence.

She was informative, too. Over home-made rock cakes she'd announced, as part of the mounting evidence of detective stupidity displayed by Gwynne and his cohorts, that they were now interviewing all the domestics, including 'that little Hopley boy'. As a matter of fact, they'd been closeted with *him* for some time.

She changed the subject to something more interesting (for her), but he felt pricked with doubts. James wouldn't say anything, would he? Surely he'd be far too afraid. Perhaps, having promised to keep a secret, he'd feel obliged to keep quiet.

And then it struck him with an awful clarity – to the extent that he half-choked on a loose crumb – that James was almost bound to reveal everything, every last detail of that final evening. And why? Because – like an absent-minded fool – George had never given him that sovereign he'd offered for his services. The next interview was going to be a disaster. He knew that for sure.

Inspector Gwynne surveyed him mournfully from the other side of the table in the library, the hollows under his eyes looking more pronounced than ever. George had decided to make a 'clean breast of it', telling Gwynne that in previous interviews he'd been tired and overwrought, anxious to avoid a scandal. ('Quite understandable, sir' was the half-convincing response.)

Encouraged by not being ticked off for wasting police time, he proceeded to give them a sanitized version of the truth. Of course he had no intention of divulging the substance of the agreement struck before his marriage in regard to his physical relationship with his wife. Nor did he care to disclose that Constance had first intimated to him – under dubious circumstances! – that Emily was having an affair, though he made a mental note in passing that it was imperative to ask her later *how* she knew. He simply mentioned that he had glimpsed a note written by Emily to Pilling which hinted at clandestine meetings, and when she had indicated she might go for an evening stroll alone he had suspected the worst. Against his better judgement he had commissioned James Hopley to spy on Emily and bring back news of her activities. This was a particularly unfortunate coincidence in view of later events.

'Well, I must say you've been very frank with us, sir,' essayed the inspector after he'd finished his account, which had been continually interrupted by questions. 'This casts a whole new light on affairs. I think we need to pay Mr Pilling a visit.'

'You don't think, do you, that he might be involved?'

'Probably not.'

'Why?' It struck him as plain stupid to rule out a main suspect.

'Simply because if he wanted to murder your wife he could have done so far more easily earlier in the evening. Why wait till she'd got back here?'

'Because – well – perhaps he wanted to make it look like me.'

It was an unhappy surmise and the lack of response which greeted it seemed in itself significant.

'You think I did it, don't you?' he blundered on.

'We simply think your wife was likely to know her attacker,' Gwynne said smoothly. 'She allowed him into her room and didn't put up much of a struggle for her life.'

'So … you think it's someone in the house? Is that the case?'

The other gave a shrug and George stiffened visibly. His wife had just died and they were playing word games.

'All right, Inspector, let's say it *was* someone in the house. Forgetting the obvious suspect for the moment, how about Mrs Proops? I mean, she had a key, didn't she? Surely her behaviour's just as suspicious as mine, roving around the house at night? I hope you've been devoting as much time to her.' His lips were turned down, eyes staring morosely. He wasn't acting naturally at all, feeling quite wretched.

'We have, yes, as a matter of fact,' Gwynne answered. 'Because you told us her job was at risk, we felt obliged to speak to her on the subject. She said she'd heard nothing to that effect – and nor had the other servants when we questioned them about it. She did admit that the subject of her wages was unresolved, but she was purposely delaying talking to your wife until her health had improved. Oh, yes, and so far as the key in the door is concerned, we've just had word that the fingerprints were indeed your wife's. Meaning that she must have opened the door from the inside.'

George put his head in his hands. Everything seemed to lead back to him.

'Perhaps you could do with a drink, sir?'

'No, I'm all right.'

'Sure?'

'Yes, perfectly. I only have the occasional glass.'

'Good, good! I can assure you, sir, you were absolutely right in telling us the events of your wife's last evening. We've already spoken to James Hopley and his story exactly matches your own. There's only one small detail to clear up.'

They'd been talking for almost six hours, clearing up lots of other 'small details', and it was nearly two o'clock in the morning.

'James informed us that when he arrived back that night you poured him out a small measure of whisky.'

'I thought it would help ward off the cold.'

'Quite so. Now he happened to notice, being a very bright lad, that the bottle was about a third full at the time. Yet when we examined your room we found it to be almost empty.'

George clung onto the table, staring with weary eyes at his accuser.

'I know what you're saying. That Emily was drinking before she died. But I swear to you. I *swear*. I didn't murder my wife.'

17

An Incriminating Letter

Clearly they thought he was guilty. The investigation had never really breached the confines of Stockley Hall. His tale involving the fleeing intruder hadn't been accepted and James Hopley's evidence had made him look a liar and a sneak. They didn't have absolute proof, of course – how could they? – but there was no question an arrest was imminent. Perhaps they just wanted to talk to Pilling, establish an alibi, confirm he *was* carrying on an intrigue with Emily – which George must have discovered that night – and only then accuse him of murder. For good measure they could even talk to Constance, extracting a confession of their stormy affair. The hounds of the press would love that.

Oh, why, *why* hadn't he admitted everything straight away? The embarrassment of others seeing his marriage for what it was? At first he'd thought he could prevent details from leaking out, but then, when Emily's death had been confirmed as murder and the police had started to probe deeper, he'd had to lie to maintain the façade. Making up absurd stories about Emily being afraid of phantoms.

And yet if he'd revealed his knowledge of Emily's movements in the first place, then Pilling, for one, would have had rather more to explain. Standing on his doorstep, grinning stupidly, as she made her way back in the darkness. Was that the twisted smile of a rejected suitor already hatching plans for her murder?

By God, if he'd killed Emily …

But who else *could* have committed the murder? If the police really wanted to make themselves useful, they should check the state of *his* shoes. See if *he'd* made any trips across muddy fields recently. Gwynne had mocked the idea of Pilling following Emily back to Stockley Hall, but then why couldn't he have made the journey? Not straight away, of course, because James would have seen him, but a little later in the evening. Perhaps he'd have known about the back door being open and calculated that, even if Emily's bedroom was locked, she'd let him in without fuss.

At all events that last conversation between them must have been critical – absolutely critical for her to leave her sickbed. Perhaps she'd decided to end their relationship, saying it was impossible to carry on, that George was beginning to suspect ...

Yes, that sounded feasible. It was just a pity there was nothing to prove his theory. If only he'd seen the rest of that letter she'd been writing on their anniversary, or any of their correspondence for that matter.

His breathing quickened and he broke out in a cold sweat. What if a letter turned up, written to Emily from Pilling, arranging that last meeting, begging for a reconciliation, full of anxious doubts about a possible return to her husband and threatening all manner of accidents otherwise? Perhaps the police would finally treat Pilling as a serious suspect.

But no, he couldn't do it. Morally it was wrong. Pilling was more than a serious suspect – good God, yes – but look where George's lying had got him already. On the point of being charged with murder.

On the point of being charged with murder. Was that justice, then? Was that morally correct? When a killer was allowed to go free?

During the course of the morning, after the long and trying interview the night before, he laboured over Pilling's letter, ensuring it had just the right tone. It began, 'My dear, sweet sister', keeping up the pretence, but its weaselly opening soon dissolved into desperation and hints of suicide. Naturally, he did not write it in his own hand, or on his own typewriter, which the police could easily check. He used an old typewriter which was languishing at the back of the attic, making sure afterwards it was trampled into a mechanical mess.

But now what? If he presented it to the police as his own discovery, it would seem far too convenient. He needed to hide the note in a place where they were likely to look – nowhere too obvious of course – perhaps dropping a hint to help them find it.

Her room was deserted when he entered it later that afternoon.

Unnaturally bright; light streaming through the windows. And larger than he remembered. All of the paraphernalia had been cleared off the floor. Evidently the police had thoroughly gone over the area and Emily's presence had been expelled. He cast his eyes round for possible hiding places, striving to avoid looking at the bed, the scene of the tragedy. The desk was the logical place to secrete his letter, one of the drawers perhaps. But surely the police would have searched there already? No, it had to be somewhere a trifle less obvious.

Ah, yes, the bookcase. Emily had her own private collection of books, separate from the library. The police were hardly likely to have gone through them all, looking for clues. The titles, the first time he'd seen them, revealed strange sympathies: Mary Wollstonecraft, John Stuart Mill, George Bernard Shaw. But this was no time for introspection. He needed to hurry. The complete collection of Thomas Hardy's works was there (her favourite author; he knew that at least) and he picked up *Tess of the d'Urbervilles*, slipping the note in the middle pages.

Now what to say to the inspector?

Once again they sat facing each other in the library for their daily war of words. The inspector, looking suspiciously happy, started, 'Well, we talked to Mr Pilling. I must say he was most helpful indeed, most helpful. A bit reticent to begin with, but faced with the information you provided, sir, I'm glad to say he gave way entirely.'

He beamed at George who instinctively smiled back. Maybe he could keep that bogus letter in reserve.

'First, though, I should point out he completely denied having an affair with your wife.'

'What! He can't!'

'He was quite adamant.'

'But I've got proof!'

The inspector gazed at him in amazement. It was such a rash outburst and George realized at once that he could not direct them straight to the letter. He'd have to think of another reason, quickly.

'Constance,' he intoned, pursing his lips significantly. 'Constance knows what was going on.'

It was a big step, introducing his 'motive' into proceedings, but

Constance was undoubtedly the key, the only person who could corroborate his story. She had hinted in the strongest terms that Emily was being unfaithful. Indeed, she seemed to assume it was common knowledge.

The inspector looked thoughtful for a few seconds and then turned to the constable. 'Tulley, see if you can find Miss Appleby. Ask her very politely if she'd mind answering one or two questions.'

His grave eyes returned to George. 'I'd be much obliged, sir, if you could maintain a silence while I talk to Miss Appleby. I'm sure your cause would be best served by allowing her to have her say.'

'I've no intention of interfering,' he responded indignantly. But before he could take issue any further, Constance had arrived – so quickly, in fact, it was difficult to believe she hadn't been eavesdropping.

'You wished to speak to me?' she said to the inspector.

'Just a few questions, miss. You knew the deceased well?'

'Yes, of course. Emily and I were at school together.'

'So you can testify to the state of her mind in the period leading up to her death?'

Constance gaped at Gwynne in astonishment. 'If you're implying, Inspector, that Emily wasn't fully *compos mentis*, then nothing, I can assure you, could be further from the truth.'

'No, no. Just trying to explore every avenue. You can't think of any reason, then, why she might wish to take her own life?'

'Absolutely not. She had everything to look forward to: a wonderful marriage, lots of friends.'

'You don't go along with the rumours that there was another gentleman in her life?'

Constance placed her hands on her hips and frowned, obviously nonplussed by this incredible line of questioning. 'That's absurd. George and Emily were one of the happiest couples you could hope to meet.'

George could tell she was grinning at him but he couldn't bear to look at her.

'I know what you're suggesting, Inspector,' she continued, warming to her theme, 'but nothing could dissuade me from thinking they weren't very much in love.'

Fortunately, the inspector ended this gibbering frenzy. 'Thank you, Miss Appleby. You've made your point very clearly.'

'Is that it?'

'Yes, the constable will show you out. Thank you again.'

She glanced at George for one last look of approval, but he kept his eyes fixed on the table.

'We seem to have a difference of opinion,' said the inspector, after the door had closed behind her.

George, red-faced, could barely contain his frustration. 'Look, Gwynne, that silly woman was trying to save me just now; preserve the memory of my marriage. But I can assure you she knows nothing about Emily. She's only lived in Eveley for the past month.' He was vaguely aware he was contradicting himself – the friend who had suspicions about his wife's faithfulness now, apparently, didn't know anything else – but he wished to make a point. 'She couldn't tell you Emily's views about vegetarianism, Thomas Hardy, practically anything. But the facts are obvious. I saw Emily writing a letter to Pilling. She went to visit him at some ridiculous hour of the night. I was cuckolded, I accept that, but it didn't prompt me to murder. If you want to investigate something, you should find that letter, and perhaps' – he waved his hand vaguely – 'other letters.'

'Yes, Mr Pilling did admit to receiving such a letter,' said the inspector slowly, 'but unfortunately he threw it away. Not that it's important—'

'Not important! Not important!' His voice was trembling. 'Why d'you always believe everyone else and not me? I've had enough!'

He stood up, tipping over his chair, and without another moment's thought stormed out of the house, heading in the direction of Potterslake Farm, the residence of Mr Edward Pilling.

18

Pilling's Story

In no time at all the house hove into view, a comfortably large two-storeyed building. He was going to find out the truth, even if he had to thrash it out of the man. The police had proved useless, Constance annoying, and it was plain that Pilling held the key to the mystery. He stood on the threshold, taking a few deep breaths to compose himself, then rang the doorbell.

'Why, Erskine, this is a surprise! Dreadful luck about Emily.' Pilling led him into the drawing-room. 'Let me get you a drink. Sherry or whisky?'

'Whisky and soda.'

The room was decorated in Victorian fashion; overcrowded, with dark, heavy furniture. The carpet was dyed in deep reds and greens, as was the wallpaper, and the crushed velvet curtains were similarly sombre. The style lent itself very much to Pilling's late wife and since her passing an air of dilapidation had settled.

'I had the police round this morning,' Pilling continued, pouring out the drinks. 'Shocking business. Very sad. I know just what you're going through.'

'No, you don't.'

Pilling looked up, puzzled by the tone in George's voice. 'Sit down, old chap, no need to stand. Here's your drink.' He made his way over to the sofa, sitting down himself and, clearly rattled, gazed up at his visitor.

'I want to know why my wife came here on the last night of her life,' intoned George hoarsely. 'I want to know what was going on between the two of you. And I don't intend to leave till you provide me with a satisfactory answer.'

Pilling took a gulp of his brandy before licking his lips. If George had been sitting rather than standing, he might have espied the hint of a smile traverse his enemy's face.

'The police must have told you about her visit,' he said ruefully. 'I suppose there's no harm in you learning the truth. But please. Sit down. That's *my* condition.'

George eased himself into the nearest armchair. His body was taut and his nerves were jangling. This was the man who had spent Emily's last evening with her, locked no doubt in an unholy embrace. He surveyed those features his wife must have adored and felt slightly sick.

'Ah, that's better. Now about my relationship with your wife. I've already spoken to that fellow, Gwynne—'

'He told me you denied having an affair.'

Pilling's eyebrows rose a fraction. He regarded the other's earnest expression for a second and then threw his head back, laughing loudly. 'Did he now? I'm so glad that *that's* been resolved at any rate!'

It was all a huge joke and even Emily's lover thought so. Had the man ever cared about her at all? Shed a single tear over her death?

Suddenly George could stand it no longer. He rushed over to the sofa, knocking over a table of sweets, and began raining his fists into his tormentor. *You fiend, you fiend. You utter, utter fiend.* Blow upon blow sailed into Pilling's head, his chest, his arms, any part of his body, the hapless recipient trying desperately to shield himself. *Make fun of his most precious feelings, would you! Well, see how you like this!*

A few moments later, hands stinging, and breathing heavily, he climbed off his hunched-up victim and returned to the armchair. Nothing happened for the next minute or so, but strangely, as he regarded the crumpled form on the sofa, he felt a certain pride in his performance. For once he had acted out his thoughts and given the fellow the beating he deserved.

His battered prey, evidently still suffering from pain and shock, gingerly removed his hands from his face and sat up slowly. His nose was bleeding and, sniffing occasionally, he pressed a red pocket-handkerchief against his face. A speck of blood was visible on his dove-coloured waistcoat.

'Finished?' he asked in a broken voice.

There was no answer.

'I shan't forget this, you know, Erskine. You can be sure if I've the chance to return the favour, I shan't hesitate to do so. For the moment, though, I shall choose to disregard your actions. I can see Emily's death has had a profound effect on you.'

George merely smiled at this, the tortuous speech of a coward. Pilling savoured some more of his brandy, frowning in concentration.

'You've made a mistake, a very grave mistake. I think you'll find the truth far more hurtful than you imagine.'

George sighed. The man really was tedious. 'Full of himself', that was the phrase. Even now he seemed to be taking an age to steady his nerves.

'I presume Emily's told you a little about her past? How she left home when she was twelve and went to live with her mother?'

'How do you...?'

'For the good reason that I was there. Emily's mother eloped with my father.'

George's face fell and a trace of pink appeared on his cheeks.

'You can examine my birth certificate if you wish,' continued Pilling, his recovery now remarkably swift. 'But it won't change the fact that Emily was my stepsister – and you and I are practically related.'

The assertion of a familial connection had a disconcerting echo from somewhere, but it was impossible for George to transfer his thoughts at such short notice.

'You weren't having an affair?'

'For God's sake, man, put that out of your mind. I hated the little witch. She can burn in hell so far as I'm concerned.'

'Go on,' said George after a pause. He was completely baffled.

'Very well. But first I need to acquaint you with certain facts about my background.' The gleam had returned to his eye. It was apparent now that, for some reason, he *wanted* to tell his story.

'The Pillings have always been well up in the order of things. Had their share of embarrassments, of course, but nothing that couldn't be covered up. That is, until dear Papa came along and entered into a dalliance with a housemaid. Unfortunately – well, fortunately, I suppose, from my point of view – she became pregnant.'

George, who had been feeling a sore point on his knuckle, ceased in his labours.

'Shocking, isn't it?' continued Pilling. 'I certainly wouldn't tell you under normal circumstances. But there it is. Owing to the awkward position your wife placed me in, arriving on my doorstep on the night of her death, I felt obliged to tell the police as well. Society can hang itself for all I care. I don't see why I should be blamed for the sins of my father.'

He polished off the dregs of his brandy, seemingly deriving little pleasure from the experience. The bleeding from his nose had now been staunched and a red smudge fanned out from underneath.

'My grandparents were in favour of letting the housemaid go, together with a suitable sum of compensation. But Father felt duty-bound to marry the girl he'd compromised. A breach in the family arose and, with the little money they gave him, he purchased a cottage just outside the estate.' Pilling sniffed. 'However, my mother died when I was two. I daresay Father would have been forgiven his lapse, but by then he was already linked with Lady Delsey.'

'Emily's mother?'

'And mine, too. I couldn't remember my first mother at all.'

George looked away despondently. On the pianoforte in the corner of the room there were various photographs in silver frames; portraits, no doubt, of Pilling's late wife's relatives.

'I was brought up with the severest economy, only vaguely aware of what was happening around me. I suppose Father thought his parents would provide for us one day, but in the meantime he was obliged to work as a bank clerk in London. Imagine that, eh, Erskine! A Pilling working behind the counter!' There was genuine bitterness in his voice. 'At least we had enough money to survive. Everything was manageable till Emily arrived.'

'She never mentioned you to me.' George had been following events with acute interest and was determined to establish the truth.

'Ah, an oversight, obviously. Well, I was nine and she was twelve when she descended upon us – and *my* recall of events is perfect. Perhaps you'd care for a Sullivan?'

He offered George his silver cigarette case, but the other shook his head impatiently. Pilling had fully regained his old chirpiness, and continued his account while lighting up.

'It was painful to see the effect of Emily's arrival on my mother, the delight with which she was received. Even at that age I realized we could ill afford another mouth to feed. The family coffers could barely support the three of us.' He leant forward, his eyes sparkling. 'But then something peculiar happened. Not suddenly, but over a period of two or three weeks, Emily retreated from life. In fact, she scarcely left her room up in the attic.'

He took a long drag on his cigarette and blew out an extravagant volley of smoke.

'Her odd behaviour became pronounced over the next few months. She'd only come downstairs once in a while, and then only to explain her eating arrangements. She preferred her meals to be left outside her door, which she invariably locked. I think she was extremely embarrassed about her size and was trying to lose weight. From what I could gather from my parents' conversations she hardly touched her deliveries of food.'

Pilling gave a crooked little smile. 'At long last, though, she presented herself to the family at dinner. I was instructed to leave the room, but listening at the door it soon became apparent, even at my age, that she was pregnant.'

He stubbed his cigarette out and, nursing his ribs with one arm and clutching his glass with the other, walked over to the drinks table, leaving his guest in stunned silence behind him.

'From the way my parents were speaking it was clear she'd been a very naughty girl; that she'd indulged in unholy practices. Dear, oh dear – and only twelve years old!'

The phrase 'naughty girl' stuck in George's mind. Where had he heard it? Why was it familiar? He definitely remembered ...

Of course, the picnic! He'd arrived ahead of the others and over-heard the same words as Emily and Pilling were laying out the meal. Which meant that Pilling must be telling the truth. Oh, the poor, poor girl. Perhaps she'd never mentioned her violation to anyone but her father, not understanding the vagaries of Nature.

'Dear Lord.' He put his head in his hands.

'Yes, it was inconvenient, to put it mildly,' said Pilling, resuming his position, glass in hand. 'Mother was particularly upset. She'd already lived in the shadow of one scandal. Another impropriety – self-inflicted or not – would bar her way in society for good.'

'*She* was upset?'

'Yes – and the guv'nor. Don't think he could accept it at all, in fact. Turned in the end to the bottle. So far as I know, the rest of our money went on a doctor who could be there at the birth and keep his mouth shut afterwards.'

Pilling gulped down a significant amount of brandy. 'On the night itself I was sent to bed early, but I could still hear Emily's screams. The next morning there was – all of a sudden – a baby in the house.'

George sat perfectly still. The colour had completely left his cheeks.

'Incredible, isn't it? A little baby boy. I was glad Emily had heaped disgrace upon herself, but the distress she'd caused the family was appalling. My dislike on first meeting her had turned into a perfect hatred.'

'A perfect hatred? Is that what you told the police? Did you tell them any of this?'

'I told them about Emily's baby, yes. Astounding what one comes out with when confronted with the gallows. As for saying "a perfect hatred", I may not have used those words precisely. But calm down, old chap. Let me continue.' He regarded George with a remnant of suspicion.

'Of course, having the baby delivered in secret didn't solve all our problems. It wasn't long before its lungs developed, assaulting our senses with its great howls. Father was no help at all and I think Mother took out her frustration a bit on Emily.'

George suddenly rose to his feet and began to pace up and down the room. 'This is awful! Don't you feel any sympathy for Emily?'

'I'd rather you sat down, Erskine. I'll be more prepared the next time you decide to throw yourself at me. Besides, there's more of my story to come. I think up to now I've been unduly kind to your late wife – for your benefit perhaps. Now please. Sit down. There's a good chap.'

George complied reluctantly.

'About three months after the birth my parents took me aside and explained that the baby had been given away. Another couple were anxious to have children and would look after him on our behalf. It was upsetting, yes, but unquestionably for the best and I wasn't to worry about it. I remember Father nodding away, merely adding that I shouldn't breathe a word of what had happened to anyone. I could certainly agree to that.'

Pilling seemed to be entering almost a trance-like state, his pupils dilating, his cheeks tinged with red.

'The night before, I'd been kept awake by the baby crying. On and on and on it went. Emily's room was directly above mine and I could hear her stomping around. She was shouting, "Shut up, shut up! Shut up or I'll kill you! So help me I'll kill you!" It made me laugh because it sounded so absurd – the sort of remarks she'd address to me rather than a baby. I was on the verge of going to Mother to complain when suddenly the noise stopped. There was absolute silence. I concentrated hard and after a while I could hear Emily saying, "Good baby, good baby" over and over. It was demented. "Good baby, there's a good baby, good baby." She was moving around, still muttering, "Sleep, sleep, my baby, sleep." Next I heard the door open and the sound of footsteps on the staircase. It was all very quiet, though, in contrast to the din of a few minutes before. I started to wonder how she'd managed to subdue the baby, then leave it without a whimper in return. I decided to go upstairs to check on the little mite. I didn't bother changing out of my nightclothes. Simply got out of bed and climbed the wooden stairs in my bare feet.

'Well, you should have seen the state of her room. Litter, food on the floor, the one thing lacking being any sign of life. It just hadn't occurred to me that she could take off with the baby directly after lulling it to sleep. I steered my way round all the clutter and stood at the window, thinking perhaps she'd gone out for a walk. Standing on tiptoes I could just make her out, leaving the house, carrying a white bundle in her arms. She walked over to the old well in the corner of the garden, held the bundle up in front of her for a full second – over the well – *and then dropped it. She dropped the baby down the well.* As clearly as I see you now I can picture that scene. She was standing there with her arms hanging by her sides, absolutely still. The dark woolly images of the night floated before my eyes as the tears streamed down my face. It was an horrific sight for a nine year old to witness and my first, perhaps my only, encounter with evil. I hurried back to my room.'

'No, no. I can't believe it. You must be lying.' George's voice carried a note of desperation.

'I believe she was on the point of telling you herself. Perhaps as soon as the day after her death, if you follow me. But we'll come to that. I'd just returned to my room, hadn't I?'

His detachment was unnerving and George nodded meekly. A shadow had passed over his face.

'Presently I heard Emily creep back up the stairs. She seemed to pause for a moment outside my door, but then resumed her progress.' He gave a little chuckle. 'The girl terrified me beyond belief. I thought she was the devil's whore, waking up every night to sacrifice her baby, sending it spinning to the centre of the earth. I prayed the baby's cries would wake me in the morning, its life recreated.

'But the next day brought no sign of life from upstairs. Eventually my parents felt the need to intervene, my mother first, then calling on Father for support. I could hear him shouting and cursing, throwing things on the floor.'

George recalled Emily's version of the same incident when they were together on the river-bank. He hadn't fully understood why Edith's lover had lost his temper with her. But now ...

'So when they told me the baby had been adopted, there was nothing I could do. It just struck me that we'd been happy before Emily had entered our lives. At least she went back to live with her father not long afterwards.' Pilling sighed. 'And so we were three again – for a while. Sadly, both my parents passed away in the next few years. I was left with my real mother's brother and his wife. I might even have forgotten about Emily but for one very unusual incident.'

19

Pilling's Story (continued)

The initiative had passed over to Pilling. It was strange that, though George had assaulted him with his fists, his rival had never really lost his self-assurance. The more he'd been allowed to talk, the more he'd pounded George with his shocking revelations. The certain jocularity which he invariably employed on any occasion was almost taunting, and the vein in which he continued his narrative indicated he'd lost nothing of his conceit.

'I've always had a way with the fair sex. I suppose neither of my parents were unattractive, but I represent, if you like, a beautiful culmination of them both. From about the age of thirteen I tortured and titillated hundreds of girls. And believe me, Erskine, they loved it.'

George refrained from comment. His mind was still trying to come to terms with the incident at the well.

'Anyhow, when I was seventeen I was seeing a remarkably doting creature called Miranda. At first her habit of following me around was amusing, especially with other people present, but I soon became bored at the sight of this doe-eyed spectre in pursuit every time I looked over my shoulder. This was a notably ruthless period of my life and I devised a rather unsubtle means of discarding her for good. I invited her on a bicycle ride and then proceeded to get lost. Of course we weren't really lost – at any rate I had a fair idea where we were – but I gradually stepped up the pace in my 'panic'. Twenty, fifty, a hundred yards divided us until she'd completely disappeared – I sincerely hoped forever.

'Directly in front of me was the garden of my youth, the ancient well standing like a gallows in the twilight. Looking at the scene after all those years, I realized the shock I'd experienced as a boy would never entirely recede. I resolved from that point onwards to get in touch with Emily.'

'Blackmail,' George muttered.

'At the time, old chap, I wasn't even aware of her circumstances – though it didn't take much looking into, I admit. Her father moved in the highest circles, while Emily herself had come out as a society beauty. Her looks seemed a natural corollary to her wealth.'

'I think it's abhorrent.'

Pilling produced his crooked smile. 'My grandparents had passed away, bequeathing their estate to my father's brother. Hence, in spite of both sides of my family – my father and stepmother – possessing substantial wealth, I'd been excluded from sharing in their fortune.'

'That's no excuse.'

'Well, my *dear* George, perhaps when you find yourself in a similar situation,' returned Pilling, 'you'll form a more sympathetic assessment. I used to plunder reports of my stepsister's illustrious lifestyle. It didn't seem fair that myself and my uncle and aunt were shut out of the same social circles as our relatives.'

A suitable breathing space had arrived and Pilling finished off his drink.

'Anyhow, the years passed by. It wasn't till she moved back to Hampshire for good, after her marriage to you, that I saw my chance. My business affairs were looking a bit shabby at the time and ... what can I say? I thought she might be interested in making a small capital investment. I waited till you'd settled in, and then introduced myself – the lost relative. The effect of my sudden appearance was splendid, Emily's eyes sparkling in recognition, then very quickly losing their lustre. ("Hullo, Sis!" I said to her.) That first conversation – fortunately without you present – was not a happy affair. She grew increasingly irritated at my demands for money and I soon needed to ask pertinent questions about the whereabouts of her baby. The reaction this produced, the shock written in her face, was very satisfactory. In the end she agreed to provide me with a share of her dress allowance, a figure she claimed you'd never question. Every month I'd receive a cheque for fifty pounds.'

George closed his eyes for a second as another memory fitted into place. No wonder Emily had taken to wearing the same dresses several times. And he'd attributed the change to a profound shift in perspective!

Pilling leant back on the sofa. 'It's quite late, Erskine. I don't know about you but I'm feeling distinctly peckish. I think you know most of the facts.'

'No, not at all,' replied George indignantly. 'I don't know why Emily felt the need to come here on the night of her death. What could be more important than that?'

'Look, old chap, she's dead. It won't do any good, you know, pursuing the matter further.'

The two men sat staring at each other for a couple of seconds before Pilling, perhaps fearful of a repetition of earlier events, renewed his account.

'Oh, very well, then. But first something to wet my throat.' He proceeded to fill his glass, talking over his shoulder. 'I daresay Emily paid up chiefly because she was worried about how you'd react to news of her past. Naturally I tried to increase her insecurity, hinting that I could destroy your trust in her at any moment. From her point of view this was obviously intolerable and I was more than concerned she might blurt out the truth to you and devil take the consequences. Thankfully, however, she arrived at an altogether different proposition.' He re-established himself on the sofa.

'One of her former tenants, Lily Potter, had been widowed several years before. Her husband had bought the freehold to their farm and they were known to possess several other properties. The implication behind Emily telling me all this was obvious. Marry Lily and I'd be rich and stop pestering her for money. I'd still possess her secret, of course, but then she'd be aware of my solely mercenary outlook.'

'You're detestable.'

'Yes, very good. Excellent. Why shouldn't a man marry for money, when women have been doing it for years? Judging by your circumstances—'

'I didn't marry for money.'

'Just a bonus, eh? Well, in my case, it made perfect sense. Don't forget I was very hard up at the time. I duly ingratiated myself with Lily – much to her surprise – and took little time in persuading her to marry me. Tragically, we only spent three months together. I say "tragically" with genuine emotion. Lily suffered from crippling arthritis. The heart attack which killed her was in some ways a godsend. *Not*, dear boy, that I was thinking about my inheritance. But when the time came to read the will I was in for a nasty jolt. Though I was named as the chief bene-ficiary – Lily bequeathing Potterslake Farm to me – it transpired that my late wife's properties weren't nearly as extensive as rumours had suggested. In fact, the number of houses she owned didn't even enter the plural.'

He took the largest draught of his brandy to date.

'This was all pointed out to me in some detail by the solicitor, an old friend of the family. Lily's first husband had indeed possessed a property in the city. But rather than being some luxurious dwelling tastefully furnished with French paintings, it was a humble, untidy studio where he'd eked out a living as a gentleman painter. It didn't even raise that much capital when he sold it, managing to pay for the freehold on their country house but leaving them with crushing main-tenance bills. I found myself with a large house full of debts.'

He gestured around him. 'That was why I decided to dismiss the servants. Your wife actually said I could have Mrs Proops if I was at my wits' end. Mrs Proops used to live here, apparently, when she was a child.'

George blinked a couple of times. Compared to previous revelations this was scarcely momentous, but the knowledge that Emily could offer up one of her father's most trusted members of staff and not even consult him about it, either! It was just as he'd been saying to the police, even if letting Mrs Proops go in such a fashion wasn't quite the same as a dismissal, and hardly constituted a motive for murder.

'But then when I stopped to think about the situation,' continued Pilling, 'the solution was obvious. Go back to Emily. Tell her she'd gone back on her agreement to marry me off to someone rich. Ask her to renew her monthly payments or else face the consequences. I was fairly sure she'd oblige, and this time I already had someone in mind. Miss Appleby, in fact.'

'Constance?'

'Indeed. I think I've alluded to my experience with women, and Constance, I can assure you, has a lot to offer. Warm ... honest ...'

'Rich.'

'The full house in other words. At least she isn't a society beauty with strong views on the roles of men and women. Anyhow, I hoped Emily would press my suit with Constance and told her that I'd like a word with her in private. She arranged for us to go to the picnic together.'

George felt a heaviness bear down on his chest. He'd been so stupid, *stupid*. Misreading everything.

'I wasn't expecting her to object to my proposal, but it turned out she wasn't nearly so sure about delivering her old friend into my clutches. I remember her saying Constance was very naïve – a characteristic hardly likely to deter me. However, she came round at last – giving me a little nod after you and the others joined us. She even came to my rescue when you were making that fuss about politics. Dragging you away and allowing me to keep the conversation suitably light.'

George's mind had already rushed on to the conversation at Tapser's Ruin. It was clear now why Emily had been praising Pilling. She'd been promoting him to Constance.

'Unfortunately, though, in spite of her work on my behalf, Constance didn't succumb to my advances, dear me, no! She was very obviously flirting with you.'

'Now look here,' exclaimed George without much conviction.

'The clearest example was after church. Not only did she decline my offer to escort her home, she flagrantly welcomed your attentions – a married man! My last view of you both was trotting off together in animated conversation.'

'That's enough!'

George's voice carried the necessary edge, but he was unable to conceal the gradual suffusion of his face.

'Curiously enough, that was my opinion at the time as well. I reasoned, though, that even if she'd developed an infatuation for you, she'd soon grow bored and come back to me. Anyhow, to be quite sure, I decided to inform Emily about your philandering ways. Ask her to tell you to stay away from Constance.'

A glitter of moisture appeared on George's brow. This was just awful. The thought that Emily's last memory of him could have been one of mistrust, suspecting him of having an affair—

'I also hadn't been given my cheque for the month. Emily normally gave it to me discreetly after church, but she didn't attend the service on the twenty-eighth of June. Nor did I see her for the rest of the week. I was particularly surprised since she'd sent word to me on the Monday that she wanted to talk about our arrangement. Either she'd had a change of heart and was avoiding me, or you weren't letting her out of your sight, not even to post a letter.'

George was silent. It was regrettably true.

'I couldn't quite believe she was prepared to stop paying me. Yet church, the following Sunday, brought only you into view and no sign of her. You told me – in the most sarcastic manner, I thought – that she was ill. But before you eloped with Constance, I told you, if you remember, that I'd call round the next day. It wouldn't be a good precedent to allow Emily to be late with her payment. I even left a message for you to pass on, saying that I'd *check* up on the little *goose*, hoping she'd pick up the reference to "cheque" and "the goose that laid the golden eggs". I'd called her on one occasion "my golden goose".'

George slumped a little in his chair. There'd been a horrible confusion. He'd deliberately withheld Pilling's message on the grounds that it was far too friendly.

'It transpired, however, that she was desperate to see me even before then. She appeared late that evening – the night of her death – traipsing her muddy boots on my carpet and looking perfectly grim. I was astonished to see her, but the reason for her visit soon became clear. She was under the impression I was prepared to divulge her secret the next day. That I'd told you I wanted to see you as well. She was so convinced of this train of events that she'd forgotten the cheque. Instead, bless her, she'd decided she was going to confess everything to you herself. She was sure you'd stand by her and that no one else would believe me if I claimed she'd murdered her son. She was sick of my blackmailing threats and couldn't be sure I wouldn't continually harass her for money. All in all, it was quite a tirade.'

'Did you mention my name in connection with Constance?' asked George, still worried by Pilling's earlier threat.

'What? I really don't remember. I think I was more concerned with Emily's exploits at the time.' He placed his glass to his lips and with a quick flick of his wrist swallowed the remaining contents. 'When she'd finished I gently pointed out that you were bound to be slightly alarmed that she'd once given birth to a son whom she'd murdered; adding that the element of trust might absent itself thenceforth. But I could see she was terribly in earnest and I'd have to let her go. The irony was, of course, that I was never going to tell the world about her loathsome past. No one would take me seriously anyhow.'

Pilling slapped his hands on his thighs. 'Well, that's it. Everything you could wish to know. I think I've been remarkably frank, don't you? And now, if you don't mind, I'd be much obliged if you cleared out.' He smiled without any pretence of sincerity and rose from the sofa.

George heaved himself out of the depths of his chair. It seemed only a few seconds later that Pilling had ushered him out into the cold evening air, his glass of whisky and soda left untouched behind him. Judging by the light it was probably about eight o'clock. The walk home would be much longer than the journey there.

Had Pilling really been telling the truth? The whole truth? His claim that he was Emily's stepbrother was supported by the 'dear, sweet sister' remark, but was it possible he'd been blackmailing Emily over something else? After all, he was the only person in that house who was still alive and it would be difficult to check all the facts. The knowledge of Emily's past which he clearly possessed could be twisted in such a way as to hurt George to the utmost degree, tarnishing his memory of her forever.

No, no, that wouldn't suffice. What about the assault which Emily had suffered? As a nine year old, Pilling would hardly have been acquainted with the reason why she should turn up so unexpectedly on his doorstep. Indeed, his calling her a 'naughty girl' may well have been based on genuine ignorance of the circumstances behind her condition.

And, anyhow, why invent such an incredible story in the first place? If he was hoping to convince the police he didn't have a motive, he was bound to fail. Perhaps his attitude, as an innocent man, was that it was better to tell everything now before it all came out later.

God, he was such a despicable creature! To think that George had once been convinced he was having an affair with Emily! He'd even gone to the lengths of writing a letter to prove the two of them had been deceiving him.

Dear heavens! The letter!

What if the police had already discovered it? He would be lost. He needed to destroy it before it was found. Almost despairingly, he broke into a run, hampered considerably by his injured knee. No time to lose ...

Hopley had scarcely opened the door before George pushed past and hurled himself upstairs. Reaching the landing, he quickly glanced round and, satisfied he was alone, hurried into Emily's bedroom, closing the door.

Breathing heavily, his knee on fire, he limped over to the bookcase. *Tess of the d'Urbervilles*, he distinctly remembered; and there it was, second shelf down. Picking it out, he leafed through the pages.

The note wasn't there!

But that was impossible! Grabbing the book by its spine he shook it violently. Nothing, still. It must have been *The Woodlanders*, then, or *The Mayor of Casterbridge*. In desperation he pulled out all of Hardy's novels, shaking them thoroughly.

'Is this what you're searching for, sir?'

The voice, so calm and measured, filled him with terror. He looked round to see the sad-eyed inspector framed in the doorway, waving the letter.

20

Superintendent Woodford

The funeral took place on the following afternoon, four jet-black horses with huge black plumes drawing the carriage bearing the coffin through the centre of Eveley. A large crowd had turned out, thronging the pavements, doffing their hats and gazing with wondrous eyes at the pageantry on display. George even noticed Gwynne and Tulley standing behind the mass of onlookers.

Only now, after her death, did he feel closer to an understanding of Emily. The rector's eulogy had made it clear he was well acquainted with the deceased, and there was no need to wonder any longer why she'd attended church. The image of the well and the extinguishing of such a young life had burnt itself into his mind. It was too soon to say how he felt about it all, but he wished they could have dealt with the problem together. Instead, she'd merely edged towards the truth – prompted into saying something by the sadist remark for instance – with the result that his suspicions had grown in another direction entirely.

But then everything could be seen in a different light. Emily's reasons for insisting on a celibate marriage, for instance, might have involved a fear of pregnancy or the pain of childbirth, perhaps even the dread of what she might do to the child if her mind was sufficiently turned. Her concern over the plight of women, too, plainly had much deeper foundations. Hardly surprising that she'd been so moved by his decision to marry his brother's sweetheart to save her from disgrace.

Her whole life had been lived in secrecy and guilt, arising from that terrible incident at the well. All the time, the hours and hours, he'd spent wondering how she felt towards him, but perhaps she'd loathed herself too much to accept love from anyone, believing he was only acquainted with the false image she presented to the world. Their last meeting, when he'd read out that poem. *In her sweet heart, so innocent.* That must have convinced her more than ever that he was incapable of accepting the truth, happy in his ignorance. But then if she'd really intended to tell him about her past, as Pilling had indicated, they'd have had to start again in any case. Perhaps in America, following her suggestion.

The succeeding weekend was surprisingly quiet and there were even moments when George wondered if the police had become bored with their enquiries. But, of course, they were only regrouping, and on Monday morning Hopley informed him that the two police officers were waiting to see him again, together with a third gentleman.

Before he saw them, though, he wanted a quiet talk with the messenger. It seemed inconceivable the man wouldn't have a view on recent events.

'Hopley, tell me, how are the staff holding up? The mistress's death must have been a terrible shock.'

'Yes, sir. Some of us remember Mrs Erskine from the day she was born. She was always such a happy personality.'

George smiled weakly. Not quite the adjective he'd have chosen.

'I know I speak for the rest of the staff,' the other went on, 'when I say you have our full support and sympathy, sir, in these difficult times. Everyone has been deeply saddened by the loss of the mistress but resolved to carry out their duties as well as they can.'

'Thank you, Hopley. I don't know what I'd do without you. I'm afraid I haven't been much use over the last week. Well, you know how it feels …'

'Yes, sir.'

The butler remained perfectly still, his arms pinned to his sides, but his expression became ever more serious. George took a deep breath.

'Forgive me if this is rather a personal question, but I feel I can speak openly to you. I know you will give me an honest answer. You didn't notice any disharmony between Mrs Erskine and myself?'

The butler looked horrified. 'No, not at all, sir.'

'I only mention it because the police seem to be under the impression that our marriage was somehow troubled.'

Again he looked suitably pained.

'Why do you suppose they want to talk to me so much?' George asked directly.

'I presume they wish to inform you of the progress of the investigation.'

'It's because,' corrected George brutally, 'they suspect me of murdering my wife.'

Hopley's jaw swung open in amazement. 'But you're a gentleman, sir.'

It was one of the few cheering moments George had had since Emily had passed away.

'It's very good of you to say so, Hopley. Naturally I'm innocent, but the police are bull-headed creatures at the best of times.'

Hopley shook his head, presumably lamenting not only the stupidity of the police but their implied irreverence for the class system – a system which would surely prevent him from believing his son and his espionage stories.

'Oh, well, better face my tormentors,' said George wearily, clambering to his feet.

A brief look of awe traversed Hopley's features before snapping back into their customary mannequin's pose. A fixed point of reference in a changing world. George followed him into the drawing-room.

There they were greeted by a little gaggle of detectives. Gwynne and Tulley were settled on the sofa, but standing next to them, small and pasty-faced, was another smart suit.

'This is Superintendent Woodford,' declared Gwynne, jumping to his feet, his face assuming an even more pronounced study in affability. 'He'd like to ask you a few questions.'

'Certainly, Superintendent,' replied George cordially. 'Would you care for some tea and biscuits first?'

'H'm, yes, that would be very acceptable,' said Woodford, seemingly surprised that George hadn't jumped on him already and started mauling his neck.

George rang the bell and they sat down, the superintendent at once bringing up the subject of his visit. His voice had a harsh, nasal quality about it.

'I am here in the hope that this will be the last time we need to interview you. We know you persuaded Master Hopley to follow your wife on the evening in question because you suspected she might be having an affair. We also know that you heard mysterious noises in the middle of the night and saw an indistinct figure rushing down the stairs. However, we'd be grateful if you would make a statement recording your views. Quite routine, you know.' A smile or a flinch briefly ambushed his features. 'You should be aware, though, that anything you say will be taken down in writing and may be used as evidence hereafter.'

He turned to the inspector. 'Gwynne, I know you're interested in one or two points, so perhaps we should dispose of them first.'

Gwynne leant forward, towering over his boss. 'Just going back to that letter we found, sir, the one supposedly from Mr Pilling to your wife. What prompted you to write it?'

George licked his dry lips. This was not going to be a friendly conference. 'I didn't think you were paying sufficient attention to Edward Pilling in your investigation.'

'H'm,' murmured the inspector. 'But surely it wasn't in your interest to make us think your wife was having an affair? It provides you with a motive, aside from leading us away from the real murderer.'

'Yes, well … How did you find that note, anyhow? I thought I'd hidden it pretty thoroughly.'

Gwynne smiled, a flicker of light passing over his long face. 'A constable happened to see you in your wife's bedroom as he was coming up the drive – though I'm sure we'd have located it in due course. One of your staff might well have come across it.'

'I think you overrate their ability,' muttered George, cursing his luck.

It was a most uncharacteristic pronouncement – he really meant *anyone's* ability – but it unfortunately coincided with the point at which the tea arrived. Needless to say, Alfred, who brought in the tray – looking very efficient in his household livery – didn't exactly receive George's last remark with the greatest alacrity. An embarrassing silence ensued until he withdrew.

'Now in regard to the bottle of whisky,' said Gwynne, changing tack most alarmingly. 'Young Hopley said that when you poured him a drink, the bottle was a third full at least. Yet in the morning it was virtually finished. Now Doctor Feltham in his post-mortem report categorically states that he noticed a smell of alcohol. We're aware that your wife had one or two drinks when she was with Mr Pilling, but do you know of any way in which she could have drunk from the bottle in your room?'

'No, it was me. All me.'

The superintendent frowned, the inspector's eyebrows travelled skywards, and the constable put his head down for some intensive scribbling.

'You have to understand,' explained George, 'that I'd just heard evidence of my wife's adultery.'

'On the night of her death,' pointed out the superintendent.

'I wanted to dull my senses.'

'Which, presumably, you succeeded in doing.'

George stared at Woodford in disbelief. Obviously the man either had a very high opinion of himself or wanted to impress his subordinates, or both. The inspector's approach was far more civilized. Thankfully, he spoke next.

'So you awoke the next morning with a bad headache?'

'No.'

George could see the superintendent in the corner of his eye shaking his head so he faced him directly.

'When you've just heard your wife's been murdered you sober up pretty quickly.'

'Hm-hm. Perhaps we should start on the full statement,' said Gwynne soothingly. 'From the beginning ...'

They started at the very beginning and immediately George found himself being interrupted every time he tried to speak. Woodford, in particular, seemed eager to poke his spry little snout into total irrelevancies. Furthermore, he persisted in asking George to repeat everything as though he were an inveterate liar. Only once did his strategy appear to reap dividends.

'So you heard your wife's door being closed,' he reiterated, 'and suddenly, even though you'd felt paralysed before – for one reason or another – you leapt out of bed.'

'The noises I was hearing sounded so peculiar I thought I might still be asleep. The door closing was the first normal sound I recognized.'

'So you knew someone was leaving or entering her room?'

'Yes.'

'And you rushed over to the staircase?'

'Yes, I've told you. I looked over the banister and saw ... the swishing of the tapestry on the wall. Ha, yes, of course! *Of course*! I've noticed it quite often, in fact. Whenever I leave my room a current of air disturbs the tapestry – it's just made of silk, you see – and it flaps off the wall. I must have thought it looked like an overcoat.'

'This tapestry is our intruder?' queried Gwynne.

'Nonsense,' muttered Woodford.

'Yes – well, perhaps, I can't be sure. I fear I've rather hindered your investigation, haven't I?'

It was not the most convenient time to remember such a detail, but then George's thoughts up till that moment had been rather dominated by later events. It was incredible how the brain played tricks with one's perception, facts that were stored away suddenly coming to the forefront. All in all, however, he felt that his little revelation had damaged him, giving the pack another morsel to slobber over. The only blessing was that Constance had recently disappeared. The last thing he wanted was her face in the same frame as his, critically assessed by Woodford.

The interview drew to a close and he started to ponder what they'd said at the beginning, about this being the last time they wanted to talk to him. Was that true? And, if so, why? The statement was read back to him by the constable. What would happen when he signed it? They would leave, presumably. And then what? Nothing? No, that was far too optimistic. They were going to arrest him, that was obvious. A tremendous pulse surged through him. But hold on. The superintendent had said that he was only making a routine enquiry. And nothing had happened to Pilling after he'd made a statement. He calmed down a little.

'If you could sign here.' Gwynne proffered a pen.

George watched his hand as it etched out his signature. Very composed.

'All done?' he queried, looking up hopefully.

Gwynne appeared almost pained. 'Yes, nearly. But I think the superintendent has something to add.'

Woodford cleared his throat. 'George Arthur Erskine. It is my duty to warn you that anything you say may be taken down and used in evidence hereafter. I now arrest you on the charge of murdering Emily Jane Erskine on the sixth of July, 1903.'

Part Three

21

Mr Samuel Minty

Mr Samuel Minty was a jolly soul. Fattened up by a succession of roast beef and Yorkshire puddings, which his wife dished up for him three times a week, and partial to the odd tipple of wine – which chugged from one cheek to the other to form a Bordeaux-coloured filigree – his personality complemented his exuberant belly.

When talking, his podgy ring-emblazoned fingers drew eccentric parabolas in the air, caressing nothing or poking at nothing in turn. He was fascinating to watch but also pleasant to listen to, taking a sanguine view of George's chances.

'Good morning, good morning. I've just been reading your case notes.'

He slapped a huge bundle of papers onto the table in front of him.

'Very nasty business, I must say. *Very*. You're denying all the charges, naturally?'

'Of course.'

'Excellent! I don't think we should have any problems here. One or two points, perhaps, need to be cleared up. But where's the evidence? Solid evidence at any rate? I wouldn't be surprised if the grand jury threw out the bill.'

George smiled lamely. Minty was obviously on his side, as he was paid to be, but since his arrest he'd fluctuated between hope and despair so often he'd almost surpassed the stage of making predictions. He couldn't remember the last time he'd had a successful night's sleep.

'Must be a terrible strain for you, even so,' the solicitor commented, seemingly reading his mind. 'The police always pin the murder on the husband. Always. The moment you admitted paying someone to follow your wife was tantamount to saying that strangling someone requires a good deal of nerve. From then on they were after you. Blinkered. Totally.'

'Right!'

'*No* physical evidence at the scene of the crime. *No* witnesses. *No* proper investigation of other leads. Just huge circumstantial dollop-ings of jealousy. Motive, my friend, is what will be bandied around the courtroom. You killed your wife because you thought she was having an affair. *That* is what we're up against.'

'But I *did* think she was having an affair.'

'Which you found out for certain on that final evening?'

'Yes.'

'Making you exceedingly angry?'

'Yes. And upset. That's why I had so much to drink.'

Minty took a sharp intake of breath, puffing out his cheeks to exhale.

'I see. Problem is we can prove your wife was being blackmailed. We have statements showing regular payments into Mr Pilling's bank account. If anyone had a motive for killing your wife, it was him.'

'So what do you want me to say?'

Another deep breath, the trelliswork of capillaries on each cheek knotting themselves into an even greater tangle.

'The truth! When it comes to motive we have a man who relied on your wife's dress allowance for his upkeep, which she was threatening to cut off; a housekeeper who felt aggrieved that she hadn't been given a pay rise since the death of your father-in-law—'

'Mrs Proops?'

'The same. And then there's Miss Appleby who, according to her coachman, took you for a long walk in the countryside the day before the murder. He'll testify to that, incidentally.'

George put his head in his hands.

'Compounding the problem,' continued Minty enthusiastically, 'I believe your wife was quite ill at the time. That kind of thing looks bad – very bad.'

'I thought you were confident of my chances.'

'So I am, dear boy. Look at it this way. You thought your wife was being unfaithful on the grounds of James Hopley's evidence. But you must have had some reason for suspecting her beforehand. The explanation you gave the police, remember? The person who suggested your wife might be having an affair?'

'Constance?'

'Yes, Constance!' His fist and the table exchanged greetings. 'And why would Constance make such suggestions?'

George stared blankly at him.

'Because she wanted to start an affair with you! Why not betray a wife who'd already betrayed you? She had the best motive of all. We need to draw out her passion for you on cross-examination – and emphasize your total lack of interest.'

'H'm,' said George unconvincingly.

'It all helps to muddy the waters. Our main worry will be the letter you wrote from Mr Pilling to your wife.'

George gazed heavenwards. God, he deserved to hang for being so stupid!

'I think we can only promote the argument that it suggests innocence as much as guilt. That you knew the police were about to make a terrible mistake in arresting you, and you wanted to divert their attention. There was a case recently involving a gentleman charged with the stabbing to death of his supposed lover. A key piece of evidence was a broken bottle lying near her head with his surname inscribed on it.' Minty was beaming. 'Yet the defence argued that he'd never have left such an obvious piece of evidence if he was indeed guilty. And – d'you know – he was acquitted!'

It all looked very reassuring. George's only qualm was the idea of treating Constance as an unfriendly witness. After all, they were taking a very aggressive defence if they hoped to pin the murder on her. If she broke down on the stand over that 'walk' in the countryside, his cause would be doomed in any case. It was certainly a delicate situation.

And yet he *did* feel a good deal of resentment at the part she'd played in proceedings. Not so much that she'd seduced him; he was equally to blame in that respect. But she'd gone on to say that she suspected Emily of having an affair – when nothing of the sort was taking place. And where had she disappeared to when the police had started to circle (although, admittedly, he hadn't been the perfect host)? Perhaps it wouldn't be such a bad thing if her already red face was given a severe grilling. She *did* have questions to answer and she could damn well answer them.

The final part of the interview covered the subject of George's counsel.

'I strongly advise briefing Sir Lionel Trefford-Letts. He's particularly adept at exploiting weak links in a prosecution case and quite brilliant at cross-examination. The only doubt remains over whether he'll accept the brief.'

'Why ever shouldn't he?' George asked indignantly.

'Oh, Sir Lionel's a very busy man. Demands very high fees. On the other hand, he *has* won some hopeless cases in the past – not that yours is, of course. Yes, I feel sure that if we can obtain his services he'll secure a satisfactory outcome.'

'I hope so,' George said with feeling.

22

The Case for the Prosecution

The trial opened on Thursday, 22 October.

Arriving at the court building in the prison van, George had been staggered by the size of the crowd and the number of policemen in attendance. Didn't they know this was all a farce? A complete waste of time? He lowered his head and tried to shield himself from the whole experience, but the shouts still reached his ears. God, this was awful. Much worse than he'd expected. Did they really think he was capable...? In spite of his assertion to Hopley that the police regarded him as the chief suspect, he'd never really believed they'd arrest him, actually charge him with murder. Even at this late stage he half expected someone to come forward and announce that a terrible mistake had been made.

Yet the judicial process had continued on its inexorable path and now at last he found himself sitting in the dock with every eye upon him. 'Wear a dark suit and look serious!' Minty had suggested the day before and, gazing around the gloomy courtroom, a banquet of marble and wood panelling, the wisdom of this advice was apparent. It didn't pay to wear anything garish for such a sombre event. Facing him was the Bench, the judge in all his glorious robes, and below his lordship, the table at which the clerk of the court, dressed in black like most of the other participants, was sitting and writing. Directly in front, on adjoining tables, sat the two protagonists in the impending drama: the Attorney-General, leading for the prosecution, and Sir Lionel Trefford-Letts, the appointed defence counsel.

The latter cut a tall and majestic figure, his full-length gown billowing out behind him every time he stood up. His voice, too, was calm authority, very respectful – 'If it pleases, my lord', the usual flummery – and yet it conveyed a sense of assurance in a case which had obviously been trumped up against the defendant. Further, not content with his own little orations, he had this amusing habit of taking a pinch of snuff whenever the Attorney-General was performing his verbal pirouettes, thus distracting the jury into thinking that his learned opponent's arguments were pure and utter humbug. Everything about him spoke of his complete belief in George's innocence – belying the quarrels they'd had beforehand about the line they should adopt (Sir Lionel reluctantly agreeing not to mention Emily's baby and her tragic past unless the prosecution first raised the subject and left him with no alternative).

Over to the left were the twelve gentlemen of the jury. George scrutinized each of their faces in turn, wondering what they might be thinking. Perhaps nothing more than their luck in acquiring seats in the royal circle. How odd it was that their lives should converge at this moment to decide his fate. That man in the upper tier with the eyebrows that moved when he blinked, which side would he come down on? And the man on the far right in the front row with the bushy moustache—

Oh, oh. Wait a minute. What was happening now? The Attorney-General, Sir Ernest Hislop, KC, had risen to his feet.

'It would be idle to suppose that most of you are not aware of the facts of the case. But I implore you to banish any impression of what you have heard or read from your minds. A newspaper report cannot always give an objective assessment and it is essential we begin with an absolutely clean slate. I hope to conduct the case temperately, with the utmost fairness to the prisoner at the bar, but at the same time carry out my duty on behalf of the Crown.'

Sir Ernest's small wig balanced precariously on top of his large head. His slightly hunched back and beaky nose, together with the grave countenance he affected at all times, gave him the appearance of a rather fat owl. His voice, issuing forth from his thin lips, was at once soothing and incisive and, as he carefully developed his case, George began to fidget in his seat. This was unbearable. That quiet voice! The mixture of truth and fantasy! According to Sir Ernest, he'd consistently misled the police. He hadn't immediately revealed that he'd paid the butler's son to act as a spy, nor that he'd been under the influence of a third of a bottle of whisky on the night of the murder. More seriously, he'd invented evidence to divert the attention of his accusers, claiming at one stage that he'd seen an intruder fleeing from the scene of the crime. He'd even gone to the lengths of writing a letter from Mr Edward Pilling to his wife hoping to implicate Pilling in the murder.

To George's great dismay, the note was then produced and read out in court. Oh, God, how could he have been such a fool! It was clear that Gwynne and company had suspected him all along and only needed another piece of evidence to realize their case. Fool, fool, *fool*! He stared at the blur of gowns and wigs before him, determined not to show any emotion, but his heart was pounding with an extra intensity. The spectators in court were waiting for moments like these, weren't they? Realizing he'd been found out and studying his every reaction. And – quite plainly – he *couldn't* control his feelings. His face was bright red, a beacon of guilt, his back wet with perspiration. After a few lines Sir Ernest was interrupted by the judge.

'I do not quite understand the purpose of this letter. Why does he call her "my dear, sweet sister", and then imply that they are having an affair?'

Sir Ernest explained patiently that, at the time, the prisoner had been convinced of his wife's infidelity and, not realizing that Mr Pilling was really Emily's stepbrother, was using the term 'sister' in jest. The purpose of the forgery was to suggest that Pilling was very concerned that Mrs Erskine might return to her husband and was hoping to prevail upon her, in no uncertain terms, to change her mind.

'I see, yes.'

Mr Justice Winstanley smiled contentedly, no pearly-whites peeping through a jaw which was clamped tightly to his bony head. His cranium, in fact, was nothing short of elephantine, especially in relation to his wizened gnat-like physique and, opposite George, he presented a very queer sight, the little black marbles he had for eyes occasionally rolling in the prisoner's direction. His voice, in contrast to Sir Ernest's, was reedy and annoying.

The rest of the letter was read, but George had already effectively surrendered. What would induce Sir Lionel to clamber to his feet?

Perhaps if he was accused of being the Ripper? Prowling the streets of Whitechapel at night as a precocious eight year old, disembowelling prostitutes as an introduction to crime? A thousand pounds he'd paid to secure the services of the man and most of it, apparently, had been spent on snuff.

Sir Ernest seemed to be drawing on every shred of evidence, even, towards the end of his opening address, referring to the subject of the victim's sepulchral state.

'Mrs Erskine was found in a very distinctive position. She was lying on the bed, covered up to her neck by a white silk sheet, her hands crossed in repose like an angel at peace. Now you may decide, of course, that there is no significance in this. But, on the other hand, you may reach the conclusion that her resting state indicates a warped sense of respect for the deceased, or maybe a last futile attempt to control her.'

They adjourned for luncheon, which George spent with his solicitor. What impressed him particularly about the prosecution case was the way all the weaknesses in the evidence against him had been accounted for, turned into proof of his guilt. His love for Emily, for instance, couldn't be genuine bearing in mind the way she treated him. Quite clearly he was the put-upon man, seething under a mass of resentment, who'd at last broken free of his wife's domination with tragic results. Indeed, that was the only conclusion the neutral observer could adopt, that he himself would adopt as a member of the jury.

'Have I no chance, Minty?'

'Of course, of course!' the other soothed. 'I think we can be more than pleased with the morning's work.'

'What work?' George asked, rather incredulously. 'I could have paid a jackass to act as my counsel with more success. At least the jury would have been more distracted.'

Minty grinned. 'Sir Lionel thought that the opening by the Attorney-General was poor. Some very tricky issues could have been raised.'

'Don't you think that they were?'

'I think that if the Crown intends motive to underpin the case, then your financial gain could easily have been introduced. We can count ourselves lucky.'

'But I'm being made to look like a blithering idiot!'

'Which is precisely what Sir Lionel wants!'

George stared at him in stupefied amazement. 'Well, he's succeeding brilliantly, then. Perhaps Sir Lionel would like me to perform some impromptu dribbling.'

'There's no need for that, Erskine. The point is that you're being depicted as charmingly naïve. The other witnesses are the unscrupulous ones: Miss Appleby was manoeuvring for your affections from the outset; Mr Pilling was blackmailing his stepsister; even Mrs Proops had a grievance against her mistress. You were blissfully unaware of these intrigues.'

'H'm.' George wasn't totally convinced, but Minty had, in fairness, made him feel somewhat better.

The afternoon session was a much more ponderous affair. Sir Ernest had disappeared from the scene – much to George's relief – and his junior, Mr de Grey, pursued a dull line of questioning with a couple of the medical witnesses.

Doctors Wetherington and Feltham both testified that Emily had been strangled. Both of them gave their opinion that it was carried out manually rather than through some artificial means such as a ligature, Wetherington kindly adding his belief that pressure on the carotid nerve must have rendered the deceased unconscious very quickly, her suffering mercifully brief. Tests on body temperature, lividity and rigor mortis set the time of death between one and three o'clock in the morning.

Wetherington's evidence ended the day. The worries George had had in regard to the Attorney-General's speech had largely subsided. Tomorrow, apparently, Constance would take the stand. For some reason he knew she wouldn't refer to that sordid romp in the barn. She would confirm, instead, her faith in his marriage, so readily imparted to the inspector. His confidence restored, he almost looked forward to the following day.

23

Constance's Story

One further witness remained to be called before Constance though, and the next morning the Home Office pathologist, Sir James Fletcher, took the stand.

Sir James, smartly turned out and speaking in a clipped Scottish accent, came across as an authority on his subject. He had detected some light bruising around the victim's neck, a deeper purpling on the left side of the voice box and a cluster of barely discernible marks on the other side, the conclusion being that death had been inflicted by a single left hand. In addition, puncturing each bruise were crescent-shaped impressions, almost certainly carved by fingernails. This seemed the clearest indication of the manner of death, but Sir James, the professional, regaled the court with knowledge concerning damage to the tongue, a fracture of the hyoid bone, and congestion of the brain.

Excitement had reached a very high level by the time of the afternoon session and the court was possibly even more crowded than the first day. It was finally the turn of one of the major witnesses to take the stand and heads were craned to see her arrival.

Constance, wearing a pale-blue taffeta outfit, was shown in by one of the attendants and made her delicate, almost timid, way across the courtroom to the witness box. She kept wringing her fingers and George noticed, perhaps due to the strain of the occasion, that her face had resumed that errant lobster colour it had displayed during their unfortunate frolics. She glanced away as soon as her eyes met his, perhaps only distracted by his proximity.

Would she hold up under pressure, defend his marriage? What was she planning? This pretence of shyness, this show of femininity, obviously hid a very subtle mind. How she had tried her utmost to separate him from Emily! And how weak and terrible he'd been to indulge in extramarital activities with the woman! His wife, it transpired, had never committed adultery – on the contrary *he'd* been the unfaithful one – and now he'd have to live with the guilt forever.

The clerk of the court asked Constance for her name and for a moment George thought he'd misheard her reply. She was no longer Miss Appleby. She was Mrs Pilling. Surely she couldn't have married Pilling in the last three months?

The first few exchanges between Sir Ernest and the witness confirmed just that. Good heavens!

Not only was she Pilling's wife, she seemed delighted to be in that role, taking umbrage when it was delicately suggested, to nullify any later intimation from the defence, that she'd experienced a somewhat precipitant romance. George regarded her mouth as it worked away, nervously chattering. So Pilling had achieved his aim. Well, no doubt he and Constance's money would be very happy. Pilling was certainly no friend of his, swearing vengeance should the opportunity ever arise.

A tingling sensation ran all the way up his spine. Oh, dear God. That business in the barn. The two of them would certainly have discussed her evidence beforehand, wouldn't they? Determined the most effective line to take? He gripped the sides of his chair to ward off the sudden desire to plunge his head into his hands. But surely she wouldn't actually...? It was in no one's interest, was it? Oh, why had she married Pilling anyhow? She'd been so damning in her comments about him after church. Clearly a person who could change her views so quickly was capable of anything. *Anything*.

Sir Ernest took her gently through her relationship with Emily, establishing their close rapport, before posing the crucial question about the nature of her marriage with George.

'I thought they were happy most of the time,' she said unsteadily. 'I know she found him a bit too serious and possessive at times.'

George looked disconsolately at the witness who was shivering slightly, as if the words had to be forced out of her. She kept her gaze steadfastly on Sir Ernest.

'And did he ever take an interest in other women?'

'Objection, my lord.' This was virtually the first belligerent move Sir Lionel had made and it was definitely a critical one. 'My client's regard for other women is surely of no relevance to the court.'

'On the contrary,' explained Sir Ernest, 'the Crown will seek to demonstrate that the prisoner's relationship with his wife had deteriorated to such an extent that he was actively seeking out other women. The question pertains to motive and predisposition to violence.'

'You may answer,' muttered the judge laconically.

'I'm sorry. Can you repeat the question?' Constance procrastinated.

Sir Ernest politely repeated himself.

'Oh, yes!' she agreed heartily. 'Emily arranged a picnic – I think it was the last Saturday in June. I couldn't help noticing he kept looking at me.'

'Kept looking at you?'

'Yes. I found it highly embarrassing, especially in front of his wife and my future husband.'

'Indeed,' agreed the Attorney-General.

George did his utmost to look composed but a touch of colour had already entered his cheeks.

'Naturally, surrounded by friends, I felt protected. But I resolved never to find myself alone in his presence.'

'And did you succeed?'

'No. There was an occasion a week later. Sunday.'

'The fifth of July?'

'Yes.'

'The last day of Mrs Erskine's life?'

'Yes.'

George bowed his head and his shoulders slumped as the air squeezed itself out of him. She was going to confess everything. Had she no shame?

'Will you tell the court, Mrs Pilling, of your experience with the prisoner on that date?'

The witness lowered her gaze, issuing a sigh.

'I was with Edward—'

'Your fiancé?'

'We were just friends at that stage. Edward asked George why

Emily wasn't in church and George replied that she was ill. He said she was bound to die before long.'

There was a gasp from the gallery. George wriggled helplessly in his chair. He vaguely remembered saying something of the sort. But for heaven's sake!

'Naturally I thought he was joking, but for a flippant remark it was in very poor taste.'

One member of the jury nodded his agreement.

'He persuaded me to leave Teddy – Edward, my future husband – and give him a ride back home. He had a limp, you see, and I took pity on him. For some reason I'd decided my fears were groundless.' She placed her gloved hand over her mouth as though what she was about to say was too shocking for words. 'We stopped in the middle of the countryside and walked over to an old barn. I know, Your Honour, it sounds incredible, but he was married to my oldest friend. And we'd just been to church!'

She began crying, gentle little sobs, her body shaking. George felt his insides turn over. Was there nothing he could do to stop this performance?

'My lord,' broke in Sir Ernest. 'My client is in a state of great emotional distress. Perhaps it would help to restore her nerves if we were to adjourn the court.'

Mr Justice Winstanley observed Sir Ernest irritably, then glanced at the clock. It was a quarter to four. Much time had already been expended discussing the relationship of the witness to the deceased.

'The court has a good deal of business to attend to,' he snapped. 'Bring Mrs Pilling a glass of water.'

The clerk rushed off.

Constance had meanwhile succeeded in recovering her composure. The Attorney-General resumed his questioning.

'Mrs Pilling, I apologize for submitting you to this ordeal, but will you tell the gentlemen of the jury what transpired inside that barn?'

Constance sniffled. 'He – the defendant – attacked me. He was like a wild animal, tearing the clothes off my back.'

'That's a lie!'

George was out of his chair, incensed beyond measure. She was trying to hang him. *Hang him*! For the sake of her honour!

The warders grabbed his arms and, with some difficulty, sat him down. The tiny chamber had erupted and the judge's gavel only just rose above the uproar.

'This court,' he boomed, 'shall *not* tolerate any disturbance. The prisoner will be taken downstairs if further interruptions occur.'

George looked at Sir Lionel and received the sternest of glares in response. He'd been utterly swept away by anger, shocking himself perhaps more than anyone else. His breathing was still frenetic, his heart desperately pumping blood around his body.

The Attorney-General, in contrast, was detachment itself. He waited patiently for the court to settle.

'Pray continue, Mrs Pilling.'

'I tried to resist him but it was hopeless. He just ... he just over-powered me.'

Once again she burst into tears, sending George into turmoil. The truth was appalling enough without listening to this. Did she actually *want* him to hang?

'Can you tell us what was going through your mind?' Sir Ernest pressed delicately.

'I just wanted it to end. It was dreadful, *dreadful*. He was so rough. Oh, it was horrid!'

'Quite,' said the Attorney-General, temporarily lost for words. 'And did you do anything to provoke him?'

'No.' She gave a little gulp. 'But I shouldn't have gone off with him in the first place. I knew about this arrangement he had with his wife. I should have realized the effect it might have over him.'

George's stomach churned. He had a terrible sinking feeling.

'An arrangement?' queried Sir Ernest.

'She told me she refused him any form of physical intimacy.'

'Objection, my lord!' Sir Lionel had finally awakened from his slumber. 'This is hearsay. My learned friend has no way of substanti-ating this claim.'

The judge looked at the Attorney-General who shrugged his shoul-ders.

'Very well. If counsel for the prosecution would care to refrain from pursuing this line of enquiry.'

It was rather late in the day: the damage had been done. George gazed at the reporters who were scribbling furiously. So! Emily had told Constance the deepest, darkest secret of their marriage while pledging him to absolute loyalty on the subject. He might have realized the worst after Sir Ernest's opening address. Hearsay indeed! Would anyone think she'd invented such an outrage?

'What happened afterwards?' continued the Attorney-General.

'He started crying,' Constance said, recovering herself. 'He kept talking about his wife having an affair with Teddy.'

'Did he show any remorse for his actions?'

'No. I think he'd forgotten about me. He was only concerned about his wife's adulterous behaviour.'

The court collectively drew its breath, astonished at such hypocrisy.

Constance looked pleased. Sir Ernest asked a few more questions about the silent journey home and then the court was adjourned. The prisoner was led away with burning cheeks and a heart beating twice as fast as usual.

How could she have betrayed him so absolutely? Why couldn't she just say that they'd gone for a walk, had a perfectly mundane conversation? Her coachman, Peters, might have had his suspicions but nothing could have been proved. Oh, how cruel! How utterly, utterly vindictive! Certainly she'd been upset at the time, but he'd assumed that they'd resolved their differences after Emily's death.

No, there was more to this. Another presence was working his evil. Because she couldn't have accomplished that on her own, oh no! Doubtless Pilling was worried that if George was found innocent, he'd become the chief suspect. So he'd told her that word was bound to get out about their lovemaking and not only would her reputation be ruined but he'd be hanged as well.

But even so, how could she? How could she?

Even Minty, this time, was no help at all. It was still only half past four, plenty of time for the jury to digest Constance's evidence; and now he'd have to wait till tomorrow, an unbearably long time, before she was cross-examined. Such was the gravity of the situation that the two men had been joined in the visitors' room of the prison by Sir Lionel himself.

'I want to take the stand,' said George, running his hands through his thinning hair.

Sir Lionel paced up and down the cramped area, scratching his chin.

'It's too risky,' he said at last. 'I can't allow it.'

'But that woman insulted me. I want to tell the jury what I think of her.'

'She's irrelevant,' he said coldly. 'At any rate she *should* be. The prosecution have nothing to relate you to the murder. They're just relying on gossip to tarnish your character.'

'Wild animal!' George muttered disgustedly.

'What would you say if called to give evidence?' he asked.

'I'd deny it!'

'Deny what? That when your wife was ill in bed, on what turned out to be the last day of her life, the two of you didn't go for a walk in the country? Didn't end up in a barn alone?'

George remained silent; supremely frustrated.

'No one accused of murder has ever successfully given evidence on his own behalf,' Sir Lionel continued. 'And in your case I think it would be highly ill-advised. You'd be fighting for your life with one of the most skilful cross-examiners at the Criminal Bar. Required to prove your sincerity to the jury while convincing them that your morals, if not beyond reproach, are at least comparable to theirs. Just consider the case of Madeleine Smith. She was accused of murdering her lover, but the crime was completely overshadowed by the revelations surrounding their sexual encounters, occurring at least once – and to the disgust of the judge – out of doors. Now if she'd been allowed to enter the box she'd have had to account for her passionate feelings, leaving her no doubt without a shred of decency. Here – catch!'

He tossed a small, circular object across the table. Instinctively, George reached out his hand, grabbing hold of what turned out to be a coin.

'Just a little test,' said Sir Lionel, smiling. 'Sir James indicated that the murderer used his *left* hand to strangle Mrs Erskine – whereas you, wholly without thinking, caught that coin in your *right* hand. Not scientific proof, of course ...'

For the next couple of hours Sir Lionel, Minty and George engaged themselves fully in a conference about tactics – all three men, by the time they'd finished, feeling much happier about the prospects for the defence. George at first had wanted an all-out attack on Constance but, as Sir Lionel pointed out, there were more subtle ways of destroying the lady's credibility. Her marriage, for one thing, gave every appearance of being contrived, in spite of the fact that she'd been very earnest on the subject earlier in the day.

No, the advocate argued, it would be a much wiser course to undermine her evidence, demonstrate that she'd produced various assertions which were quite unsustainable. If she was claiming, for example, that George had torn her clothes off her in a passion, then what, to her knowledge, was torn? Or was this 'wild animal' some sort of squirrel? And could she really claim that she was overpowered by George when by all accounts she was a strapping woman and he was a rather diminutive man? (George was not so impressed by this last argument.) Furthermore, why did she kindly drop her assailant off at home and not go directly to the police? And why, too, did she comfort George after Emily's murder and help with the funeral arrangements if the thought had crossed her mind that he might be guilty?

Yes, there was every likelihood with careful questioning that Constance – meek, gentle Constance – would be completely demolished. She'd overplayed her hand, wavering, for some vindictive reason, away from the truth. But now – well, now she would be justly punished. George appeared to be closer to an acquittal than ever.

24

Mr Peters

'Call Mrs Pilling!'

At last the wait was over. The muscles in George's stomach tightened almost to the point of pain. As Sir Lionel had pointed out, Constance's examination-in-chief really concerned a separate issue, unrelated to the matter at hand, but of course the jury wouldn't have seen it that way. Anyone capable of assaulting a lady would be perfectly capable of killing his wife. Thus it was absolutely critical that the woman was held up for shame and ridicule.

'Call Mrs Pilling!'

The clerk repeated his summons and all eyes turned in the direction of the door through which the witnesses entered the courtroom. Where on earth was she? An attendant disappeared to check the waiting-room before returning, red-faced. There'd evidently been a mistake of some sort.

'Mrs Pilling does not appear to be present, Your Honour.' He gazed round nervously; his pronouncement had caused quite a stir.

Judge Winstanley frowned heavily, then turned brusquely to counsel for the prosecution. 'Sir Ernest, have you any idea as to the whereabouts of your witness?'

The look on the Attorney-General's face was answer enough. He climbed reluctantly to his feet. 'None at all, my lord.'

'Well!' The lines on the judge's face had crosshatched into an expression of great vexation. 'Are you aware then of any just excuse why Mrs Pilling cannot attend this morning's session?'

Sir Ernest wasn't aware. The judge appeared quite exasperated. From his vantage point on top of the raised platform, he gazed down upon the Attorney-General with all his authority. He was, as he pointed out at length, most unhappy about the situation. He had always been informed in advance of the non-attendance of witnesses and never, *never*, had a witness failed to return to court in the middle of giving evidence. It was too early, without any sufficient grounds, to think about contempt, but he was offering the defence the opportunity to adjourn the case. In the meantime, he would serve notice on Mrs Pilling to attend at the earliest possible time.

Sir Lionel, responding, thanked the judge for his offer, and declared that although he was anxious to interview Mrs Pilling – in fact, he regarded it as essential – he was quite prepared to wait for the time being. Without saying anything specifically, he implied that there was good reason for the witness's non-appearance, and indeed many of his remarks were directed at the jury – who were no doubt drawing their own conclusions – rather than the judge.

The well of George's patience, however, was almost dry. To have the cross-examination planned so meticulously and then still have to wait! Every few seconds he'd glance at the door and then rub his neck or tug on a sleeve. *Calm.* Somehow or other he had to remain calm. But these chairs! Like sitting on concrete. And the day had only just started ...

The next prosecution witness was Constance's coachman, Harold Peters, a thickset man with a pugnacious expression who strode purposefully to the box and identified himself to the court in a deep, conclusive voice.

'Take the Bible in your right hand,' instructed the clerk. 'Do you swear by Almighty God that the evidence which you shall give shall be the truth, the whole truth and nothing but the truth?'

'I do, so 'elp me God.'

The first question came from the judge who leant across to ask Peters if he possessed any knowledge as to the whereabouts of his employer, receiving yet another response in the negative. Sir Ernest then asked him some preliminary questions about his job and his opinion as to the character of Constance – who, naturally, he defended – before proceeding to elicit various details in regard to the jaunt in the country. It was all painfully matter-of-fact and George could tell that the jury implicitly believed the man's every word. It was obvious now that it would be a terrible mistake for him to give evidence. The

Attorney-General would crush him over that frightful episode in the barn.

Sir Lionel did not attempt to discredit the witness, contenting himself with a few simple questions.

'How would you describe Mrs Pilling's mood when she and the defendant set off that day?'

''Appy. Oh, yes, sir. Very 'appy indeed.'

'Not in the least worried or concerned?'

Peters shook his head.

'You must answer the question,' the judge pointed out.

'No, not at all worried, your lordship. She appeared in the best of spirits, if I may say so.'

'And whose decision was it to stop at one point in the journey?'

'That'd be the mistress's. She said, "Peters, stop. Stop right 'ere, Peters."'

Some subdued chortling escaped from the gallery. Here was a witness they obviously liked.

'It was her idea? She desired to go off with the prisoner alone?'

'Well, it looks that way from where I'm standing.'

The judge sighed. 'Just answer yes or no.'

'Yes,' said Peters.

'And what did you do, Mr Peters?'

'What did I do?' answered Peters, inadvertently finding the perfect response to irritate the judge.

'Yes, what did you do?'

'I watched them till they went out of sight.'

'Did you notice any friction?'

'What? Them rubbing against each other?'

The judge gazed despairingly at the ceiling. Everyone else, though, laughed.

'My object,' said Sir Lionel with a smile, 'was merely to establish if in your opinion Mrs Pilling and the prisoner were still on good terms.'

'I'd say so, yes,' said Peters. 'They went off arm in arm, chatting, saying, "My, what a gorgeous day!" and that.'

'And when they came back?'

'It wasn't a gorgeous day any more. They were like two black clouds, not talking to each other. I tried whistling to cheer them up, but it didn't make a jot of difference.'

Peters proceeded to whistle to illustrate his point.

'Yes, yes!' rasped the judge. 'The court is aware of what a whistle sounds like.'

'How upset did Mrs Pilling appear?' Sir Lionel persisted.

'Well, I wouldn't say she was upset as such. Just a bit downhearted. Normally when she returns she's 'appy as you like.'

'What do you mean, "*normally* when she returns"?'

'Well, the two or three other times she's taken young gentlemen out they've always come back looking very pleased with themselves. Like the cat that's got the cream, you might say.'

Peters gazed round the courtroom, seemingly unable to understand why his last remark had caused such amusement. Sir Lionel asked a couple of further questions about the frequency of Mrs Pilling's visits to Stockley Hall after Mrs Erskine's death, and then they adjourned for luncheon.

Minty, though disappointed as well that Constance had not appeared, still managed to seem ebullient in front of George.

'Sir Ernest shouldn't have called Peters. He was more use to our side than theirs. When Mrs Pilling finally turns up we can really press home our advantage.'

'What if she doesn't turn up?' asked George, to whom the prospect was beginning to appear increasingly likely.

'But she must! She could go to prison for up to three months.' Minty fell silent for a second, a thoughtful expression etched on his face. 'It would be bad for us, though, if she adamantly refused to testify. The judge might rule a mistrial, but that would only mean you'd have to be tried again. And all of her evidence has already been circulated in the press.'

There wasn't much more for them to discuss. What on earth had happened to Constance?

25

Mrs Proops

In the afternoon Constable Tulley took the stand, giving evidence on behalf of James Hopley – who was suffering from influenza – followed by Inspector Gwynne who answered questions about James's statement and the investigation. There was a hushed and heavy air to proceedings; a feeling of drowsiness. The dull roar of traffic could be heard on the street outside; the occasional scratching of a quill.

It was quite late by the time the last witness was called. The gas jets were turned on and a faint hissing sound accompanied Mrs Proops as she made her way to the stand. She was wearing pince-nez, partially obscuring her dark beady eyes, and her thin sable hair was scraped back fiercely off her forehead. Fittingly, she was dressed in black, her face a paragon of misery.

Yes, she replied, in response to the Attorney-General's first question. She had known Mrs Erskine very well; had always been on very good terms with Lord Delsey, whom she had served for many years; and was familiar enough with the deceased to call her Emily and be addressed as Matilda in return.

'Now, Mrs Proops, I ask you to cast your mind back to the morning of Saturday, the fourth of July. Did anything of interest occur on that date?'

'Mrs Erskine was taken ill during breakfast. Her face was very pale and she was running a high temperature. I immediately sent Mary to the kitchen for some mustard and hot water, and told Mr Hopley, the butler, to call for Doctor Wetherington. I tried giving her coffee, then brandy, but everything she swallowed came straight back up again.'

Why had nobody told George about this? He'd believed at the time that Emily had merely been acting.

'What was the attitude of the prisoner?' asked Sir Ernest pertinently.

'I never saw him. I think he must have left shortly after breakfast.'

'His wife was seriously ill and he took no notice?'

'Not to the best of my knowledge, no.'

The Attorney-General nodded sagely, letting this idea sink into the minds of the jury.

'Did he visit her at all?'

'I saw him the next morning leaving her room. I don't think he could have seen her on Saturday without me knowing. Mrs Erskine was very particular about whom she let into her room after ten o'clock at night.'

'Not even her husband had access to her private quarters?'

'No.'

'Didn't you find that rather odd?'

'It was Mrs Erskine's decision.'

She lifted her chin a fraction and George was sure that if he were closer he'd have heard a sniff. Good old Proopsy! Gossip, at any rate, wasn't one of her faults. Sir Ernest was left to survey his notes, with no other reason apparently but to gain time.

'So on the Saturday,' he reiterated, 'the defendant did not visit his wife during the daylight hours, to the best of your knowledge, and could not have seen her late in the evening. Is that correct?'

'She could have allowed him into her room overnight, I suppose.'

'Unlocked the door?'

Sir Lionel interrupted. 'My lord, I must object. This is pure conjecture.'

The judge agreed. But, again, the point had been made.

'When you saw the prisoner on the Sunday morning, Mrs Proops, leaving his wife's room, how would you describe his mood?'

'He was exceedingly cheerful, laughing a great deal. He seemed delighted that he hadn't suffered any ill consequences himself.'

George bit into his fingernails. There was no question that Mrs Proops was telling the truth – at any rate her version of it – but she was making him look uncaring in the extreme. Sir Ernest pursued the theme for a while, entering into the details of their conversation outside Emily's room, before proceeding to the evening of the same day, asking Mrs Proops to relate to the court her experiences at the time.

'I locked up as usual and then went to bed. I was about to lie down to sleep when I noticed a light under the door. My only thought was that I must have forgotten to turn down one of the lamps. I rose from my bed and went downstairs to find Mr Erskine in the process of closing the door of his wife's bedroom. It was my impression he wished to make as little noise as possible. He turned around and looked very startled to see me. We stared at each for a moment. Then he walked back to his room.'

George looked over at the jury. They were all sitting upright, seeming to appreciate the importance of this last statement. Such was the tension and closeness in the courtroom that his underclothes were wringing wet.

'He did not offer any explanation of what he was doing there?'

'No.'

'What time was this?'

'About eleven thirty, I would say.'

'Did you check Mrs Erskine's room?'

'I didn't see any reason to disturb her again. I went back to bed.'

'And what happened the following morning?'

Mrs Proops shuddered. Her long fingers clasped the wooden rail of the box.

'Mary and I knocked on her door at eight thirty with her breakfast tray. There was no response so we knocked again, a little louder. I called out to say that her breakfast was ready, but there was still no answer. After waiting a minute or so I decided to unlock the door. To my surprise, though, it was already open.'

She drew a long breath.

'Mrs Erskine was lying on the bed. She was covered by a white silk sheet, her arms resting on top, one hand holding the other. I touched her cheek and said to Mary, "She's cold", and Mary dropped the tray.'

George cast his eyes down, his hands resting limply in his lap. The scream he'd heard then was presumably Mary. A rushing of feet had followed and then Hopley had made that comment about 'some sort of accident'. Poor man, he didn't know what else to say. And poor Mrs Proops! Not only did she have to live with her shocking discovery, she was obliged to testify to her experience in a court of law, the Attorney-General now pressing her for a more detailed description of Emily's final resting position. How ghastly it all was. There were times when he could almost persuade himself that the 'Mrs Erskine' referred to in court was someone else – another victim – but there were other occasions when it was simply impossible.

At last, though, Sir Ernest resumed his seat and it was the turn of Sir Lionel to address the witness. Rather than throw doubt over her evidence so far, he confined himself to such questions as who, if anyone, locked the back door at Stockley Hall every night, Mrs Proops claiming it was Mrs Hedges' responsibility. Didn't she think as well that George's apparently indifferent attitude to his wife's illness could be explained by the fact that he was convinced she was getting better at the time? Sir Lionel, at any rate, thought so. He also managed to persuade the witness to admit that George might not have been leaving Emily's room on the night of her murder, merely opening and closing the door.

The court was adjourned. The day had been overshadowed by the disappearance of Constance – about whom nothing more had been heard – and, even more frustrating, since it was Saturday, there'd be another day to wait before the trial resumed on Monday. With little to comfort him, George was led back down to his cell.

26

An Offer

'You have a visitor.'

George gazed with tired eyes through the bars of his cell at Graves, the warder. Minty again! It would be his third visit this evening.

'A Mr Edward Pilling is here to see you.'

He raised himself from his prone position, a little electrical surge going through his body.

'The gentleman has already obtained permission from the governor,' continued Graves, lacking an immediate reply. 'Shall I tell him you're asleep and don't wish to be disturbed?'

George smiled grimly. 'Thank you, Graves. You're a good fellow. Can you please ask him why he wants to see me?'

Graves departed and George remained sitting on the bed, biting on his lower lip. Maliciousness, that's all it was. Pilling wishing to state how pleased he was that George was in his current predicament and to express a hope for a guilty verdict.

Well, not if he refused to see him ...

A minute later the warder returned. 'Mr Pilling says it's essential he speak to you. Something to do with the death of his wife.'

George's heart took a sudden leap. Constance? Dead? He stared at the other for a couple of seconds to ensure the man was being serious.

'Shall I take you to see him?' asked Graves.

George stood up. There was no question now about seeing Pilling. The warder unlocked the cell door and led the way to the interview-room.

They arrived to find Pilling, dressed in a morning coat, hair swimming in brilliantine, seated on the other side of a glass screen. George sat down opposite, still slightly dazed and unsure what to say, leaving Graves standing in the corner. Pilling looked very solemn.

'How d'you do, Erskine? You've been told about Constance?'

'Just now. It was a great shock.'

'H'm, yes, to all of us.' Pilling, in spite of his drained appearance, did not look especially upset. 'It was suicide, I'm afraid.'

George instinctively raised his hand to his mouth. This was absolutely terrible. The despair she must have felt, perhaps brought on by his own actions.

'She left a note stating her reasons. It's not easy for me to talk about.'

'I can imagine.'

'Trouble is, you see, certain matters have come up. To be quite blunt, the note didn't refer to my prospects at any point. I've been talking to solicitors for most of the day.'

A cold feeling enveloped George. 'You mean you haven't benefited financially?'

He was hoping that he'd misunderstood Pilling's last remark and would be immediately corrected. But the other merely shook his head.

'It's a bad business, that's all I can say. Constance was leasing Eveley Manor from Colonel Morecombe. When her father died he left her and her mother over seventy thousand pounds in stock and securities. However, they were persuaded by relatives to execute a voluntary settlement protecting their fortune, which was then managed for them by a family trust headed by Constance's uncle. Her mother, up to her death a few weeks before the trial, was receiving a monthly income from the trustees which paid in part for the lease on the house. The settlement meant that if Constance died intestate her wealth would be inherited by the next of kin under the Statute of Distributions. In other words,' concluded Pilling, mistaking George's expression for one of sympathy, 'unless she left a will in my favour, I'd receive nothing, not a shilling.'

He bowed his head.

'Didn't you care for her at all?' asked George.

'Oh, yes, certainly!' Pilling looked up, somewhat surprised. 'Her death was a shock, a terrible shock. Shall I tell you what happened?'

George gave a little nod, but he was feeling distinctly ill at ease.

Why had Pilling troubled to pay him a visit? Was it possible he regarded him as a friend? Under the circumstances he wouldn't have been surprised if the other had blamed him for his wife's suicide, but this calmness of his was almost inhuman. At least Constance in all her mad passion was understandable. Even her display in court could be attributed to hurt feelings. No emotion existed in Pilling's voice at all.

'Last night, after the business of the trial, we dined as usual and I retired to the drawing-room to read. At about eleven Constance came to tell me she was going to take a stroll before turning in. She was used to walking at night, enjoying the peace and quiet, and I said she should go ahead by all means. Feeling tired myself, I went to bed not long after.

'Anyhow, this morning I discovered that she'd disappeared. At first I presumed she'd gone for another walk, sending Peters on to the trial in the belief that she'd arrive a bit later. But the minutes ticked by, then the hours, and by luncheon I was beginning to feel uneasy. In a bid to do something I walked to the end of the drive.

'Almost at once I saw a horse and cart turning the corner, travelling at speed. I moved to the centre of the road, but Willoughby, the driver, only seemed to notice me at the last moment. He looked in a complete state and I had to spend some time trying to calm him down. At last, though, he managed to explain that there'd been a horrible accident. He'd gone into his barn and discovered Constance hanging from the beam, a rope around her neck.'

Pilling fell silent, closing his eyes and holding the bridge of his nose between his thumb and forefinger. Graves stepped forward.

'Visiting time is over. I must take the prisoner back to his cell.'

Pilling looked up. 'No, wait! Ten more minutes!'

The warder sighed, nodded, and returned to his corner.

'There was a letter addressed to me, marked "Strictly Personal", in the valise of her bicycle. She used a bicycle to balance on, you see, to reach the noose. The police wanted me to divulge the contents of her note. But I told them she was just saying goodbye.'

He leant forward, speaking in a whisper. 'I know what happened between the two of you in the barn, Erskine. Constance has confessed to seducing you and trying to destroy your marriage. She's revealed everything.'

George looked at him in utter bewilderment, quite unable to believe what he was hearing.

'There are other details which I'm not prepared to enter into for the time being,' continued Pilling. 'The point is that if the note is produced in court, you'll be acquitted for certain.'

'Do it then!'

'Ah, my friend, if only it was so easy!' Pilling leant back, his arms outstretched. 'There's my late wife's reputation to consider. Remember, too, that her financial situation wasn't as – how shall I say? – felicitous as I'd imagined.'

For a moment George was mystified as to Pilling's meaning. 'What d'you want?' He gritted his teeth.

'Very direct. I like that. I could quibble about the tone but we're apparently pressed for time – at least, *you* are. Now, what do I want? Oh, yes! Your home, old fellow. Stockley Hall … and the estate.'

'What!'

'Yes, a swap, you might say. I have some ties with the family, remember? You could say I'm merely asserting my ancestral right.' He smiled broadly. 'Not that I'm an unreasonable man. I'm quite prepared to allow you to move into Potterslake Farm. Believe me, I've thought about this matter at some length. A solicitor could draw up the details immediately for you to sign—'

'You're quite serious, aren't you?'

'Perfectly.'

'And justice? Does that bother you at all?'

'This *is* justice – for all concerned. If you like, we can discuss this further after your release, perhaps while you're showing me round my new home.'

George wanted so much to tell him to go to hell. All it needed was the strength to say the words.

'Why should I place any trust in you?'

'Well, what choice have you got, old chap? Constance's death has pretty much sealed your fate, if you'll excuse the hackneyed expression.'

The reason for Pilling's visit – the point of his seeing George on the day of his wife's death – was now laid bare. Minty had already outlined how Constance refusing to testify would damage George's chances of being released. But then to succumb to the threats of this blackmailing scoundrel!

'Oh, and by the way,' Pilling added, 'if you're thinking of reporting to anyone that I've a certain note in my possession ... don't. It'll do you no good. It's very well hidden and I can at any moment destroy it. I'll only come forward with the new evidence when we've reached an agreement.'

George lowered his head. It was the most terrible dilemma. And yet he already knew what he was going to do. Pilling's offer was quite repugnant, but a small sense of hope was working within him.

27

A Confession

Sunday. It had been a strange day, not at all as George had imagined when he'd left the courtroom the previous afternoon. A telegram had reached him at nine in the morning, from Messrs Penderbury and Ashurst, his solicitors, frantically requesting further information and confirmation of the proposed property transaction. He'd already written to Mr Penderbury the previous evening, in Pilling's presence, stating that he wished to sell his house posthaste, but now he wrote another note emphasizing how vital it was that his wishes were carried out as soon as possible. After handing this missive to Graves there'd been no further correspondence and he could only imagine that the lawyers concerned were busily drawing up contracts and examining title deeds.

In the afternoon Minty and Sir Lionel had arrived to discuss Constance's death. George, following instructions, had not informed them of Pilling's visit and his subsequent offer, not wanting to run the risk of the suicide note being destroyed, and from the mood of the two gentlemen it appeared his decision was justified. Even though, as Sir Lionel admitted, the situation was not beyond salvation, Constance's death had certainly not improved their hopes. The advocate advanced a theory that the suicide might have been engendered by feelings of compunction over committing perjury, but this was not wholly convincing. In any case, their line, as expected, would be to apply to the judge in the morning to discharge the jury and order a retrial. Naturally, this course of action didn't guarantee George his freedom.

In the evening Pilling had presented himself once more. The legal work had gone smoothly and he wished to thank George for his assistance. It was an unhappy interview from the latter's point of view,

Pilling still refusing to be drawn as to the exact contents of the letter, knowing full well that George had little choice but to agree to his proposal. The prisoner noted how smartly the other was attired compared to himself – and now the cad would be moving into his house! Potterslake Farm was still a sizeable residence, and he was really exchanging his cell – and ultimately his life – in return for living there (assuming, of course, that the letter significantly helped his cause). But the greed of the man! The death of Constance had obviously been nothing more to him than a financial transaction. George remained fairly quiet throughout and was pleased to see Pilling leave.

That night, unable to assuage his guilty feelings over Constance's death and his acquiescence in Pilling's plans, a series of images entered his sleep. Pilling had killed his first wife, Lily, and inherited the farmhouse; strangled Emily after she'd threatened to cut off his allowance; then murdered Constance with a view to acquiring the manor. It was Pilling all the time. Pilling had killed all those women …

He sat up, sweating profusely. What a terrible mistake it had been to see the man. He would now die in the knowledge that Pilling had won, playing his nasty and cold-blooded games. The letter had been a hoax – of course it was! – and he'd been duped into believing that he might be saved. He was going to be hanged – *hanged* – and all his possessions would be lost to his greatest enemy. God, he'd been such a fool. Worse, a coward, desperately clinging on to life. He buried his head in his hands and let out a little moan. Oh, why couldn't it all end now…?

The dawning of a new day, however, brought a touch of much needed calm to his thoughts, and his confidence had somewhat restored itself by the time he was fetched from his cell. If he was to be found guilty, then he'd bring Pilling down with him. Tell the world of the man's blackmailing activities. No news had arrived from Minty and Sir Lionel and he could only presume that they hadn't been approached about the suicide note. And if that was the case – well, Pilling would pay….

He was led up the stairway to the dock, taking his place, unusually, before the arrival of the judge, to find the courtroom in a ferment of excitement. White-wigged barristers were locked in animated discussion and people were whispering urgently to each other. Presumably news of Constance's death had just been received. Only the lugubrious figure of Inspector Gwynne, seated on the table set aside for the police, did not appear caught up in the new spirit. Naturally enough, of course. It was his investigation.

A loud knocking on the door, followed by a cry of 'Silence!' from the usher, quietened the chatter. The court rose to its feet as the judge, donned in scarlet and ermine, accompanied by the sheriffs in their violet costumes, entered the court. Mr Justice Winstanley's head was framed by a very large horsehair wig which, draped over his shoulders and combined with his solemn features, might have made him look faintly ridiculous in other circumstances. Carefully folding his robes about him, his lordship took his seat, pausing only to fire a warning glance upwards at the spectators in the gallery.

The court settled and Sir Ernest, nervously rearranging the papers on his table, climbed back to his feet.

'My lord, I would beg to draw the court's attention to the subject of Mrs Constance Pilling who gave evidence on Friday. As your lordship is aware, she died under the most tragic circumstances ...'

The Attorney-General briefly described the events of Friday evening, so far as they were known, lending his condolences to the friends and family of the deceased.

'Unfortunately the prosecution had planned, this morning, to call Edward Pilling as our last witness, but for obvious reasons Mr Pilling feels too distressed to take the stand.'

The judge, looking more aggrieved than ever, asked about the likelihood of the witness attending on the next occasion, were he to adjourn the court, but was greeted with the vaguest of answers. He would not, however, allow a deposition to be read out of Pilling's evidence at the committal proceedings. He had already, he felt, given sufficient leeway to the prosecution. The Attorney-General, in lieu of further witnesses, said that in that case he had finished giving evidence.

George took a deep breath, allowing himself to relax a little. The prosecution could hardly frame a case against him if several of their witnesses had not testified in court. The last few days had been tremendously worrying, but Constance's death had eventually worked out in his favour.

Sir Lionel had a brief word with Mr de Grey and then stood up to address the court with even more of his customary swagger. He sympathized with his learned friend's difficulties during the course of proceedings. The death of Mrs Pilling was an unusual as well as tragic element of the trial, but though she was a witness for the prosecution, he did not want her testimony to be discounted. Indeed, he wished to take the opportunity to thank Sir Ernest and the police for their prompt disclosure—

'My lord.' The Attorney-General had risen from his seat. 'I must object to certain evidence which I understand my learned friend desires to introduce.'

George felt his pulse quicken. They could only be referring to Constance's suicide note. Pilling must have gone to the authorities with her letter. But what objection could there be to its introduction?

Mr Justice Winstanley's face creased in frustration. The trial had already produced more than enough problems. Both counsel, though, stressed that a very important point of law had arisen.

The jury, looking completely bemused, were instructed to leave the court, and the stage was set for a great legal debate.

Sir Ernest stated that a letter written by Mrs Pilling – he did not question its authenticity – could not be admitted as evidence unless it was against her pecuniary or proprietary interest. He accepted it was against Mrs Pilling's *penal* interest, but the *Sussex Peerage Case* was very clear in regard to declarations exposing the maker to criminal prosecution.

So much for the Attorney-General. Perched on the edge of his seat, George strove desperately to fathom the arguments. They *must* accept the letter!

Sir Lionel countered by stating that since Constance had clearly intended to take her own life, her statement could hardly be used against her in any future proceedings, and that as she had written her letter under a settled and hopeless expectation of death, her motive to lie was considerably diminished.

No, Sir Ernest retorted – much to George's dismay – the opposite was true. The letter could have been written a day, or a week, before the suicide. In his opinion, the reference to the trial in the note did not outlaw this possibility. And *R* v. *Bedingfield* demonstrated that statements 'after the main act was concluded' allowed the witness time to invent a story. In any case, knowing that she was going to die might have induced in her a desire to rescue the defendant.

George watched helplessly as his legal representative crossed swords with his opponent over what he'd assumed was a fairly straightforward issue. Slowly but surely it became clear that there was a good chance that Constance's letter might not be admitted as evidence; not providing, apparently, an exception to the hearsay rule. Sir Lionel's tone was becoming increasingly desperate and, in contrast to Sir Ernest, he was flapping his arms about more and more frantically. Evidently, he was losing the debate and, so far as George could remember, he had not, as yet, quoted any previous cases to bolster his arguments.

Damn the law! What had it to do with real people, real life, anyhow?

It was with a tremendous sense of relief when Mr Justice Winstanley finally pronounced, 'If I am to decide whether Mrs Pilling's statement is admissible against interest, I must know the nature of the declaration. Would it be possible, Sir Lionel, for you to read out the letter in question to the court?'

It certainly was possible, and it was apparent from the sudden shifting in seats that the packed courtroom thoroughly approved of the judge's decision as well. Minty twisted round in his chair and positively beamed at George. Reading the letter – even with the jury absent – was part of the battle won.

Sir Lionel cleared his throat and began to read in a loud clear voice.

'"Eveley Manor, October 24th.

'"Dearest Teddy, I am writing these lines because I feel I must tell you the truth about myself. You've no idea how debauched and immoral I really am. I don't deserve you as a husband."'

Not a sound could be heard apart from Sir Lionel's voice.

'"The evidence I gave at the trial is a lie."'

A lady in the gallery gasped.

'"I said those things because I was resentful at the way George had rejected me. He told me before the funeral that Emily was irreplaceable. Now I feel disgusted at my behaviour."'

A loud murmur had begun which was immediately silenced by the judge.

'I must insist that this court observes the proper decorum at all times. Pray continue, Sir Lionel.'

'"I led George to the barn. He didn't attack me, quite the reverse. I wanted to seduce him, make him mine. I thought that by providing the warmth and affection which didn't exist in his married life, he would love me, find me appealing."'

George was more aware than ever that eyes were trained in his direction. Constance had appeared fond of him, certainly, but to describe her feelings in such a way! And then to take her own life ...

'"At the picnic I saw him for the first time in years and instantly felt a great attraction. In the past I'd admired him tremendously, but now I knew he was the one person who could fulfil all my hopes and expectations. When Emily told me her marriage was platonic I was sure George would be happier with me. I even hid his bicycle hoping I could stay behind afterwards and help him look for it."'

Oh, God. He'd completely forgotten about the missing bicycle. Attached no significance to it whatsoever. And Constance had been so keen to help him look for it!

'"Over the next week I couldn't stop thinking about him. I couldn't sleep, and cycled to his house every night, just to be near him. Once I even threw gravel at his bedroom window. I was madly in love."'

Yes, the gravel! That would have been the night of his anniversary. Just as he was dropping off to sleep after standing for so long at the window ...

'"After church on the day of Emily's death my dreams were realized. I spurned your offer, Teddy, to walk me home so as to be with George. We were going, I told him, for a drive in the country and I purposely withheld our destination."'

Sir Lionel briefly paused to sip from a glass of water.

'"In the barn the two of us enjoyed intimate relations. I was ecstatically happy, in the arms of the love of my life. After we'd finished, I insinuated that Emily was betraying George behind his back and, fully convinced he was now mine, attributed his tears merely to dented pride, the coming to terms with a failed marriage."'

Sir Lionel carefully placed the first page of the letter back on the table and continued reading from the second. The tension in the courtroom was exceptionally brittle.

"'It was important, I determined, that Emily learnt of our love for each other. If she agreed to release George, all of our problems would be solved in one shot. In a state of great nervous excitement I cycled to Stockley Hall, arriving at about a quarter past one at night. Everyone, it appeared, had gone to bed. Quite unnoticed, I crept up the staircase and knocked, very softly, on Emily's door. There was no response, so I knocked a bit louder. I could hear her getting out of bed and then walking over to the door. 'Who's that?' she said. 'It's me', I told her. 'I need to speak to you.' 'Are you on your own?' she asked. I assured her I was, and then I heard her fiddling with the lock. She opened the door, dressed in her nightclothes.'"

The colour drained from George's face. What was she saying? *What was she saying?*

"'She looked very shocked to see me, but before saying another word I stepped into the room and told her to close the door. After doing so, she turned back to face me and asked what was the matter. Almost at once I confessed my love for George and told her that we'd had intimate relations. 'You're mad!' she said. I told her she could never give her husband the love I was offering. 'Get out, you slut, get out.' I stood up, clutching my coat. 'You need more time.' I'd tried to talk to her but it was hopeless. 'Come on! Out!' she cried. She grabbed my arm, dragging me in the direction of the door. 'Out! Out!' She was practically shouting and in a vain attempt to stifle her voice I tried to place my hands over her mouth. But she kept struggling, flinging my arms aside and almost pushing me over. In desperation I charged at her, forcing her back onto the bed. I merely wanted to stop her squealing, force her to be quiet. I had my hand on her throat but she was still gurgling, 'Get off me, get off me!' Her arms were flailing, beating at my arms and chest. 'Be still', I begged her. 'Please be still.' I didn't think that anything horrible …

"'Oh, God, Teddy. It was me, not George. *I* killed Emily. All I can say is that it was wholly unintentional, an appalling mistake. Please, please forgive me.'"

The second page had ended. The sweat was pouring from George's brow; he was in a severe state of shock. The courtroom listened in fascinated silence as Sir Lionel read from the final page.

'"So I've decided to take my leave of the world. I certainly don't deserve another fate. My appearance is as horrid as my vile nature and the rope will need ... "' Sir Lionel hesitated, either through emotion or because of the slightly ungrammatical nature of the sentence. '"The rope *must* be strong to support my heavy load. Farewell, my darling. You were a fine and noble husband. Shed no tears on my account. – Constance."'

Sir Lionel let the paper drop to the table. For a couple of seconds nobody spoke, the silence suddenly broken by a shout from the gallery:

'Set him free!'

A storm of applause greeted this outburst. The court was the scene of pandemonium. George, whose mind was still fixed on the murder, the terrible picture of Constance strangling Emily to death, was dimly aware of smiling faces, a sea of happiness swimming before him. An usher shouted 'Silence! Silence!' but it took an age to quell the cries, the release of tension which had been waiting to burst forth. The judge's voice could scarcely be heard above the clamour. On the third attempt he ordered the court to be adjourned for luncheon.

George was led away to the sounds of cheers and friendly voices, too shocked to really comprehend anything around him. Constance – *Constance* – was the murderer! Minty, who joined him a few minutes later, finally shook him out of his reverie. The solicitor was absolutely jubilant.

'We've won, dear boy. The afternoon will be a formality. Sir Lionel is in the judge's chambers at the moment discussing with the Attorney-General the best way to end the case. There's such over-whelming support for you I can't believe the judge won't bow to the pressure. There'd be a national scandal.'

For a second George imagined the few disgruntled letters in *The Times* lamenting the sentence of death passed upon him and then dismissed the thought from his mind. It was difficult to accept the shadow of the gallows had completely vanished, but Minty must know – surely, he must – what he was talking about.

28

The Trial Ends

The court reassembled after luncheon to listen to the judge's decision.

'I have decided to receive Mrs Pilling's letter into evidence. The declaration was written *in extremis*, with every knowledge of her approaching fate, and no motive to misrepresent what she knew. My only proviso is that such evidence should be treated with the utmost caution because it is subject to no cross-examination.'

A feeling of elation encompassed George. Surely nothing now could prevent his acquittal?

The rest of the day was spent calling defence witnesses, a procession of friends and acquaintances testifying to George's character. Mrs Wetherington, Mrs Hedges, Arthur Hopley, as well as a host of others, were all generous in their conviction of his innocence. The judge closed proceedings by announcing that he would sit to any hour the next day in order that a verdict might be reached.

The following morning, in consequence, the courtroom was even more crowded than usual, spectators contorting themselves into ridiculous shapes to preserve their places. One of the principal doors had been blocked by a row of seats and special tickets of admission had been issued by the sheriffs. In the adjoining corridors non-ticket-holders swarmed with increasing desperation, unable to gain entrance, while a small multitude, preparing to cheer an innocent verdict, had already begun to gather outside in the street, overseen by twenty mounted policemen. It all seemed removed from the ordered conduct of events inside the court, where each advocate knew instinctively just what his role demanded.

In Sir Lionel's case that meant a short and incisive attack on the police. They had not explored the possibility that an intruder had entered the house through the back door. And since Mrs Pilling's note had not been queried on any question of detail, there was no reason for thinking that with virtually her last breath she had not told the truth. It was essential, therefore, that George Erskine should be acquitted. Sir Lionel's face, his manner, his tone of address were all indignant, and when he sat down and mopped his brow at the end of his peroration he looked very indignant indeed.

George, in contrast, just wanted the trial to end. During Sir Lionel's attack on the police he'd watched Inspector Gwynne lower his head, apparently in shame. How unfair it was to heap all this criticism on his shoulders. After all, he was only doing his job. The walrus moustache, which had been carefully sported hitherto, now looked as though it had recently passed on. It was now quite impossible that the jury could do anything else but acquit him. The Attorney-General had a hopeless task in front of him.

But if there was no point in Sir Ernest presenting his arguments, he certainly seemed unaware of it. George listened despondently as he droned on in a calm, dispassionate voice. The suicide note, apparently, was the desperate attempt of an infatuated woman to save her lover. There were, in fact, a hundred explanations to account for the letter. The jury were invited instead to consider the weight of evidence against the prisoner. The fact that his wife was scared to leave her door open at night, his unexpected presence outside her room after the house had gone to bed, the letter he had forged from Edward Pilling, the amount of alcohol he had consumed, the number of lies he had told the police.

The courtroom was becoming increasingly stuffy and George began to feel the same disquiet he'd experienced during the prosecution's opening address. Sir Ernest had been talking for at least twice as long as his opponent – surely there were rules about that sort of thing? – and it was clear he'd placed too much faith in Minty's optimism and Constance's letter, swayed by the cheering of the spectators. In the end, only the jury mattered, and it was apparent that they were listening to the Attorney-General's closing remarks with the gravest interest. Not only did it look as if he *might* hang, it was looking increasingly likely. More than likely, in fact. Oh, God. Oh, dear God.

This was horrible, ghastly. He imagined the reporters' assessment of his appearance. *The prisoner, indifferent to his own counsel's eloquence, could not conceal the colour in his cheeks as he listened to the Attorney-General's brilliant elucidation of the case against him; writhing and squirming in the dock as, point by point, the foundations of his defence were clinically dismantled.* No, it would not pay to show his feelings. He immediately adopted an expression of profound incredulity.

But Sir Ernest did go on. God, was he never going to stop? And everyone treated the man with such unholy reverence. There was absolute silence in the courtroom, not one little cough. The open-mouthed mob were too engrossed in listening to a sermon which suggested, very politely, that he should be hanged.

Only the judge's summing-up remained, upon which everything hinged.

A high-pitched and desiccated voice drifted through the stale air, Mr Justice Winstanley's prune-like head bobbing in time with his staccato points. Finally it was his turn to speak, and revelling in the knowledge, perhaps only fully understood by himself, that he was cleverer than anyone else, he carefully explained to the jury the meaning of reasonable doubt, an explanation rendered only slightly less dull in the light of his subsequent exposition on the difference between direct and circumstantial evidence, the former invariably proving more valuable than the latter.

For the last time the evidence was dredged up. The forged love letter, the involvement of Mrs Pilling and the validity of her 'confession'; the infuriating fact, mentioned two or three times, that the defendant did not undergo a cross-examination – 'stating on oath, before a jury, his innocence, and therefore exposing himself to questions that might naturally arise about points of difficulty in his story'. Words, words, and yet more words!

By now George was sweating profusely and, looking around, he could see he wasn't the only one suffering. More and more handkerchiefs were on display, conducting a variety of mopping-up operations. Pushing on into his third hour, the judge divided the case into four different aspects – two for the prosecution and two for the defence – which the jury might wish to use as a framework. Offering some last instructions, he finally asked them to retire to consider their verdict.

George rose groggily to his feet but was informed by Graves that it was customary for the prisoner to remain in the dock while the jury deliberated. So while most people trooped out of the court for a dose of fresh air, he sat on, scrutinized by a handful of reporters. Gas jets flickered round the chamber, which was as short on air as ever. The atmosphere was unbearably close, with only the clock to keep him company.

6.45 p.m. Half an hour passed. It had begun to rain outside and a drip-drip-drip could be heard from a gutter. The crowd inside the courtroom were beginning to filter back and the odd cough broke the tense silence, the tapping of fingers. One of the female spectators was furiously knitting, as she had been all day, and the sound of her needles bore into the prisoner's brain.

Another twenty minutes elapsed with painful reluctance. 7.35 p.m.

George could see a reporter out of the corner of his eye sipping a drink. People were now starting to shuffle impatiently – there was the occasional muffled shout from outside in the street – but, statue-like, he stared resolutely ahead. So this was fear. Real fear. It felt as though his heart would collapse with the strain.

Then, startlingly, the distant cry of 'Jury!' could be heard. Footsteps everywhere. Great agitation. The court quickly filled to the brim with people.

The cast was the same apart from a figure in black standing next to the judge: the chaplain. His function would be to place the black square of silk – the 'black cap' – on the judge's wig should there be a verdict of guilty. George knew that his face looked extremely flushed. Wouldn't it be terrible if he fainted? No, he resolved to be a man.

To draw out the agony, the clerk painstakingly read out the names of the jury. George scanned their faces frantically, looking for some indication of his fate, but they all appeared extremely sombre. Then – was it time already?

'Gentlemen of the jury, have you agreed upon your verdict?'

George was tapped on the shoulder and made his way uncertainly to the front of the dock. He felt the blood rush to his face.

The foreman of the jury rose.

'We have,' he answered.

'Do you find the prisoner at the bar, George Arthur Erskine, guilty or not guilty of the wilful murder of Emily Jane Erskine?'

The foreman paused. Everyone held their breath.

'Not guilty.'

For a fraction of a second, there was silence; then a huge cheer erupted, followed by a prolonged ovation. George was still staring at the foreman in shock, tears streaming down his face, tears of joy and relief, all the tension in his body subsiding. All around him women were crying or waving their handkerchiefs, men tossing their hats in the air. The judge's voice briefly rose above the hubbub.

'This conduct is an outrage! A court of justice is not to be turned into a theatre by such indecent exhibitions ...'

Outside the court the crowd which had only just received the verdict provided an enormous echo to the cries of celebration which had convulsed the court. George felt on the point of collapse. The judge was saying a few words to him, but he did not hear a single one. A number of people surrounded the dock, pressing forward to shake his hand, sharing in his happiness ...

An hour later, George, Minty and Sir Lionel were led by a cordon of police through the tremendous crowd which had gathered outside the court, the traffic brought to a standstill. It was too soon for the papers to publish a full account of proceedings, but a good deal of copy could be written and, as the trio entered a hotel for refreshment, the cry of a newsboy could be heard:

'Eveley murder – trial and verdict. Read all about it!'

Part Four

29

A Visit from Inspector Gwynne

Three weeks had elapsed since the end of the trial. At the outset George had been inundated with letters and telegrams – including even one proposal of marriage – but now the furore was beginning to die down. In the press there had been much discussion about the performance of the police – Inspector Gwynne had been singled out for especial censure – and some of the papers had frothed at the mouth over the savage and wanton behaviour of young women in society. But George, of course, had been lauded as the hero of the hour. Although news had leaked out about the exchange of properties between Pilling and himself, leading to more specula-tion as to the circumstances behind the move, the public had, by then, another murder to command their interest. Emily had been murdered by her friend, Constance, who, in remorse, had committed suicide. The 'Eveley Mystery', as it had been called, was, in most people's minds, closed.

George had taken up residence at Potterslake Farm with little enthusiasm. He'd been glad in one respect to leave Stockley Hall, once the scene of such happy memories, but it had been odious to hand over the estate to Pilling, and he'd tended to avoid that smug gentleman whenever possible. Surprisingly, perhaps, he'd been joined by Arthur Hopley and Matilda Proops, both of whom had been summarily dismissed by their new master – apparently for reasons of expense. Even though George's financial circumstances were scarcely cause for celebration, he'd re-employed his old servants, agreeing to keep them on before they found more suitable arrangements. (Mrs Proops was accepted in a particularly weak moment.) With the last member of the press gone and sightseers rare, he spent much of his time writing to thank well-wishers, and was in the process of going through his letters one morning when Hopley appeared in the doorway.

'You have a visitor, sir. One of the policemen, Mr Gwynne.'

The butler's opinion of the new arrival was clearly indicated by the change in title. George laid his paperknife aside and rose from the table to greet Gwynne as he made his embarrassed entrance.

'Ah, Inspector, welcome! No trusty constable as well?'

George instantly decided to treat him kindly. It certainly took courage for Gwynne to show his face.

'No, sir. Tulley is up at the Hall right now, conducting enquiries.'

'Oh dear. Nothing serious, I trust.'

'Possibly not.'

There was obviously more to this remark, but since Gwynne fell silent George continued in his genial manner, 'Well, sit down, my good fellow. I'll order you some tea. Hopley!' The butler had disappeared – probably in disgust that George hadn't at once given orders to dismiss the visitor – but was now passing the open doorway. 'Will you tell Mrs Proops to prepare a pot of tea and some slices of cake? Thank you.' He turned to the inspector. 'Now, Gwynne, to what do I owe this visit?'

The inspector licked his lips nervously. Since Hopley hadn't relieved him of his muffler, he draped it over one of the arms of his chair.

'I'll try not to take up too much of your time, sir. I wonder if it might be possible to talk with you in private?'

George forced a smile, taking up a place on the sofa. It was obviously too much to hope that this was purely a social call. Still, it was decent of the man to continue to address him as 'sir' in spite of his straitened circumstances.

As Hopley brought in the tea tray, they chatted about recent events in the news, most particularly the American government's recognition of Panama as an independent state and the proposed building of a canal.

'Will that be all, sir?' said the butler, having righted himself.

'Yes, thank you, Hopley. Oh, Hopley!' he added, as the other was leaving. 'Can you make sure we're not disturbed? Tell Mrs Proops if you would.'

'Yes, sir.'

The butler quietly closed the door.

'*Now*, Inspector.'

Gwynne took a bite out of his cake. His features looked wooden and a little despondent.

'Sorry to go over old ground, sir. Just one or two questions, if I may, about the trial. I wouldn't trouble you, I promise, unless it was strictly necessary.'

George gave a weary smile. He'd discussed the case now hundreds of times.

'This would be for the last time, Inspector?'

'I hope so, sir, certainly. Just the odd point to clear up, that's all. Mrs Pilling's letter, for instance. If I could start with the way it was revealed to the court. Your life hung in the balance and yet Mr Pilling didn't come forward for quite some time – even allowing for his sorrow over his wife's death.'

George sat forward to dispense the tea. The inspector was right to be suspicious, of course, but it hardly mattered since the letter had eventually been produced. Gwynne continued to speak in his relaxed fashion.

'The thought struck me he might have tried to see you in advance, and so I spoke to all the warders on duty at the time. One of them, Graves, said he was present at a meeting between yourself and Pilling. He told me he'd heard everything that passed between you.'

George stopped pouring the tea. No. Impossible. Graves had been standing in the corner, too far away.

'Not everyone is aware the interview-rooms are designed so that even whispers can be picked up.' Gwynne gave a little smile. 'Graves heard Pilling say his wife had owned up to seducing you. He also heard him say he'd only pass on such information to the authorities provided you gave up your estate.'

George paled. What was the implication behind all this? Blackmail had been hinted at in the press, but this was proof, absolute proof.

'I – I don't see that I can help ...'

'You could press charges against Mr Pilling.'

For one ghastly moment George had imagined that he might have to be retried – on the grounds of tainted evidence or something of the sort – but the purpose of Gwynne's visit was now revealed. The police were certainly a dogged bunch. They hadn't discovered Emily's murderer in their initial investigation but were still prepared to tackle a lesser crime. Not exactly a piece of detective brilliance – an overheard conversation – but then Gwynne obviously didn't possess enough imagination to progress any further. It was quite depressing on the face of it. No wonder the fellow looked so mournful.

'You have to understand I gave my word,' he responded. 'Whatever my personal feelings towards the man, the fact remains he *did* save me from the gallows. Besides, I can't in good faith object to something I signed and which is strictly legal.'

'Yes, but you only agreed to it under great duress.'

'I'm sorry, Gwynne. I know you've got my interests at heart, but I'd prefer to let the matter drop. I very much want to put the past behind me.'

'I quite understand, sir,' replied the other, as though he'd expected such a response. 'If you would bear with me a while longer, I was hoping to ask you what you thought of Mrs Pilling's confession.'

'Well, I was as shocked as anyone else.'

The inspector was absorbed in a piece of cake and some crumbs had strayed onto his waistcoat. The desire to brush them off was intense.

'You don't think Mrs Pilling an unlikely murderess?'

'Well, obviously—'

'H'm! I'm afraid I found it all very difficult to accept. Especially that suicide note.'

Gwynne's jawline stiffened and suddenly George regarded him in a different light: a policeman who'd been doing his job for many years and, near the end of a probably unblemished career, had made the most hideous mistake, one which he couldn't now come to terms with.

'Well, yes,' he replied. 'Fortunate for me, though, Gwynne.'

'I just knew something was wrong with it, you see. The wording. *Something.*'

George shifted uncomfortably in his seat. Perhaps it had been a mistake after all to invite Gwynne into his home. The man was a bore, an unfeeling one at that, and he'd obviously misjudged him. He was on the point of diplomatically ending the conversation when Gwynne announced, 'It was my granddaughter, would you believe, who finally provided the solution.'

'The solution? I don't quite follow you, Inspector. The solution to what?'

'The case.'

George nearly spilt his tea. 'I thought "the case", as you call it, had already been solved.'

Gwynne shook his head, his moustache curling up at the edges.

'Are you telling me, Inspector, a four-year-old girl has succeeded where doctors, lawyers and policemen have all failed?'

'Not exactly solved everything, but provided the initial clue, certainly. We've strong reason to believe that Edward Pilling murdered his wife.'

George let out a laugh. The charge was a gravely serious one, of course, and Gwynne looked so sombre – but really! Another wife-killer in Eveley! Would the police ever give up?

'I'm sorry, Gwynne. I don't know what came over me.'

'Perfectly natural, sir. Especially after everything you've been through. I can assure you, though, we've looked into everything very closely. The barn in which the hanging took place was the same one, in fact, that Mrs Pilling took you to. I imagine it was chosen because Pilling knew it held significant memories for his wife. He was the only person who saw her leave the house that evening—'

'Hold on, hold on, Inspector. What about the suicide note? Are you saying Pilling was responsible for that?'

'I am indeed.'

'No, no. You're quite wrong, I'm afraid.' George's brows were knitted in concentration. 'If Pilling murdered Constance for her money, there'd have been no need to leave a suicide note.'

'Perhaps he wasn't murdering her for her money.'

'No, no.' It was bad enough that Gwynne was a poor investigator without being a poor judge of human nature. 'I know this man Pilling. He cares for nothing else except money. If he didn't murder Constance for that reason, he didn't murder her at all. You might have garnered the rough details of our conversation in prison, but I can tell you it was a great shock to him when he found that Constance wasn't leaving him anything.'

'Unless that was the impression he wished to convey. Do you suppose he didn't look into all the provisions of her will some time beforehand?'

George frowned heavily, debating his reply.

'No,' Gwynne continued, 'Pilling knew he'd inherit nothing. His mistake had been made earlier when he married Miss Appleby. I daresay he discovered her financial situation shortly afterwards.'

'So what are you saying?'

'That he was after *your* money. Whatever else one can say about the man, he certainly doesn't suffer from a lack of nerve.'

This time George did not laugh. Gwynne was plainly talking nonsense, but it was disconcerting nonsense nonetheless. If he was right … but it was hardly worth contemplating. The other continued to speak with the same conviction he'd shown thus far.

'After his wife died I was frustrated that he wouldn't show us the note she'd left behind, but it wasn't something I felt I could press him on. Nothing at that stage, you see, indicated foul play. By the time he did come forward, I was beginning to have my suspicions, but then why hang on to a piece of evidence which cleared him entirely? It was a complete masterstroke, that's why! Of course he didn't mind me or anyone else having all sorts of doubts, which could be resolved later. He needed the letter to blackmail you.'

'But it was written in Constance's handwriting. How do you explain that?'

'Ah, yes.' The inspector didn't look even slightly perturbed. 'I'm afraid I don't have the letter to hand, but handwriting experts have proved, almost conclusively, that it was written by Mrs Pilling.'

'There you are, then.'

'Exactly so. But we know that the chief beneficiary of Constance's death, eventually at any rate, was Edward Pilling. So it might be that we're approaching the problem from the wrong direction. Let me give you another version of what happened. What *actually* happened.'

30

The Rope Must Be Strong …

George rather doubted the entertainment value of what was to follow. Naturally he was prepared to listen to what the other had to say, but there was no earthly way he was going to stand by while the police arrested another innocent man – even Pilling. At least he'd been assured at the beginning of Gwynne's visit that this would be the last time they'd discuss the case.

The inspector began his résumé.

'Constance has already told Pilling what's happened between the two of you in the barn. She's incredibly frank, saying that she developed an infatuation for you, and even paid visits to your house overnight, throwing gravel at your bedroom window. In all likelihood she's redirected her passion from you to him but wants him to accept her for all her faults.

'The tragedy is she's telling all this to someone whose pride is not only hurt but who sees an opportunity to exploit. Any feelings he once had for her, I imagine, have gone for good. In the days that follow, he convinces her that you took advantage of her in the barn, persuading her to claim that she was somehow attacked. Easily dominated, particularly by men, she agrees to this suggestion.

'By testifying in court, however, to this version of events, she has unwittingly signed her death warrant. Pilling has prepared for this moment and it's vital he acts now before his scandalous activities come to light. Why subject himself to public condemnation over the accusation of blackmailing your wife?'

'Yes,' George said slowly, 'I can see that her death occurred at a convenient time for him.'

'That night, after they arrive home, she's naturally anxious about testifying the next day. Sleep or an early night is out of the question. Pilling therefore suggests a late night walk to calm her nerves. The two of them head off, unseen, discussing the trial.

'As soon as they're a fair distance from the house, Pilling's mood changes. He's been leading her in a certain direction, but now he compels her to go that way. When they reach the barn they find a rope, a fountain pen and several sheets of paper – oh, and your bicycle.'

'My bicycle?'

'Yes, rather a neat touch, that. Constance claimed in her letter that she'd taken your bicycle, but during the game you played at the picnic, if you remember, Pilling was the catcher. Thus he had plenty of time, more than anyone else, to steal the bicycle while everyone else was hiding. Though Constance probably spent all of her time with your wife, nobody'd be able to confirm that fact after your wife's death.'

'But why should he steal the bicycle in the first place? I don't understand.'

'I can only imagine he was frustrated that your wife wasn't paying him quickly enough, and wanted to take something of yours in compensation. In the end it proved very useful to his purposes.'

'So in the barn ...' – George moved on to the most difficult part of the inspector's theory – 'presumably he forced her to write that note.'

'Yes.'

'No one in their right mind would write a note like that knowing they were certain to die.'

'I agree with you entirely, sir, but that's where Pilling was cleverest of all. He begins by accusing her of fornication. Asking her exactly where it happened. Did she realize she'd turned him into a laughing stock? Was she in love with you even now? You can see how awkward he could have made her feel. Ordering her to drop to her knees, he thrusts a piece of paper in front of her and tells her to write him a letter confessing her guilt. He tells her that to aid her memory he's already written a note which she can copy, and places a page – just one page – down on the floor. (It's possible, of course, that Pilling might have dictated the letter but this method seems more probable.) He's just given her the part of the letter, you see, containing the admission of what happened in the barn.

'Scared witless, she copies the note, but her handwriting is smaller than his and there's quite a gap at the bottom of the page, a valuable clue. He's still not happy, though, and continues to berate her, saying she was jealous of your wife. That she murdered her so she could have you to herself – an accusation she vehemently denies. Probably, to persuade her further, he strangles her with the rope, without taking her life, or grabs her hair. We found a lot of her hair on the floor of the barn. By whatever means, he forces her to write another page confessing to the murder of your wife. She probably reasons she can deny it later, but towards the end, perhaps, starts having doubts.

'He asks her to sign the two–page confession and she asks him what will happen to her afterwards. Fixing her in the eye he says, "You know what will happen." He already has what he needs and feels he can be more open about his intentions. She says, "You're going to kill me." He replies, "No, you're going to kill yourself." She is petrified. "This is a suicide note?" she queries. "I haven't mentioned anything about suicide." "Well, here's your chance," he sneers, and hands her another sheet of paper.

'Desperately trying to think of a way to show she's being murdered, she pens a few lines and then signs the third page. He picks up the third piece of paper, reads it – he's thoroughly read the other pages as well – and is satisfied. However, her clue remains.'

'She's left a clue?' George's voice rose in astonishment.

'Yes, a brilliant clue.' Gwynne extracted a note from his pocket which he unfolded. 'Before I came here I took the trouble of copying out a line from the critical third page. In the original she'd written, "The rope will need to be ..." which she'd crossed out and substituted, "The rope *must* be strong ..."'

'"Will" or "must". Is it really that important?'

Gwynne stood up and walked over to where George was sitting, handing him the note on which he'd jotted down:

The ~~rope~~ must be strong

George studied the words, without seeing anything significant, while Gwynne returned to his armchair.

'I sat in my study, staring at the letter for hours, while Caroline, my granddaughter, played around me. I just knew there was something there, some clue, if I looked hard enough. It was impossible to concentrate, though, with Caroline shouting at the top of her voice, and I'm afraid I lost my patience with her at one stage. I told her to stand in front of me to receive a telling off, and it was then, as she was looking down at the note from the other side of the desk, that she said, "Murder. Murder, Grampy, look!"'

George turned the piece of paper upside down and let out a gasp of surprise. 'Oh! Well, I'm blessed!'

'Pretty, isn't it? There's a certain artistry in her last written words.'

'Incredible. Just incredible.' George slumped back on the sofa, turning the paper round and round. 'She did mention she had a talent for mirror writing. But ... well!'

Gwynne took a sip from his tea, which had been left for ten minutes and must have been cold.

'Now that Pilling has obtained her written confession, he can end her life. Standing behind her, he uses the rope to strangle her to death. This produces quite different results from hanging, incidentally, a point which wasn't sufficiently appreciated when Mrs Pilling's body was first examined. Although the furrows in her skin suggest the same rope was used, the post-mortem report indicated that there was a groove running round the entirety of her neck. This could only have been caused by a running noose which would have tightened on impact. But Pilling, who could hardly be expected to know about such things, had constructed a fixed noose. Had she died from hanging, she would have been pulled up by the suspending rope, forming an inverted "V" shape, and leaving a patch of unmarked skin on the back of her neck. Her injuries were more consistent with the fact that she was garrotted.'

'So Pilling really did murder her,' George said in a quiet voice.

'The letter containing the word "murder" is proof of sorts, but the forensic evidence puts the matter beyond doubt. For Pilling, it's now only a question of applying the finishing touches. He slips her suicide note inside the valise, together with the pen, making sure he's retained his copy of the letter. Then he leaves the barn and heads back home. Everything is in place.'

'Wonderful! You've got your man, Inspector.'

'Not quite.' Gwynne flattened his hands on the arms of his chair. 'Ever since your trial there's been enormous pressure on the police not to make another mistake. The powers-that-be have made it clear we must collect every shred of evidence, and only proceed with an arrest when we're quite sure of our facts.'

'But, Gwynne, you are sure of the facts.'

'No harm in amassing more, I suppose. That's why Tulley is over at Stockley Hall at the moment. His excuse is that he's closing the enquiry into the murder of your wife, but what he's really searching for is the original letter which was used in the barn. My personal feeling is that, if there was one, Pilling will have destroyed it some time ago.'

'So what if nothing is found? What will you do then?'

'Well, I was rather hoping you'd help us out there, sir. You see, if the suicide note *was* composed by Pilling, then Constance's confession doesn't count for anything. She could still have murdered your wife, of course, but assuming she didn't – and certainly if we can prove she didn't – it throws even more doubt over that note.'

'I see, yes.' George's enthusiasm had wilted a little.

'So I was hoping that if you thought back again to the night of your wife's murder, you might be able to remember something else of significance, something that would indicate Mrs Pilling couldn't have been the killer.'

'Well ... I suppose I can try.'

'I've spoken to James Hopley. He says he didn't see anyone else in the vicinity of Stockley Hall that evening, or notice anything suspicious. I was wondering if you might have reconsidered that story about the tapestry. Decided it was an intruder after all. Perhaps remembered the coat the murderer was wearing...?'

'Um-m ...'

Gwynne chuckled. 'I have to confess, when you told us about glimpsing that coat, that was when I first really began to suspect you. Such a slender chance! It wouldn't disgrace a three-and-sixpenny novel! One second earlier and you'd have been able to recognize the murderer. One second later and you'd probably think you'd heard nothing of significance at all.'

'Yes, Inspector. Most unfortunate. But then I changed my story, remember?'

'Oh, indeed.' Gwynne smiled disarmingly. 'And I quite understand, sir, how vexing it must be to have me raise the subject again. You've every reason, I know, to wish to forget that evening. The point I was making was that our memories can play strange tricks. By your own admittance you had a fair amount to drink that night, aside from being in a state of considerable disturbance.'

George did not offer a response. Gwynne's sad eyes appeared even more mournful in the dark room.

'In my time as a policeman I've seen enough people worse the wear for drink to know how it can alter one's perceptions – indeed, alter one's whole personality. I expect you were exhausted as well at that time of night. It's a wonder, really, you managed to hear anything at all.'

'H'm,' agreed George vaguely.

There was a pause. The atmosphere seemed to take on a new and oppressive seriousness.

'Well, that's about it for the time being,' said the inspector, rising to his feet. 'Sorry again for disturbing you, sir. I'm sure you appreciate the importance of these new developments. And if you do happen to remember anything else ...'

'Of course, Inspector.'

George stood up. The other man was already heading towards the door.

'Oh, hold on, Gwynne. You forgot this.'

He picked up the muffler which had been left on the armchair and offered it back to its owner. Gwynne reached out his hand, but seemed to take an extra moment to secure it into his possession, displaying the same little smile as before.

'Thank you, sir. I expect we'll see each other again.'

Without waiting for assistance he made his way out, leaving George standing in the middle of the room, gazing after him and frowning slightly. What an abrupt end to their interview! Naturally, there were still questions to be asked in regard to Emily's death, but Gwynne had appeared to invest his last remarks with an extra meaning. All that guff about repressed memories and the effects of alcohol.

And what was that business with the muffler? Gwynne had been staring at George's hand as if there was some significance ...

His left hand ...

George's knees nearly buckled from under him. Emily had been strangled by someone who was left-handed. Sir Lionel's experiment with the coin hadn't really proved anything and he'd kept quiet at the time because ... well, because he'd wanted them to think he was innocent, wanted to believe himself that he was innocent ...

But Gwynne hadn't been fooled. Gwynne knew. Why make a special point of visiting him in the first place, breaking off in the middle of an investigation and sending his subordinate onto the Hall? Everything he'd said showed it. He didn't have enough proof at the moment, but he wanted George to know that he was on to him. Encouraging him to come forward and confess. Even providing him with a way of explaining himself, implying that George might have convinced himself that he didn't kill Emily, that he might have heard someone or something instead. At one point on the night of the murder he'd found himself on the landing, but how had he arrived there?

The tears rose in George's eyes. The inspector had brilliantly dissected the events of that night. It was just as he'd described: the jealousy, the drink. Yet he couldn't remember killing Emily, he really couldn't. One nightmare had succeeded another, dreams about knives and screams, the lack of any physical affection, and perhaps ... perhaps he'd blocked out the memory of her murder. He'd killed Emily, the dearest creature in the world. How could he have committed such an act? How could he?

31

The Truth

The room was spinning around and, taking a step backwards to regain his balance, George collided with the tea things, sending the tray with all the cups and saucers crashing to the floor.

'Oh, I'm sorry!' he said automatically.

Mrs Proops came rushing in to deal with the mess, shortly followed by Hopley. George dropped to his knees beside the housekeeper, but she clearly didn't care for his assistance, snatching at items he was about to pick up. He'd always been an idiot, always been lacking in *savoir-faire*, but now he'd turned into a murderer. The exercise of tidying up seemed to take forever and he watched in a sort of dream as Mrs Proops bustled about with her usual efficiency.

The inspector was right. Of course he was. No one could drink that much without it having an effect. This wasn't the first time in any case he'd forgotten an event owing to the amount he'd had to drink. Henry Beakston, his friend from the early days of Emily, had once or twice regaled him with tales of George's exploits after a particularly heavy evening. Oh, Lord, and all the time he'd thought Beakston had been joking …

Mrs Proops finally departed and he found his way to the armchair and slumped down, gazing at his hands, his murderous hands, bending the fingers towards him—

Hold on a moment …

Suddenly he was all alert, eyes staring in concentration and face glowing with wonder. He held up one hand, then the other. But yes, it was perfectly true. Of all the…!

He looked up, surprised to see Hopley still in the room, standing beside the table, awaiting further instructions.

'I didn't do it,' he said with a beaming smile. 'I didn't do it, Hopley.'

'No, sir. But, with respect, you were the only one in the room at the—'

'Not the tea tray for goodness' sake! The murder – Emily's murder! Look at my fingernails. Look!'

The butler took a couple of steps forward and inspected the hands held up for his perusal, a natural tact precluding him from commenting on their shocking state.

'See! Bitten to the quick!' said George. 'The pathologist at the trial said that there were crescent-shaped impressions on Emily's neck, almost certainly carved by fingernails. So you see I simply couldn't have ...'

He brushed away a tear, unable to stop smiling. Oh, wonderful relief! Just an attack of nerves, that was all. Thinking Gwynne possessed mystical powers when all he was trying to do was trick him into confessing.

'I'm sorry, sir. I understood that Mrs Pilling had owned up to—'

'No, no, Hopley. Everything's changed, the inspector's just been telling me. Here, sit down – on the sofa.'

The butler hesitated, no doubt concerned about the breakdown of the master–servant relationship which such an act entailed.

'Sit down, man. I want to talk to you. Protocol be damned!'

Hopley moved over to the sofa and gently lowered himself onto what might have been – judging from his expression – flaming hot coals. Over the next twenty minutes George reiterated Gwynne's theories about Pilling and how ideas about Emily's death had been thrown into doubt. He spoke quickly and excitably, inspired by the inspector's detective work and his own latest discovery. God, he'd been asleep all this time. Positively asleep! Emily's death had naturally been a terrible shock, but he'd largely assumed that Pilling – and then Constance – must be to blame, never really considering any other possibilities.

'There's no reason why we can't solve this ourselves, Hopley. Very few people – very few – could have committed the murder. And we know far more than the police about the daily running of the house – at least you do.'

A resolve was establishing itself in his mind. Find Emily's killer. Dedicate himself henceforth to tracking him down. Apart from anything else, the person responsible was likely to be left-handed, a characteristic which immediately narrowed the field.

'I still hold to the view, sir, that it was an outsider.'

'Very well, then, let's discuss it. If you're right, there seem to be only two people with a credible motive – Edward Pilling and his late wife. Agreed?'

Hopley frowned in concentration. 'I must say, sir, that Mrs Pilling appeared unusually happy at the time of the mistress's death. Upset in your presence perhaps ...'

'Yes, but would she have committed murder to achieve her ends? That's one aspect that's bothered me since the trial. There'd be no guarantee she'd become the next Mrs Erskine.' George stroked his chin thoughtfully. 'No, I think we can discount her. That suicide note doesn't say how she got into the house. Nor does it mention using a pillow as a murder weapon. And there's no mention of making the bed after the murder.'

'Begging your pardon, sir, but I thought Mr Pilling dictated the note.'

'Yes, and he was drawing on every detail she'd given him in order to illustrate her guilt. Mentioning throwing gravel at my bedroom window, for instance. But if she'd really confided in him he'd surely have asked her how she gained entry into the house. Yes, yes! And if *he'd* committed the murder he'd have been able to provide such information himself. In any case Emily would never have let him into her room.'

George was sitting upright in his chair, his eyes sparkling. Gwynne would no doubt have reached this stage as well, concluding that George himself was the killer. But of course he had an advantage over Gwynne, being able to deduct the list of suspects by one ...

'Someone in the house was responsible, Hopley. No other solution presents itself. Didn't you think that your mistress's illness came on very suddenly? Remember when she left the breakfast-table? I thought at the time she was shamming.'

'Oh, no, sir. Mrs Erskine was very unwell. The doctor said it was food poisoning.'

'Yes, poisoning,' he said significantly. 'The police showed me a medical book of mine which always fell open at the entry for arsenic. They probably thought I'd been looking at other ways of killing my wife, but the truth is I was only pursuing a harmless interest. Besides, I'm very careful how I treat books. No, Hopley, the only explanation is that someone else was looking at that section. Maybe for innocent reasons, maybe not. Did we keep any poison on the premises, do you know?'

'Well ... um ... I know Mrs Bridges kept rat poison in the kitchen. And Mary used flypapers – to improve her complexion or some such nonsense. Oh, yes, and Mrs Proops also—'

He suddenly averted his gaze. George turned in his chair to see the housekeeper framed in the doorway. Her appearance, just as her name was mentioned, was more than a little fortuitous, but then perhaps she could help in their deliberations. She entered the room, her black gown gliding along the floor, and stood, hands folded, looking down on the butler.

'I'll thank you to mind your own affairs in future, Mr Hopley.'

The target of this rebuke, perhaps laboured by his seated position, didn't respond directly, and George felt obliged to intervene.

'Hopley is merely helping me to understand the everyday workings of Stockley Hall, Mrs Proops. We think, or at least I do, that my wife's illness at the breakfast-table may have been deliberately induced. You were standing next to Alfred at one point if I remember rightly. Did you notice anything suspicious or out of the ordinary?'

'No, I did not.'

'These flypapers used by Mary ... do you know anything about them?'

'No.'

'Oh, come, Mrs Proops!' said Hopley.

She remained unmoved, eyes at their most inscrutable, as she continued to look at George.

'I'm afraid we need to know as much as possible, Mrs Proops, however embarrassing it might be. You didn't use arsenic for cosmetic purposes?'

'Certainly not.'

Hopley coughed politely. 'Mrs Bridges informed me that—'

'Mrs Bridges is a silly, unreliable woman.'

George sat back in his chair and gripped the armrests in an attempt to control his feelings. Mrs Proops had been ruled out of the investigation because she'd possessed a key to Emily's room and thus wouldn't require her mistress's assistance in opening the door. But even by her standards she was being unhelpful.

'All right, let's not argue among ourselves,' he said. 'How about your mistress, Mrs Proops? Was she mistrustful of anyone after she fell ill? I know you spent some time with her.'

'She had no fears of that nature – none she admitted to me at any rate.'

'You told the police she seemed preoccupied.'

'Yes, she was.'

'Well, do you have any idea what might have been troubling her?'

Mrs Proops sniffed, not answering immediately.

'Please try to remember. I know it's hard, but any thoughts or confidences she passed on could be of the utmost importance. Were you aware, for instance, that she'd offered your services to Mr Pilling?'

At last he'd broken through the façade, her mouth producing a little gobbling motion.

'I wasn't aware of that, no.'

'Really? That's odd. She didn't say anything to you about it?'

Mrs Proops reverted to a sullen silence. A stand-off was developing and George strove to keep an even tone to his voice.

'Look, all I'm interested in is ascertaining the truth. We no longer believe that Constance Appleby – Pilling, sorry – killed my wife. However, there's a certain amount of circumstantial evidence which implicates you, Mrs Proops, and we just want you to clear your name.'

'Am I supposed to be on trial?' she sneered.

'No, no, of course not. But I did see you, didn't I, that evening on the stairs?'

'I saw you.'

'Yes, you saw me, that's quite so. You saw me ... open and close Emily's door. Yes, of course you did!' He sat forward in his chair, buoyed up by another line of enquiry. 'So you'd believe she hadn't locked her door, that you wouldn't need your key to gain entry. Yes, that's right, isn't it? You wouldn't know she'd gone out.'

'Are you suggesting that I killed Mrs Erskine?' she asked.

'No, no, forgive me.' He brought himself up, constrained by her icy calm. 'I was just thinking of something Gwynne referred to, about you wishing to use your own key to avoid waking your mistress ... oh, I don't know what I'm saying! I don't suppose it makes any difference, not if the door was locked later in the evening.'

He rested his elbows on his knees and covered his face with his hands. Of course someone *could* have stolen into Emily's room beforehand. But then how would that person know her door would be open, or when she might return?

'Unless ...' He emerged from the depths. 'Unless Emily's room was unlocked the whole night long. Perhaps she left her key in the door before setting off and forgot about it later – never opened her door to anyone at all. Tell me, Mrs Proops – just so we're absolutely clear – why were you at the top of the stairs at half past eleven? You said at the trial you noticed a light under your door, yet so far as I recall, everything was dark.'

'A lamp was still burning on the upstairs landing.'

'So you turned it down and then heard me. But how? I was as quiet as possible.'

She did not respond and the doubts in his mind moved ever closer to certainties. She was left-handed, wasn't she? Hadn't most of the tea things been picked up with that hand? Then the position Emily had been found in could simply have been someone anxious to make things appear as normal as possible – but overdoing it, possibly as a last snub to her mistress.

'Why did you come downstairs, Mrs Proops? Why?'

Even as he was asking the question an answer suggested itself.

'Because Emily had dismissed you, hadn't she? That's why she offered you to Pilling. You'd been complaining about your wages and she'd had enough. You were going to remonstrate with her one last time.'

Good God, it was her. She'd killed Emily. Furthermore, she knew he'd found her out, a touch of red on her cheeks giving her away, even while her lizard-like eyes remained impassive. The desire to press on with his attack was immense, but a voice inside his head told him to be quiet. She was obviously wavering, thinking about something to say. A semblance of a smile hovered around her mouth.

'She told me to pack my bags in the morning and go. Thirty years I'd been in service – thirty years of looking after Stockley Hall – and she wouldn't even provide me with a character.'

'Now, now, Mrs Proops,' said Hopley. 'That's not the way to speak—'

'I'm not like you, Mr Hopley,' she turned on the butler. 'You were born into this life. It's in your blood. I was brought up in a household where I was one of those waited upon. My father was a successful man, on good terms with Lord Delsey. That's why I was treated differently to the rest of the staff, why I commanded a certain influence. Who do you think persuaded his lordship to keep you on after your marriage? Your wife came to *me* to plead your case. She was aware of my standing in the house, even if you weren't.'

'Your standing in the house?' George queried. 'What are you referring to?'

She looked across at him, her face full of disdain.

'Your standing,' he repeated. 'Was that an issue you raised with Emily, along with your wages? You waited until she'd fallen ill – until she was unable to avoid your company – and then ...' His eyes widened at the thought that had just occurred to him. 'No! I know what happened. You didn't wait. You poisoned Emily, didn't you? *Didn't you?*'

She didn't reply immediately and he started to his feet in a sudden fury, advancing one step before Hopley placed a restraining arm around his chest. Mrs Proops backed away until she was standing next to the table. Her dark, sunken eyes peered at him from the white mask of her face and her jaw stuck out defiantly.

'Very well! Very well, then, if you want the truth so much! Yes ... Yes is the answer to your question. I didn't use much. Not enough to risk serious harm. I wanted her to see how much she relied on me, how important I'd been to the family.'

'You poisoned her just so that you could talk to her?'

A sense of desperation gripped him, taking hold of his stomach and squeezing it with painful intensity.

'It was the only way,' she went on in the same even tone. 'I'd tried speaking to her before but she'd always brushed me aside. I wanted her to listen. To hear what I had to say. We had words on the Sunday, not long after your visit. I told her that her father had broken off a promise to marry me when she arrived back from her mother. But she accused me of telling lies. Trying to take advantage of his lordship.'

George was breathing heavily, looking at her through a haze of despair. Constance had hinted that Delsey and the housekeeper might have had an affair. But for heaven's sake. For heaven's sake …

'Her whole attitude – the way she dismissed my account – was quite intolerable. Who looked after Lord Delsey when she and her mother left him all alone? The truth is that he cared for me immensely. That was why he wrote me into his will, why he left me this house – this house where I spent my childhood.'

'This house once belonged to … ? Oh, yes. Of course …'

Pilling had told him that Mrs Proops used to live at Potterslake Farm. But then – a flush crept over George's face – he should have known the facts already, involved himself more in the servants' affairs. Perhaps if he'd taken heed of Emily's remark about Mrs Proops pressing for a house, her death could have been avoided.

'When his lordship sold it I knew it would never be mine. But he assured me that he'd made provision for me. That he hadn't forgotten.'

'He changed his will, didn't he?' said George, recalling the scene on the river-bank when Emily had mentioned the subject. 'He changed it after his daughter returned.'

'I didn't know he'd changed it until after his death. Just imagine that if you can. Imagine all that time … To be promised a house, with my own servants, and then end up with nothing.'

'But to kill Emily …' His voice rose in exasperation. 'Your grievance was with her father.'

'No. She could have corrected his mistake. Recognized my role within the family. To just dismiss me like that, leaving me nowhere to go. My life was over then. Or, rather, it's over now.'

She suddenly transferred her attention to the table, grabbing the paperknife and bringing it round. Hopley's arm fell away while George raised a hand in entreaty. He was mesmerized by the knife which she was turning in an arc, exposing her long nails. A vague sense of what she intended to do came to him, but the blade was already pointing—

'No, Matilda, no!' shouted Hopley.

She plunged the knife with enormous force into her chest, allowing her hands to drop, still gazing at George with the same lack of expression. He rushed to her side, guiding her down onto the floor, supporting her head and shoulders. A strand of her hair had come loose on her forehead and she gave a choking sound. He reached out to remove the knife but she pushed him away.

'No, leave it,' she said, quite calmly.

His whole body was bathed in perspiration and the panic showed in his eyes as he looked to her for confirmation. Oh, what had she done, what had she done? This was Geoffrey all over again, lying dead beside him in the battlefield. He didn't want her to die like this – not even her – but then it was probably already too late to do anything. He laid her down as gently as he could on the floor and took off his frock coat, rolling it up into a pillow. She seemed more comfortable now, taking measured breaths, her gaze never leaving his face.

'I want to die,' she said in a quiet voice. 'To die here, in this place.'

She took a huge gulp of air. Her skin was so thin, blue veins showing on her forehead. So frail ... and yet somehow she'd killed Emily, killed the person who meant more to him than any other. For a moment her eyes turned away from his, up at the ceiling, fluttering – oh, God, she nearly went there – but now she was back from the edge of the abyss.

'This was my house ... my father's house.' Her voice was a strangled whisper. 'Lord Delsey promised ... promised it to me.'

Her breathing was becoming more and more laboured. Tears started in his eyes at the cruelty of Nature. Was this how it was for his mother at the end when he was all those miles away? Fighting desperately against the pain, the increasing suffocation as life seeped away? The seconds drifted by with an agonizing slowness. Mrs Proops gave out another breath, more of a gasp. Her lips parted as if she were about to say something, stretching into a ghastly smile. Then – at last – her black eyes glazed over.

'Gone ... She's gone.'

Her face had assumed a serene expression. He sat up as his own breathing recovered, exchanging a look with Hopley, before turning back to Mrs Proops – finally at peace. A moment passed and then he took hold of her hands and rested them one over the other as she'd once done with Emily.

Epilogue

The trial of Edward Pilling for the murder of Constance Pilling née Appleby took place during the first week of February 1904. A verdict of guilty was returned and the following month his appeal was dismissed. On the morning of 22 April Pilling was dragged across the prison yard to the shed where the hanging was to take place, crying and wailing. Standing on the trap doors while the executioner adjusted the noose, he proclaimed, between sobs, 'I am innocent before God and King!' – his final words.

In years to come he and Mrs Proops were to make a very distinct and unusual couple in Madame Tussaud's, where they became a main-stay attraction of the Chamber of Horrors. The arrogant expression displayed by the man seemed well-suited to the dress of an Edwardian dandy, while her stern features, framed in a black bonnet and stole, lost nothing by being immortalized in wax. Even though the house-keeper was not much taller than many of the children who came to visit, she was still able with her disapproving eye to send them scur-rying home to their nightmares.

Inspector Gwynne's success in bringing Pilling to trial met with very qualified approval. Significantly the judge did not commend the police for their part in the investigations, the implication being that it was a terrible oversight to have arrested the wrong man initially – an attitude also adopted by the press. The superintendent, however, *was* impressed by Gwynne's conduct and made it known to his superiors that he considered the inspector a little unfortunate.

George Erskine was able to reclaim Stockley Hall but quickly sold it and emigrated to America. He never married again, but by all accounts enjoyed a long and happy life, shrewd investments allowing him to become a rich man and also a noted philanthropist. The past was never forgotten, of course, but he was not plagued by it as Emily had been, and indeed he was able to address the odd outstanding issue. Before he left England, for example, he left a large sum of money for James Hopley's education and made sure to keep in touch with his father as to his progress. The other regular correspondent of his, perhaps surprisingly, was Inspector Gwynne, the man who had arrested him for murdering his beloved wife.